A young rake soon to inherit an impoverished estate…a lonely widow unable to produce an heir…a love they must forsake.

"Mistress, I've made it quite clear that I wish to learn from you. I believe you wish to teach me as well. I—you…"

He blushes beautifully. She sat back, interested to see where he would go with this line of thought, content to let him stammer, while she attempted to keep her libido from finding the nearest set of restraints—those curtain ties would work—and having her way with him.

He arched a brow at her recline, realizing her intent. "You know of what I speak, Mistress. I was thinking that for every five words I teach you in Latin, you could teach me something. It would not be possible to learn the whole language this summer, but I think at that rate you'd make significant progress."

She was impressed that he'd already planned his approach and was ready to barter. However, she thrived on dickering and refused to make this easy. "And, just to be clear, what would I teach you?"

"Mistress." He sighed out, sounding exasperated.

"William, if you cannot say it, then I daresay you are not ready to learn it." She grinned.

Trade Paperback ISBN 979-8-89044-405-9
Digital ISBN 979-8-89044-406-6
Cover by *Lisa Dawn MacDonald*

Charlotte's Control

by

Maggie Sims

The Control Series
Book One

Chapter One

William Stanton, heir to the Earl of Harrington, guffawed at his cousin Percy's latest tale of late-night antics. The group of young men occupied the corner of William's first ball. At nine-and-ten, just home from his second year at Oxford, he was an unusual sight at formal events. He'd hoped to have until he reached his majority before giving in to the formalities of society.

From the corner of his eye, he caught a few heads turning toward them at the loud laugh. Their small group was drawing attention from the row of seated matrons against the ballroom wall. Still chuckling, he turned his head and froze, gaping.

Standing alone, an iceberg with the sea of ball-goers flowing around her, was the most beautiful woman he had ever seen. A cliché perhaps, but undeniable. Unlike the married ladies in chairs, who leaned toward each other to gossip, or the twittering nests of girls new to the marriage mart, this creature was solitary and serene. Her plum-colored ballgown stated that she was married, but she appeared closer to his age than that of those lining the room. The honey curls pinned high on her head gleamed with youthful lustre, unlike the gray streaking most of the mamas' heads.

She was also staring back at him, her expression

unreadable.

His mouth was still open from the laughter he had stopped mid-breath, and he snapped it closed, straightening an inch and squaring his shoulders. He pivoted to face her fully, even as one of the other young men in the group nudged him.

She arched a brow before breaking eye contact and turning to peruse the dance floor.

Percy's friend, whom he had met an hour ago, asked, "Who's the lady? Do you know her?"

"Not yet. Who d'you think could introduce me?"

"I've no idea. Our host, I suppose."

He had just been introduced to the earl whose home they occupied that evening, so he could not waltz up and ask about a woman who could be a duchess for all he knew. Disheartened, William turned back to the group of young, mostly-idle aristocrats in his cousin's set. Balls held no appeal to him. He'd rather be out with his childhood friends than making small talk with strangers, and he was years away from hunting for a wife at such events.

He had planned only to gain introductions to a few members of the House of Lords who Percy knew, lingering just long enough to do his duty. Thanks to his father's irresponsibleness, he was trailing his cousin around, learning the politics of an earldom for the remaining weeks of the Parliamentary Session instead of the usual post-matriculation activities like a Grand Tour or frequenting gaming hells like most young aristocratic men. He was lucky his mother had salvaged enough funds to get him through the next year to graduate Oxford.

At some point, he would need to think of marriage,

if for no other reason than to replenish the family coffers. But after a mere hour at one ball, he'd become bored with the vapid misses in pastel. They simpered and primped, opening and closing their fans and peeking at him in some mating ritual he neither cared about nor understood. Until he'd spied this paragon of poise.

The goddess who stood apart did not flutter or flit, nor did she whisper to a companion behind a fan. Composed and confident in her solitude, she held herself apart and observed. What must she make of the yapping pile of earls-in-the-making he lingered with? Did she see them the way he viewed the girls his age?

Only she could answer that question. He broke away from his circle and strode through the crowded room toward where he'd last seen her, determined to forego propriety and introduce himself.

Spying a flash of purple skirts disappear around a tall couple who'd just arrived, he maneuvered in that direction. A simpering miss, apparently feeling quite daring or the effects of the champagne, stepped into his path and fanned herself like it was an Olympic sport.

He sidestepped. She matched it. Sighing, he bowed. "I beg your pardon, miss. I was looking for a friend, if you'll excuse me."

Turning, he found a different path to the ballroom entrance and peered at the stairs where the ladies' retiring room lay, then at the front hall and door. The lady had vanished. He hadn't seen her speak to anyone, and he could not even ask someone her name.

Gritting his teeth, he returned to Percy to learn his duties for the future. He'd ask his cousin about her tomorrow, or his friend South would have ideas. South was always creative at circumventing society's rules.

* * * *

William woke early the next morning, as was his routine. Throwing clothes on without a cravat or jacket, he made his way to the library to meet with his mother for an hour before breakfast. Entering just after him, hair a shade lighter than his due to gray streaking the gold, she stood almost as tall as him. They shared the same long, lean build and not-easily-ruffled demeanor, unlike his sister, Emily, who was younger by three years and took after her father in creativity and temper.

William contemplated his mystery woman's age. It was likely midway between Emily's and his mother's, but just as his mother did not look her age, mystery woman's appearance left a wide margin for error.

His mother grabbed some documents from her desk and moved to the seating area, the rust cushions and curtains offset by touches of yellow, a thick patterned rug with similar colors beneath them.

"Mama, what do we need to accomplish today?"

"Who did you and Percy meet last night at the ball and the club?"

He and his cousin had headed to White's after the ball, to discuss the bills currently under review in the House of Lords. An off-night for Parliament was most often used for squiring wives, sisters, or daughters to a ball—or looking for a wife depending on one's situation—followed by political machinations at White's, one of several private men's clubs favored by Peers of the Realm.

William ran through the members he had spoken to, and the topics covered.

When he had arrived home last week from university for the summer break, he'd been looking forward to continuing to learn the earldom bit by bit and spending evenings with his closest friends. Instead, his mother had pulled him into the library, brackets around her mouth indicating her worry. "William, I have had to step in and keep an eye on things. Funds are tight. We have enough to get you through university, but I need your help in maintaining the business of the earldom, please."

His father's over-indulgence in drink had been apparent to everyone for a long time, but he had not realized it had become that out of control. In the blink of an eye, his summer plans were forgotten. His concern was for his mother and family, as well as the dozens of servants and tenants who relied on the earldom for rent and food. "Mama, you know if you need me here, I'll stay. I can finish Oxford later, or read the books in my own time."

She hugged him. "I know you would, my son, but I do not want that for you. And there is a limited amount any of us can do with your father still the earl."

He nodded. "But how will you manage when I'm away? Summer break is less than two months."

"Percy is three-and-twenty, if you recall. He's been managing his own household for two years, and before that was learning in preparation to manage it. He stops by and helps me. We review whatever paperwork we can before Fred awakes. Then we review the most important items with him at breakfast, before he leaves for his club. And just between us, I've had to sign for your father on a few things. Even if he was asked, he would not recall whether he'd signed something or not." Her eyes shuttered and the grooves around her mouth became more pronounced.

"Mama. I wish you had more things in your life that

made you happy." He'd make it all go away for her if he could. After their initial conversation about expediting his learning, he'd noticed how tired she'd looked. Before, she'd just been mama. Now she was his business partner and his responsibility as much as he was hers.

"My boy, *you* make me happy." Her smile chased the tired look away, at least for a moment. "Knowing you'll finish university and be ready to take your place in the world thrills me. I see so much strength and compassion in you. You are already a gentleman I am proud of."

Her words strengthened his resolve to alleviate her burden as much as he could. "Right, then. How can I help?"

Thus began the summer of shadowing his mother and his cousin to safeguard what he could of the earldom and its coffers, while other young men his age learned from their fathers. His father was lucky he was not around much. Once William saw the shambles of the family ledgers due to mismanagement and poor investment, his ever-growing anger might have gotten the better of him.

This morning, his mother's question about who they'd met brought back his Plum Lady in a rush. He needed to find time to discover her name and station.

"William? Are you quite all right?"

Coming back to the present with a start, he shook his head. "Sorry, Mama. Did you ask me something?"

"Did you meet the Earl of Peterborough?"

"I do not believe so." He ran through the names and faces to whom his cousin had introduced him. "Shall I send him a note asking if he'd be willing to meet me at White's one morning?"

"That should work." She nodded. "As I mentioned, I have heard his politics align with ours, despite

Peterborough having quite different industries up north. But tread carefully. Consider taking Percy, as he has more experience in these matters."

As usual, his mother's request came more like a demand. He was accustomed to it, and did not mind. She was more intelligent than many of the men he knew and was juggling her role as a countess with having to be Merlin to his father's sotted King Arthur. William's strength of character came from her. Stifling a sneer for his father's weakness, he wrote the requested note, specifying morning to avoid his father as the man rarely rose before noon, and William avoided interactions with him as much as possible. When Percy arrived, he'd bring up the subject of the gorgeous mystery woman.

* * * *

Percy hadn't known who Plum Lady was, either. Frustrated, William sped through his work and granted himself a reprieve to spend time with his two closest friends. He'd met South and Nate at boarding school.

The day was gray but dry as he strolled the few blocks to Luke Lynwood's family townhome, also in Mayfair. Luke—or South, as they'd dubbed him in opposition to the title he'd one day inherit—was heir to the Earl of Northumberland. From South's, they grabbed a hack to get to Nate's forge.

Nathaniel Follett neither lived nor worked in Mayfair. Nate had not been a student; rather he'd been the son of the other boys' housemaster.

The students surmised that he'd know how to have the most fun in the area, as well as how to circumvent house rules and not get caught. The three quickly grew close. William helped Nate with his last years of studies before apprenticing to learn a trade, and Nate helped them "borrow" boats to row on the town's lake, among other activities to expend some of their youthful energy.

The unlikely trio had been separated the past two winters with William and South attending Oxford, while Nate journeyed to London to pursue an apprenticeship as a blacksmith. Now South was in London for a fortnight before his father planned to adjourn the family to their country seat, giving the three a limited time to reunite.

While the other two had been at university, Nate had formed a partnership with Robert and Beth Orford to make leather and metal accessories for sexual play. The income from that allowed him to need only one year of apprenticeship before saving enough to open his own shop. The smith Nate apprenticed with had used a play on his last name and his hobby—crafting intricate items like nipple screws—and dubbed him Folly. Despite his teasing, he'd been very supportive of Nate's growth, introducing him to the Orfords and helping him strike out on his own.

The smithy was located in Soho, located just to the east of Mayfair. The neighborhood included a mix of businesses, immigrants, and working class folks who lived above their storefronts, as Nate did. Aristocratic visitors were infrequent but not unheard of, given the goods and services offered there.

Clambering down and paying the hack driver, they strolled in to find Nate hunched over the fire with the smallest tongs in his hand, droplets of sweat sizzling as they hit the flames.

"Oh-ho, it seems Folly's finished his real work for the day and is making more toys," South mock-whispered to William.

"My hands are full, but please consider yourselves

gestured at rudely," muttered Nate. "I am nearly done."

"Will you show us the piece if we wait quietly?"

"Not a chance in hell you'll succeed at that, so no."

William snickered, and promptly received an elbow jab to the ribs.

"Hey, now." South faked outrage, but strolled around patiently.

"Don't—"

"I know, I know. Don't touch anything." South finished Nate's oft-spoken warning.

Ten minutes later, William and South claimed their favorite corner of the public room while Nate ran upstairs to rinse himself off and put a dry shirt on.

Mugs in front of all of them, South asked again, "What were you working on?"

"You know I'm not going to share until I am certain the pieces are finished and usable." The Orford partnership and resulting catalogue were Nate's passion and he was protective of their designs.

William's few sexual encounters had been quick, half-dressed, and rare. He'd only dallied with serving girls who threw themselves at him at school and was still at a loss as to what all the fuss was about. The girls were eager and seemed easy to please. While he enjoyed himself, he wasn't all that interested in prolonging it with contraptions. Anyway, he had more important things to worry about. "South, did you see the lady in the plum gown last night?"

"Plum?"

"Purple." Nate clarified, rolling his eyes.

"Why do you both call it plum when purple will do just fine for any self-respecting man?"

William gritted his teeth. "Did you or did you not see

her?"

"Nah. I had my eye on a cheeky little miss in yellow. Oh, excuse me…" South searched for a word. "Lemon. Wait, why do you want to know?"

Nate turned to look at William for an answer as well.

"She caught my eye, but when I looked for her to introduce myself, I could not find her. She was…intriguing." He was not going to tell his profligate friend she'd been the most beautiful woman he'd ever seen, as well as the most composed.

"Well, if she was wearing 'plum' then I can see why. Sounds like a perfect opportunity for a dalliance with a matron for the summer before heading back to university." South wiggled his brows.

Nate interjected, "Why do you assume that?"

"The marriage-minded misses are all in pastels. It's like marking them for slaughter."

"Lovely," Nate said with a snicker.

"What do you suggest?" William was about to knock their heads together if they did not stay on the point.

"Send a note to the host?" South offered.

"And ask what, exactly?" William huffed.

"Attend more balls." Nate's voice was matter-of-fact.

"Ugh." Although, he'd be attending them anyway. At least the hope of seeing her and actually getting to talk to her would make them more palatable. Perhaps Plum Lady would be at the Earl of Cheltenham's ball. Percy had said it was one of the most widely-attended.

Chapter Two

Charlotte poured herself tea from the pot on the breakfast table. She preferred a minimum of servants for breakfast, for her sake and theirs, and she was perfectly capable of pouring her own drink. Thus, there was no buffet on the sideboard, just a plate of toast before her with a jar of strawberry preserves at hand.

The rustle of skirts at the door made her look up.

Her friend Isabella Rossi threw her hood back and placed her basket of flowers on the far end of the dining room table before removing the cape and handing it to the butler who'd followed her in.

"Belle!" Charlotte rose to exchange cheek kisses.

Her friend's glossy sable locks were pinned back in a simple chignon, and her dress was plain, high-necked, and brown, stark against the rose walls above the wainscotting.

Isabella was a courtesan. As a flower seller was one of several ways her friend visited, insistent on disguises and the servants' entrance to protect Charlotte's reputation.

Charlotte's late husband, Charles, had introduced her to Isabella once upon a time, and they'd become fast friends despite their varied upbringings and stations in life. It helped that they were close in age, with Belle only two years her senior. As a countess, Charlotte had followed along with Isabella's disguises to protect Charles' reputation with his cronies, but as a widow she'd become impatient. So once in a while, she liked to surprise Belle with a visit at her apartment. In broad daylight.

After kissing her on the cheek, Charlotte requested coddled eggs from the footman, as they were Belle's favorite, and a larger pot of tea. Sending the servant to the kitchen also meant they could eat and talk without an audience.

"How was the ball?" Isabella leaned in, holding her tea with both hands, elbows propped on the table.

Charlotte waved a hand. "They are all the same. Well, Cheltie's is likely to be different, but still…" Evan Gardner, the Earl of Cheltenham and Cheltie to almost all who knew him, was one of Charlotte's closest friends.

"Still a wallflower?" Belle's lips pursed.

"I am simply out of practice." She shrugged, attempting to make light of the awkwardness she'd experienced.

Reinserting herself into society as a widow was more effort than she'd like, but she'd been alone for more than a year, mourning and adjusting to being alone.

Charles's younger brother Edward had married last year, which had been as sudden as Charles's succumbing to a fever. But Edward had fallen in love with a country miss who loved horses as much as he did. It worked well for all, as Charlotte had no interest in the dower house at the Peterborough estate, and the couple preferred the country over their London townhouse. Therefore, he'd signed the city residence over to her. If he hadn't been married, Charlotte would have continued to help their steward manage the various properties and households, but Edward's new wife, Sophia, had been happy to step in. That was both a blessing and a curse, as it left her with too much spare time.

Charles had tutored her on his Cambridge curriculum, and they'd enjoyed the active social and intellectual aspects of the city, attending lectures, soirées, and musicales as well as balls. When she'd lost him, she had withdrawn from all of that. She'd gone to visit her brother in the south once, but they weren't close, and her parents were dead. With the additional free time, she focused on her second interest beyond learning—investing.

Months later, when she complained to Belle of loneliness, her friend insisted that meant it was time to assimilate back into the London social scene. Charlotte had balked, but Belle had insisted she try a few outings, so this Season, she'd ventured back into Ton circles.

She'd expected the anonymity of balls might be easier than the smaller lectures with Charles's closest friends, but she'd forgotten that almost everyone was paired at balls—or else looking to be paired—and those looking for partners were as much as a decade younger than her eight-and-twenty years. The isolation of her aloneness hit her hard.

"You are simply off your game, and that is why I pushed you to attend these. 'Twill be the same with sex. The first time back in the saddle may feel strange—hopefully a good strange, though. Then you'll practice and it shall improve."

"Belle! One step at a time, please. Let me ease into re-establishing relationships with friends." Still struggling to exchange social banter after eight years of marriage and a year and half of widowhood, she could not imagine the deeper conversations needed to become more intimately acquainted with someone. Nor could she picture the dialogue needed for the bedroom play she preferred.

"Oh, bother. You'd be much more relaxed about renewing acquaintances if you'd had a few orgasms. After all, you are still young." At Charlotte's chastising look, she demurred. "Right, then. What is your plan?"

"I'll see how Cheltie's ball goes. I need to go early to speak with Althea about the Bath partnership." Belle had met Cheltie's new wife, Althea, when she'd come to Charlotte as an investor in expanding her apothecary before he'd managed to win her hand in marriage.

"How is the competition going?"

Much of the reason Charlotte sought knowledge on as many topics as possible was to inform her choices of investments. She and Charles had garnered a staggering level of wealth after she'd found she had a knack for identifying successful investments and businesspeople. Cheltie was in a like position and they had both turned their efforts to helping women who otherwise would not have access to investors, making it a friendly rivalry.

Belle had benefited from Charlotte's investment groups where she pooled women's funds to funnel into investments she handpicked, and had a sizeable fortune of her own.

Now Belle replied, "Ah, yes, the lovely Cheltenham. I still wish I had had a chance to sample those goods before he stupidly fell in love and stopped working his way through the Ton and the demi-monde."

Charlotte shuddered. Empirically, he was attractive, but he was a brother to her. "That reminds me, Leah

Godwin is due to visit next week with a new round of her flock's savings."

"Excellent. I'll join you." Belle had introduced Leah to Charlotte. Leah was a retired courtesan around forty years old, who maintained relationships with younger women in similar roles and taught them survival skills, including saving and investing—through Charlotte now.

The work was Charlotte's passion and was part of why she'd re-entered society. If it was just her future, she needn't worry or invest further. She needed a purpose again, not to mention showing up Cheltie, and to do that, she needed to keep up with the new innovations and investment opportunities.

"I almost wish this was one of Cheltie's you could attend, too." Charlotte said. She tilted her head, considering the opportunities at Cheltie's wilder fêtes. He had always dabbled in the more risqué underbelly of the Ton, his looks and wealth—and sheer maleness, she suspected—allowing him to get away with it. The attendees were likely to have as much wealth and knowledge as the more sedate Ton balls. Certainly when she was ready, she'd have better luck finding a suitable bed partner there who would not be looking for marriage and heirs.

"Even so, Cheltie's parties are not to be missed. I'll bet it can help you address both socializing and pleasure."

Charlotte again directed a quelling glare at her friend, which only resulted in laughter.

Chapter Three

Despite this being her second outing in a week, Charlotte was not prepared for how loud the ballroom was. The chatter of dozens of people, announcements of new arrivals, and clatter of dishes as servants replenished refreshments were underlaid by the chords of violins warming up.

She'd had tea with Cheltie and Althea before the guests arrived, but once the orchestra had come to set up, both hosts had to direct staff. The contrast between quiet conversation in their library and this made her head hurt. Only for her close friend would she venture into this chaos. Where was Cheltie, anyway?

She again bemoaned the social structure of a ball. Gaggles of débutantes quacked and ruffled their fan feathers at the edge of the floor, just as she had at that age. The girls peered at the eligible men, hoping to be asked to dance. Men huddled together on the other side of the room, some lustful, some hopeful, reflecting the scrutiny. Matrons gossiped and lounged in the background.

She sighed. Charles had found her and culled her from the herd; she'd hoped that would be her happily-ever-after. Widowed before thirty, Charlotte was too young and too childless to be a matron, and too old—and too wise—to be a débutante.

Feeling conspicuous as she always did at these events, she fiddled with the stylized heart pendant hanging on a delicate chain just below the hollow of her throat. Men did not have this issue. They spoke in groups of varying ages, clustered by political alliances, alma maters, or familial connections.

She watched the litter of would-be rakes, tossing their fashionably short curls back as they tried to outdo each other with tales of outlandishness. The one who had caught her eye at the first ball had been in such a group, standing long and lean, his narrow hips pulling her hands like a magnet. When he'd thrown back his head in laughter, his working neck muscles had called to her tongue. Shocked at her thoughts, she'd frozen, staring, until he turned and caught her.

Snapping out of her fantasy, Charles had come to mind and she'd fled, guilty tears clogging her throat. In the darkness of her carriage, the inappropriateness of her interest was apparent, and her guilt became tinged with self-directed anger. He was at least five years her junior, and he looked even younger than that.

Despite echoes of that anger, she scanned the rake puppies, trying to be a tad more circumspect in her search for the delectable young man, even as she tried to talk herself out of it. When she spied his profile, desire jolted her again, shocking her. His hair was the color of the peach roses in her garden, containing blonde, gold, and ginger highlights. Straight as straw, he wore it parted in the middle, and cut to shape around his ears, with sideburns. The fringe had a tendency to make parentheses on his forehead before he'd brush them back toward his hairline. His clothes were plain, dark colors with only the waistcoat being bright—tonight's was black and red paisley on a gold background—and fit him well. Her pulse leaped, but she managed to restrain herself from scanning down to view his hips from the front, along with whatever might be showing between them.

His hips? Really, Char? What business do you have ogling a man's hips at your first few balls without Charles? Much less on someone who probably hasn't reached his majority.

She blamed Belle. Her friend was outrageous, even to Charlotte's liberated mind. Charles used to say that Belle's views on sex were more progressive than most of his university friends'. But even Belle would not go so far as to leer at a callow youth, not even old enough to become a Member of Parliament. Or would she? Who was she kidding, Belle would be encouraging her to touch as well as look. Certainly, her friend would never have made it a year without intimate relations like Charlotte had. But until her first sighting of this gentleman, she hadn't missed it, her focus on losing Charles had been more emotional and intellectual, despite their fulfilling bedroom activities.

Oh la, he is pretty, though, she conceded.

She clenched her fists, moisture pooling in her mouth, as she fought to pull her gaze away.

He turned and froze as he caught her gawking again.

Turning her back to the group, she watched the doorway for Cheltie to come in from greeting guests.

Cheltie was over six feet tall, and she spotted him as soon as he entered the ballroom. Plucking a glass of champagne off a passing waiter's tray, he sipped and scanned the crowd. When his gaze landed on her, he grinned and plowed into the sea of clothing, perfume, feathers, and fans.

Unsurprisingly, he was stopped every few feet by a guest. In addition to being the host, Cheltie was perhaps the most easygoing and approachable earl she'd ever met, at least on the surface. Most did not realize that he allowed only a select few into his inner circle. It included his two closest friends from Oxford and her, and Charles once upon a time. In part, his walls remained up because he was one of the wealthiest men in the country. Hence their competition.

After long minutes, he was beside her, tugging on her hand for a finger squeeze.

"How are you faring?" he leaned in so she could hear him.

"I shall be fine." Perhaps if she said it, she could will it to be so. She pressed his hand before intertwining hers at her waist. "But I do appreciate you checking on me. Now go enjoy your fête."

"Never fear, I plan to. You know me, though. I like to ensure that everyone enjoys it. Even guests who are just dipping a toe back into the cesspool that is polite society." He said the last words in a mocking lilt.

"Hush." She shook her head at him with a smile. "Do I need to be wary of rooms upstairs or salacious invitations, or is this one of your tamer parties?"

"Define 'tame'…" Cheltie trailed off on a teasing note. "I'm joking. I would not have thrown you to the dogs in your first Season back without warning you."

His phrasing made her glance over to the cluster of men, especially the one from the last ball whose hair was one shade lighter of gold than her host's. To her surprise, the young man was almost to them.

"Stanton. Good to have you here. How is your family? Is your cousin with you?" Cheltie asked as the young man bowed.

"Yes," the stranger gestured behind him.

"Good, good. If you'll excuse me, Charlotte." Cheltie started to step toward the group of young men, jerking back when Stanton cleared his throat.

"Lord Cheltenham, would you be so kind as to introduce me to your lovely companion?"

"I beg your pardon. Of course."

Charlotte snickered at his quick agreement. Cheltie was always too casual for his own good, and his parties were likewise structured. It was no surprise when he shortcutted the introduction.

"Charlotte, may I present William Stanton, heir to the Earl of Harrington." He waved a hand and William bowed. "Stanton, Lady Peterborough. Now I must find the other Stanton for a moment, if you'll pardon me."

At her title, William's gaze shuttered. How odd.

As the earl rushed off, William bowed over her hand. "'Tis lovely to meet you, Lady Peterborough. My mother asked me to find you tonight, if possible."

Charlotte's brows rose in polite question, masking her disappointment that he was there on orders from his mother. How singularly disappointing when she was fighting physical attraction to him.

"Well, she bade me to find your husband, in truth. I understand our political views—"

He cut off when Charlotte choked and put a gloved hand to her mouth. Shocked, she could only stare at him in horror for a moment. She'd thought she'd done her mourning and was ready for any and all questions from the Ton. However, this felt like a horrible prank someone was playing, pretending Charles was alive, and it threw her.

"Lady Peterborough?"

"Is this a joke?" she hissed.

"Not at all. Why do you ask such a thing?" He tilted his head with a small frown.

The young pup must not know the Ton gossip or the Parliamentary players. Or perhaps his mother was not up on such things. Regardless, she found herself on the edge of tears again and stepped back. "I'm afraid you'll have trouble getting answers from my husband. Charles died over a year ago. Now, if you'll pardon me."

His mouth opened and closed but no sound emerged.

Charlotte did not wait for him to decide how to proceed. She twirled and strode toward the terrace, scaling the steps to the garden to find a dark corner and compose herself. After a breath of cool evening air, the stab of sorrow turned to anger. How dare the young pup. Did he not understand the rules and protocols of social interactions? And what on earth had she been thinking, allowing herself to feel an attraction.

Playing it back in her head, she realized he must have thought she was the current countess. Damn Cheltie and his casual approach to all things. If he'd introduced her with her full title, the Dowager Countess of Peterborough, this would not have happened.

On the other hand, the term "dowager" made her feel twenty years older than she was. Until the last hour, she had hated when people used her formal title.

She laughed. There was just no winning with her.

Had William obtained clarification? She supposed she owed him an apology for her brusque retort. Hmph. His visage had created the first stirrings of sexual desire she'd felt in over a year, but up close his youth was even more apparent. She'd be surprised if he had completed his university studies. Given her inappropriate attraction, she should just stay away.

* * * *

A shoe scraped on stone. Then a thud and rustling of leaves.

She dared a quick glance along the path. His persistence alone should cure her of her infatuation. After all, she liked to be in control. Yet, her lips curved in a small smile when she saw him.

William—why was she thinking of him by his first name?—had spied her around a bend in the walk and now hurdled a low group of bushes. Barreling to a halt with his shoes almost touching her dancing slippers, he gave a shallow bow. "Please, Lady Peterborough, allow me to apologize for my faux pas."

He must have asked their host or someone for clarification. She shook her head, admitting, "'Twas not your misstep. Frankly, it was Cheltie's, and I plan to tell him that next time I see him. He tends to be lax on protocol, if you aren't aware."

"I wasn't. But I am duly warned now, thank you, my lady. However, my approach was rather more abrupt than it should have been. I am still learning—" He choked on his words.

She suspected his cheeks would have heightened color if she could see them.

"May I sit with you for a minute? Please?" he begged.

Not wanting to be found here with him in case it was construed as a liaison, she vacillated. As she owed him an apology and perhaps assistance in finding Edward, the current Earl of Peterborough, she gestured beside her.

"Thank you." He sat closer than polite manners allowed, his left thigh trapping the edge of her skirt.

She caught her breath at his proximity, inhaling spiced rum and the garden. Was that him or a flower? She again had the intense desire to lick his throat and find out.

Inappropriate, Char! "Lord Stanton—"

"William, please, my lady."

She nodded. Permission for his name was helpful as she had almost called him that a second ago.

"William, as you seem to know now, I am the Dowager Countess. My brother-in-law Edward is the new earl. However, he and his lovely bride Sophia prefer to avoid London when they can. As you referenced politics, it may help you to know that he sends his votes through his friend the Earl of Suffolk. Nicholas is also Sophia's cousin."

"It is a pleasure to properly meet you, Lady Peterborough." He paused.

He was hoping for reciprocal permission to address her by her first name. Knowing she needed to keep all proprieties between them to remind her how inappropriate her body was acting, she waited him out.

He continued, "Thank you for the context. I shall have to see if Lord Suffolk is here tonight and arrange an introduction."

She expelled a tiny sigh and dropped her shoulders. When he made no move to rise or return to the party, she capitulated and offered her own amends. "William, we've discussed Cheltie's and your error in etiquette but not mine."

He went to speak, but she raised a hand.

"My response to your innocent inquiry was unnecessarily harsh, and I apologize. Whilst this is one of my first social events since Charles's passing, I should not have attended if I was not ready to be polite."

"Lady Peterborough…" He held his hand out as though asking to hold hers.

Did he not recall formal etiquette? There could be no handholding between them. Ack, he might not have learned it yet given his youth. Well, this she could handle. She glanced down at it, then pointedly back up at his face.

Dropping his hand between them, further pinning her skirts, he did not seem to realize that it brushed her thigh.

The audacity of the puppy! Straightening her spine an inch, she raised her brows at him.

"No apology is needed, to my mind. However, if you feel it necessary, my response is that allowing me to sit and bask in your beauty erases all memories of faux pas from my thoughts." He smiled, leaning in.

She snorted, ignoring the spurt of pleasure in her chest to shake her head side to side. "Oh, please. Try that on someone your own age." Had she thought him audacious? Impertinent was more like it.

"I beg your pardon, my lady. I was being truthful. I could stare at you all night." His hair flopped onto his forehead again, as he leaned toward her.

Charlotte remained silent, staring at him and trying to ignore the thump of her heart and spurt of heat between her legs. Nor did she want to catalogue the pull of his jacket over his muscled shoulder and biceps as he twisted, or the strain of his breeches around powerful thighs. His eyes were deep pools of liquid darkness, his lips plush and parted.

He moved his hand on the bench an inch, the pinky pressing against her then retracting. "May I…may I hold your hand please, Lady Peterborough?"

The impact radiated down to her toes, curling them in her slippers, and up, tightening her nipples and bringing heat to her cheeks.

Oh my, he is potent.

Belle's wager came to mind. Of course, her first challenge had been to re-enter society and renew the friendships she'd ignored the prior year. In one of her darker moments, Charlotte had bemoaned her belief that she'd never find another man who fit the needs that Charles had introduced to her, and Belle had promptly bet she'd find someone to pass a miniature bondage test within a year.

She did not answer William, instead turning her head away with another snort.

Her skirts loosened and she caught his hand lifting out of the corner of her eye.

Snap. She smacked his knuckles with her folded fan. Impertinent *and* audacious, she amended her earlier thoughts. At least she wasn't the only one being inappropriate this evening.

"Lord Stanton. You do not have permission to touch me."

"Lady Peterborough. 'Tis William please." He rushed on, "You have my apology. Will you forgive me? Please?"

She gave a small sniff, still fighting with her conscience over Belle's suggestion. Did she dare?

His next question answered that. "How may I make it up to you?"

At his words, the devil in her reared its head,

overriding her conscience. She'd been lonely this past year and a half. While Belle insisted that she could meet someone who fit her sexually, she was not so sure.

Belle had pointed out that she had not had, or at least known of, her own inclinations when she'd married. Belle ought to know, as she had been the one to train Charlotte at Charles's request.

She'd met him at a musical soirée at some earl's home. The performance, given by the earl's daughters, was terrible, and they had both chosen to linger at the back of the room near the punch bowl. From that evening on, he had wooed her with art and music dates, with offers of books and scientific presentations. They shared a quest for knowledge and culture, and she had quickly fallen in love.

Their first months of marriage were as expected. She ran the household and helped with correspondence, he managed the earldom and all its holdings and participated in the House of Lords. She found their bedroom activities nice, albeit not quite as exciting as the romantic novels she occasionally read had intimated. Her experience also did not quite match with her friends' newlywed tidbits, either. But she was happy, and Charles was the kindest, most loving and encouraging partner she could ask for.

Until he came to her with a request. Would she be so kind as to visit with someone from his past? Someone who might help them find more excitement in the bedroom. He confessed that he wanted her to take the lead in their intimate relations, he loved feeling as though he was doing exactly what a woman wanted. But as a new wife, she might not have the repertoire to draw from that would benefit them both. And while he could tell her what *he* liked, he preferred to attend to what *she* liked. A woman's perspective might help.

He assured her that his relationship with Isabella had ended before he met Charlotte, and that she was a good person, courtesan or not. Charlotte was intrigued and curious. Thus, Charlotte's sex education began, and now here she was, contemplating something wild and foolish. Of course, her little test would not work on such a bold and brash young man, but it could be a good rehearsal for when she met someone who might suit.

The breeze shifted, and his scent floated to her. Tempered sweetness of spiced rum with something else she couldn't name after being alone so long. No matter, it was delicious.

She tilted her head and ran her gaze up and down his form, her pulse racing. Lingering for a moment on his lap, she licked her lips before forcing herself to continue searching. Her gaze settled on his neck, before raising to his.

"Remove your cravat."

"Charlo—Lady Peterborough?"

"You heard me. And you do not have permission to use my given name. It is Lady Peterborough. Or—" she sucked in a breath, trying not to pant as she attempted to rein in her inner devil. But it had slipped its lead and was running wild. "—Mistress P."

His eyes bulged and his throat moved on a swallow. He lifted his hands hesitantly to his cravat.

Gracious, he was actually following her command. She'd been sure his reaction would be insulted dismissal, or worse, laughter. Another hot wave of arousal washed over her.

Undoing the pin and knot, he slid the cravat from

around his neck to hold it across his lap. "What now, Mistress P?"

"You may make amends by keeping your hands to yourself, and I shall help you do that." Charlotte reached over and slid one end of the cravat through his loose hold. She pulled it from under his hands to his wrists, crossed the two ends, and raised his hands using the linen.

He shifted and opened his mouth as though to protest.

She glared at him through her lashes. "Hold still."

With his hands between them, she leaned forward an inch and wrapped the ends under his wrists, around to the top, and under again. As he watched, mouth open, she tied the ends into a loose double knot over the wrapping, well out of reach of his thumbs. It would take him a minute or two to figure out that she had left it loose enough for him to bend one hand and get his fingers to the knot to pick at it.

Still amazed at his willingness to sit still for her ministrations, she schooled her features. All of this open-mindedness could simply be lack of maturity. However, she could still take her fun. Before she straightened, her inner devil—she liked to think it had Belle's voice—made her lean in further, closing that gap, to brush her breasts against his knuckles, inhaling his scent again.

He jerked. "Lady-Mistress P?" he asked, his voice a croak.

Ah, youth.

"Just testing that you have learned not to grab people without permission." She smirked.

"Absolutely, Mistress P." He was gasping.

Her inner devil preened. She'd not been allowed out in so long, she was enjoying this tiny show of power.

"Er, now that you have me at your mercy, what will you do with me?" The upward lilt of the question sounded hopeful.

"Remind you to play with children your own age." Charlotte winced internally. Harsh, but she deemed it necessary. The young pup apparently had trouble reading more subtle signs. She ignored her conscience telling her she needed the reminder of their age gap as much as he did. Standing, she shook out her gown and leaned over him.

He held her stare, unblinking.

She gave him credit for keeping his eyes on her face, as she knew the pose offered a tantalizing glimpse of her cleavage.

"Good night, Lord Stanton. Sweet dreams."

His eyes widened as she turned. Her skirts swished as she sauntered out of sight along the path to find her carriage. She might be ready to handle these balls after all.

Chapter Four

William stared at his bound hands, replaying his conversation with the woman who had given him leave to address her as Mistress P.

She was magnificent. From her parting comments, she seemed to think she was too old for him, but he doubted more than a handful of years separated them. He probably wasn't the best judge, particularly as her beauty had eclipsed all thought of age. Her flawless skin was unbroken by wrinkles, her hair held no gray. Beyond that, her bold fathomless eyes held him captive. Her gown was a deep bronze with a square cut neckline and puff sleeves, both trimmed in ivory. A shade darker than her hair and eyes, in low light it might appear brown until she moved and the light caught the amber sheen. Even if she was older than he guessed, he cared not a whit for what society thought.

Now, though, he had a name and a correct title, and he could pursue her, convince her that society's stupid rules did not matter. He'd never chased a girl before, never saw the point. Now, he did; he was beginning to understand why his comrades at Oxford were always looking for a new conquest, and why Nate spent so much time conjuring accoutrements to extend pleasure. All from one conversation.

Well, and this. He smiled down at his crumpled cravat. The memory of her breasts brushing his knuckles made him squirm. He'd gone hard as soon as his hand had hit her skirt on the bench, as soon as her décolletage raised and lowered with her breath, as soon as he'd stared into her dark eyes that matched her dress. He'd stayed that way throughout their conversation. The whisper of her gloved hands on his thigh when she grabbed the cravat had made him throb in his breeches and catch his breath. Then with the brush of her breasts, she'd given him a tiny taste of their lush softness.

He groaned aloud, then flicked a quick glance around to check no one was near. He'd have the devil of a time explaining being trussed with his own cravat.

Testing the binding, he twisted a hand. Deciding to expedite matters, he raised his wrists and worried the knot with his teeth. It came apart easily, which he was certain she had planned. He sighed, refusing to analyze whether he was disappointed or relieved.

"Stanton? Will?"

"Over here." He threw his cravat around his neck as his cousin strolled the path.

"What—? Who were you out here with?" Percy asked, examining his untied neckcloth.

"A gentleman never tells." He grinned.

"You do realize 'twould not be a simple matter to wed before your majority, right? You also have another year of university." Percy eyed him.

"Yes, yes. I'm not barmy." He added under his breath, "Just too young for everything, apparently."

"Right, then. Best be careful who you waylay in gardens then. If you compromise some deb, there will be a whole host of problems to deal with that neither you nor your mama want right now."

William nodded. His cousin was trying to help. "I understand. You know I'm not looking for marriage for the foreseeable future. I'll take care."

"Come, then. I want you to meet another MP."

He trailed after his cousin, pausing when they hit the circle of light from the house to have Percy check how terribly he'd retied his cravat.

An hour and several important negotiations on bills currently in the House of Commons later, the Earl of Cheltenham found him.

Leaning in, the host murmured, "I've just sent Percy to collect your father. The earl passed out in the smoking room and Percy and a footman are helping him to your carriage. He asked that you meet them out front."

Oh no. He hadn't anticipated the added burden of being responsible for his father as he attempted to navigate the business his father should have been handling. William's face flamed for the second time that night. "My lord, you have my apologies."

The earl swept his apology away with a hand. "Come now, young Stanton. You are not even through university yet. Your father is a grown man. If he can't handle himself, 'tis no one's fault but his own."

William nodded, gulping a breath.

"Perhaps next time you two younger Stantons will forget to show him the invitation, eh?" Cheltie said with a chuckle and a wink.

He managed a weak laugh before excusing himself to help get his father into their carriage.

Lying in bed later that night, the embarrassment faded, and the new names he had learned were overridden with thoughts of Charlotte…Mistress P.

He had so many questions. Why truss him and then leave? Having Nate as a friend meant he understood in theory that some people enjoyed being bound or binding their partners. Was that her preference, or was this just to reprimand him for wanting to touch her? Given that his cock had been hard until the cravat was undone, long minutes after she'd left, was it his preference? He did not have enough experience to know for sure, but he was willing to try it.

While he'd never before pursued a woman, Percy being four years older and William's attendance at several stifling balls meant he'd observed some of the mating rituals. However, after their interaction in the garden, he suspected those might not work with Charlotte.

He'd simply have to find his own path.

* * * *

No balls were scheduled for the following night, and William escaped to meet South and Nate for drinks at Nate's neighborhood pub. They planned to go to a gaming hell after that.

He threw himself onto the bench next to South and reached for an ale they'd already ordered for him.

"Rough day, chap?" Nate asked.

"Well, I wasn't standing over a fire trying to bend metal to my will for hours on end, Folly, but yes." It was his standard answer, an attempt to recognize that Nate's job was harder than his on any day.

"Ah, but I love what I do. Can you say the same?"

"I like parts, and I think I'd like it more if it were fully mine so I could enjoy the fruits of my labor. 'Tis all a bit overwhelming at the moment."

"Eh, time enough for that, old man." South clapped him on the shoulder and waved his own drink. "Now's the time to enjoy life. I can't wait to show you the new spot I've found. The serving wenches are practically in chemises."

Nate's steady gaze encouraged William to expound, despite South's dismissiveness.

"Right now, I am cleaning up a giant mess that I didn't make, having to drag my drunken father out of balls, and trying to keep Emily out of trouble—"

"Emily?" Nate's voice was sharp. "She's barely seventeen, what trouble can she get into?"

"Shall I mention the most recent prank of filling Father's pipe with weeds and lighting it to stink up the library—where I spend more time than he does? Or switching out the whisky with cold tea steeped to a matching color? I'm afraid to let her go on social calls with Mama, not that Mama has much time for that."

South was snickering, but Nate was frowning. "Does she not realize how much you already have to manage?"

"I'm trying to be patient. After all, I was up to no good with you two at that age, we were just away from home." William changed the subject, looking for ideas.

He was unwilling to share too much of his conversation with Charlotte. He wasn't looking to wed, but nor was she a possible casual conquest.

Deciding to keep it vague, he threw out, "I have a question. If you want to woo a lady—"

The other two hooted. South murmured, "About time."

He gave them a withering look and continued, "but cannot risk compromising her, how do you go about it?"

Nate leaned back. "Are we talking Ton or no?"

William's lips twisted. "Yes. And you know Mama requires that I finish university."

"I doubt I can help then, old man."

William leaned forward, intent. "I seem to recall you telling me once upon a time that a woman is a woman is a woman. Even if she was not Ton, if you could not risk discovery, how would you approach it?"

South interjected, "I'm confused. If you are trying to avoid wedded bliss until after Oxford, aren't you simply looking for a tup?"

Nate pointed at him and nodded. "Fair question."

"First, this is a theoretical question." The other two snickered, but he ignored them and continued, "And can't a man woo without it leading to marriage banns in short order? Do you not want to ensure you are compatible before you get leg-shackled for the rest of your life?"

South responded. "You and your puritanical views of marriage. Most of the Ton ignores the 'for life' bit, chap."

"You get my meaning." William waved a dismissive hand.

"The romance novels often have the man risking life and limb to get to the girl. Like climbing trellises or trees to her bedroom window." Nate threw in.

South skewed a side glance at him. "And you know this why?"

"Research." Nate grinned.

All three broke into laughter and clinked their beer glasses in a toast.

Did Charlotte have a handy tree or trellis by her chamber? He'd won time with her through boldness once, why not again?

* * * *

The following afternoon, after a few discreet inquiries, William stared at a slip of paper noting Charlotte's address.

After her gentle setdown, he daren't be too forward. Instead, he scribbled a note and sent a calling card requesting permission to call upon her. With a grin, he addressed it to "Mistress P" and signed it "Your humble servant, William Stanton."

The footman returned promptly with a response which read, "I hoped you'd learned to play with children your own age."

Having anticipated such an answer, he had a reply waiting. His beyond-forward behavior could hopefully be attributed to the brashness of youth or not knowing all of society's rules. "No, but your parting wish came true. You gave me very sweet dreams. I politely requested permission and I did not see a "no" in your reply, thus I look forward to seeing you in an hour."

Directing the servant to inform Charlotte that he was out on the Town and not available for a response, he strolled to his club to count the interminable seconds until the appropriate time to call.

Her townhome was also within walking distance of the club, which aided an inconspicuous arrival. He slowed his steps as he ascended her front stairs. Despite his bravado in writing, he was uncertain of his welcome, and cognizant of the ubiquitous rumor mill centered in Mayfair. While his reputation could withstand a black mark, women were judged more harshly. However, nothing would dissuade him from pursuing this never-before-felt interest sparked by her. Her serenity, her standoffishness, and her independence were Sirens to his

Odysseus.

As he neared the door, it opened. A butler gestured him in, taking his hat, coat, and gloves before showing him into the parlor.

"Thank you, Austin. Please ask the kitchen to bring tea," Charlotte stood across the room several feet from a front-facing window, as though she might be trying to hide the fact that she'd watched his arrival. Her rose gown matched the accents in the primarily-blue room. "And I am not at home to other callers."

William caught Austin's arm give a slight jerk, but he inclined his head and his voice was as calm as a pond on a windless day. "Of course, milady."

She turned to him. "Lord—"

"Ah. We'd established that it's William, please." He grinned at her, too happy to worry about possible chastisements. He added cheekily, "'Tis lovely to see you, Mistress P."

She narrowed her eyes at him, her lips pressed together, as he approached.

When she did not offer her hand, he bowed, having learned his lesson to not touch without permission, at least for the time being.

"As we—and by we, I mean I—am on a first name basis, I feel it is acceptable for me to ask this. How old are you, William?"

"Does that mean I may ask you the same question?"

She shook her head slowly in the negative, then arched a brow.

Steps approached in the hall, and he gestured to the seating area with a tilt of his head.

Charlotte walked past the silver and blue patterned settee to lower herself into a plush navy chair with a sigh.

He bounced to the edge of the settee closest to her.

After she poured and passed his tea, she sipped hers and stared at him.

"Thank you for receiving me." Suddenly shy, he was at a loss for conversation topics. He'd rather hoped she'd take control as she had in the garden.

"I asked you a question, William."

"I am nine-and-ten, Mistress." He'd be twenty within a sennight, but felt no need to prevaricate about his age.

Shaking her head once, she set her teacup on the low table between them, nudging aside a book. She clasped her hands in her lap and narrowed her gaze at him to reinforce her next words. "Just as I suspected. You are years away from reaching your majority. You have no business being here. For heaven's sake, if you are in university, which I hope you are, you have no business calling on any woman, least of all a widow nearly a decade your senior."

"May I ask why you hope I attend university?"

"Really?" She glared at him. "That is what you took from my words?"

"I understood the others. This, I'd like clarification on. If it pleases you, Mistress."

She sucked in a breath.

Ah, she liked that. Was her reaction to the moniker or the pleasing her part? He'd have to test that.

"I hesitate to explain as so often it is a waste of breath. Men do not comprehend the privilege of being able to attend an institution of higher learning. There are no such opportunities for women who desire to learn beyond tutors or whatever schooling they are allowed. Every youth who is accepted and has the funds should not only attend university, they should also pursue that education with their entire focus."

Her vehemence took his breath. Her thoughts were similar to his mother's, which is why Mama had fought hard to ensure they had the funds. "What about those who pursue it but then use it to further persecute women?"

She slashed a hand. "There will always be those who do so, whether out of fear or tradition or ignorance. But the more we can educate people—ideally, men *and* women one day—the more we eradicate at least two of those, and establish a new tradition."

"I agree. That is a tenet held by my whole family, in fact, which is why I asked you for your reason."

She deflated on a sigh. "You do?"

"Yes, Mistress." He smiled. "Except for the part about me not having any business being here."

"That is not for you to say, young man. My house means my rules. Do your parents know you are here?"

He almost rolled his eyes. Her intimation that he was still a child was her putting up walls, but he ignored it as he had her note. "No. However, I know you shan't mention it to them."

"What makes you say that?"

"First, you do not move in the same circles, or I would have met you before now. And trust me, I would remember the most beautiful woman I have ever seen." He grinned, and she blushed. "And second, ratting on me would show less maturity than even my tender years, and give me the advantage. I have the feeling you would not like that."

"Don't be so sure—about the circles. Anyway, the point is moot." Her voice turned frosty. "From today forward, I will not be at home to you. I shan't have rumors flying about me entertaining a man-child, nor do I wish to tarnish your reputation when you'll have need of it in a few years."

"Mistress, please. I simply want to talk to you. I apologize for causing any risk to your reputation." Begging, he searched for what would delay the inevitable and recalled a phrase that had sparked her interest the night in the garden. "How may I make it up to you?"

She sucked a breath, and his hopes soared as he tucked away the knowledge of the opening in her armor. She lifted a hand to a delicate gold pendant at her throat.

Then she dashed those hopes, shaking her head and rising. "There is too much risk to both of us. Now, if you please."

He was dismissed.

In the hall, the butler fetched his outer garments. William lingered, hoping Charlotte would leave the parlor and he might determine which side of the house held her room.

Finally, he was forced to depart without her appearing, but made sure to check both sides of the house for trees and trellises, seeing options along both walls. The trick with his Mistress seemed to be balancing boldness and supplication. If he could get to her bedroom, he could supplicate, implore, and outright plead.

Chapter Five

With no social commitments that evening, Charlotte sent a note round to Isabella to see if she was entertaining or if Charlotte could come by. She needed a sounding board regarding her underage would-be rake dilemma, even if she wasn't sure she could define the issue. And even if she worried Belle's reaction would be unadulterated enthusiasm.

Given Belle's over-developed sensibilities regarding Charlotte's reputation, her reply was not a surprise, requesting that Charlotte set an extra place for supper.

As their meal was served and wine poured, Belle asked about Cheltie's ball. "Are they becoming more comfortable?"

"No, and I managed to embarrass myself and a young man."

"That sounds promising." Belle arched a dark brow.

Charlotte described the botched introduction, her trick with William's cravat, and his subsequent note and visit.

By the end of her recitation, Belle was leaning forward open-mouthed in her seat, elbow on the table so her palm could support her chin while the other hand held her wineglass.

"Tell me how can I help. Or…do you not need any

help? Is there a rake slithering down the trellis as we speak?" Belle arched a brow.

"I would not call him a rake. Perhaps a rake-in-training. He is very young. Younger than I remember any gentlemen at balls. Upon reflection, I do not know how he came to be there. Another reason I need to call on a few people. I am quite out of touch with all the Ton gossip."

"Ohh…how young? This is delicious." Belle leaned forward, nearly putting her left breast in her potatoes.

"Nine-and-ten. I asked him today." She braced herself for the reaction she knew was coming. Belle was as predictable in her outrageousness as Charlotte was in her circumspection.

"And he pursued you and called you beautiful? Gracious, that is perfect. A young rake-in-the-making. So trainable. So biddable. And the enthusiasm and stamina at that age." Her eyes rolled back in her head as though at a memory.

"Belle. That would be totally inappropriate. It would also interfere with any chance of finding another partner like Charles, who I could share a life with. He's the son of an earl, which also means he needs heirs." Her lips flattened in a grimace.

"Ohh, which earl?"

"His surname is Stanton. I think Cheltie said…Harrington?" She should have asked Belle about him as soon as she arrived. Her friend was an excellent source of information.

"Now I understand." Belle's lips twisted. "Lord Harrington has spent more time in his cups than sober for the past decade. William's cousin has recently stepped in to help with the estate."

"Yes. Percy, I believe. He was there."

"'Tis likely William is learning the trade so to speak."

Charlotte was thinking of her own earl. What would Charles think? Her fingertips caressed the heart at her throat again, a gift he'd given her with the endearment, "My heart is yours to keep." She pursed her lips as she considered the matter. Her kind and devoted husband would tell her to find love again. He would support whatever she wanted, just as she would have for him. But what did she want? Not a young lord who would need heirs one day, she'd already failed on that count. She imagined how different her life would be if she'd given Charles children. No, what she wanted was companionship but independence. Charles was a rare breed, allowing her to take the lead on a number of subjects, including investments, and helping her learn subjects not available to most women.

The Ton, however, was another matter. She knew exactly what they'd think if she even looked twice at a man a year younger than her, much less a decade. The gossip would not be kind.

Belle disagreed. "Hmph. You must recall all the on-dits from when you socialized. Everyone is doing everyone, no one cares. I know you aren't looking for marriage, and while I maintain the lack of children in your marriage may not have been your fault, I understand your concern. However, there is no reason not to enjoy the vigor of youth in the meantime. You have far more to offer him than those simpering misses who only want to be married and would not know a cock if it was waved under their nose."

Charlotte gave a reluctant bark of laughter, before

shaking her head. "Your test to judge someone's predisposition toward my—" She glanced toward the footman by the door. "—preferences did not work."

"I beg to differ. It seems to have worked quite well from what you've just told me about the rakelet. *So delicious!*" Belle sat back, mock-fanning herself with her hand.

"Belle! Stop it. I meant to dissuade him."

Her friend straightened in her chair and put her glass down, her smile fading. "Char, all joking aside, what I am hearing is that he was open to being tied, willing to call you Mistress, bold enough to pursue to a point, and has an innate understanding that you need to take it from there. How is that not everything you want?"

"He is barely more than half my age."

"You were his age when you married Charles."

Charlotte clamped her mouth shut. She hadn't thought of that. William seemed so young. Had her husband seen her the same way? How difficult it must have been for him when he'd been looking for someone to take charge. She shook her head. "You know it's different for women, at least in the Ton's eyes."

After letting Charlotte contemplate that comparison for a long silent moment, Belle added, "As I said, I'm not pushing you to wed him. Only to tup him."

Charlotte broke down in laughter, meeting Belle's glass with her own in a giggling toast to that idea, even if she daren't follow through on it.

"When and what is your next sojourn?" Belle asked.

"The salon. A talk on a new industry. I think the smaller group will help me renew acquaintances better and be less distracted. I've had enough of feeling like an oddity at balls for a bit."

Her friend always had to have the last word. "Distracted by rakelets. I can't wait for the next ball. This is better than a play."

* * * *

Charlotte surveyed the small group. When Belle had pushed her to re-enter society, she sent notes to the couples that she and Charles had spent the most time with. Several of them had responded, inviting her to call upon them. The hosts of tonight's event had sent an invitation to tonight's gathering.

In addition to being more confident she'd know people here, she also enjoyed the lack of a ball's marriage mart ambiance. Here, no matter how many people she did or did not talk to, she would get to learn something new.

Tonight's lecture featured a speaker about the steam engine locomotive invented up near Leeds a few years ago. Science was not her strength—she'd much rather read poetry—but this was an opportunity to re-engage her brain in learning new things with others similarly inclined, and research possible investments. The steam locomotives had already proven invaluable to northern commerce, and she wanted to ascertain the appropriateness and safety for ships. This could mean the difference between back-breaking labor—and labor on their backs for some—and the ability to stop working at a reasonable age for a number of women in her and Leah's investment pools.

Her hair, too long for the current trend, was pinned up in curls again to try to replicate the currently popular shorter looks. It was uncomfortable, but the gathering would not last as long as a ball, so she'd make do. Her gown this evening was a mint green with rose embroidery. She was still getting used to evening gowns again with their lower décolletage, and her hand kept inching up to trace her collarbone and Charles's pendant.

Already feeling exposed, she shivered, her skin pebbling, although there was no draft. She glanced around and found eager chocolate puppy eyes staring at her from a corner. She refused to believe that she had sensed him, instead telling herself a chill had made her nipples perk up. Frowning at him, she then smoothed her brow and looked forward again, moving away from the door to find a seat.

Another friend waved at her from across the room and turned to point her out to his wife. Charlotte returned the greeting and started toward them. They were drawn into conversation by other guests then, and she diverted to a row of empty chairs.

Spiced rum heralded William's arrival beside her.

"Mistress P, may I take this seat?"

"You already have—and that form of address is not suitable in public, Lord Stanton."

"My apologies, my lady. I dared to sit here because I cannot believe such a setting will risk your reputation."

She stared ahead.

He continued, unfazed by her silence. "What prompts your interest in steam power?"

Surprise flickered through her. He assumed she was here for the content, the learning.

"I am considering investing." She waited for the inevitable question about her solicitor handling such things, but it never came.

Instead, he asked, "What do you think of the locomotive line then?"

"It sounds like an efficient way to get coal from the

mines to the towns in the area, one less weather dependent than the roads. It makes me wonder what else could be transported thusly, if the railway lines were expanded." She had discussed this with her brother-in-law months ago, as Peterborough was well-placed to benefit from such an expansion.

"I agree. I should like to hear your thoughts after the talk." He changed the subject. "I noticed you were reading Homer the other afternoon. Are you enjoying him?"

She shot him a sharp look. He was very observant. Threading the needle in not taking her note as a "no" had proven that, and his comment now reinforced it. He was also bold to reference his call when she'd admonished him about the risks. She should discourage such behavior, but a kernel of excitement ignited in her; it had been too long since she had discussed intellectual pursuits with someone like-minded. "Oh, yes. The layers of Telemachus coming of age, Penelope's perseverance, and Odysseus's travels and trials are excellent."

"Was it perhaps Calypso enjoying holding Odysseus her captive?"

Oh, mmm. At that image, her cheeks heated and she glanced away from him. A different sort of warmth low in her belly made her want to squirm.

He raised his hand to skim her bare arm above her glove for a millisecond before returning it to his lap.

Her head snapped around, and she glared at him, saying under her breath, "Did you not learn your lesson about touching people without permission?"

He grinned, responding at a similar volume. "I beg your pardon, *Mistress*. You should smack my knuckles with your fan."

Deciding to accept his apology for that delicious image alone, she simply replied, "Sadly, I do not have a fan."

"Right. Well, then, you shall simply owe me one." A dimple formed as he gave her a cheeky lopsided grin and a wink. "Of the non-deity characters, whom do you like the best?"

"Hmm. Not really fair, as you likely know I would have said Calypso or Athena…"

He nodded, still grinning.

She considered the question. "I think Odysseus's opportunity to travel and see the world makes me envy him a bit. But ultimately, the women, including Penelope, seem stronger than the men, do they not?"

"I agree. I was glad you had found it, as I thought it might suit. Do many countesses read Homer then? I wouldn't have thought so."

She snorted. "Honestly, I'd have no way of knowing, but I doubt it."

"Yet you chose it. And you're here learning about steam engines. With only a handful of other women."

His comment drew her gaze around the room, making her realize the women were quite outnumbered. She'd never noticed or cared when she had come with Charles, but now felt conspicuous. Thankful it was a small crowd, which included more people she knew than the ball had, she shrugged.

"I admire that."

Gracious, the puppy eyes were back, and they were affecting her. Heat bloomed in her belly as she recalled the last time he had looked at her that earnestly, and she shifted on her chair.

Just then, the host came to the front of the room to

introduce the guest speaker, and to remind everyone that there would be refreshments served afterward.

Needing to nip the rakelet's pursuit in the bud and get a grip on her own interest, she managed to slip out when the gathering broke for refreshments.

Chapter Six

The following night over a solitary dinner eaten at her desk, Charlotte reviewed her notes from the articles she had read on steam powered locomotives to compare them to her notes from the salon. She was fascinated by this particular invention, but still struggled with the science.

Might William share his learnings from university with her, as Charles had?

Gracious. She had no business wondering if he would share education with her. They were not going to spend enough time together for him to do that. Besides, he likely hadn't even taken classes that would allow him to explain the science to her, he was so young.

Forcing herself to concentrate on the documents, she put William from her mind. Soon, however, the diagrams and her scribbled notes with arrows were replaced by visions of hands, slender with youth, ensnared in a cravat. That eager gaze, staring up at her as she leaned over. Her nipples hardened, and she shifted on her chair, tilting her hips as though to grind herself against the wooden seat. For a moment she allowed herself to imagine straddling those slim hips, rubbing up and down the hard length between them, building a delicious friction for her and—*No.*

She refocused on learning the new technology, only to begin the daydream again.

Giving up, she abandoned the remains of her meal and took her wine with her upstairs. After changing for bed and fluffing the pillows, she lay down and opened Homer. In her first few months of widowhood, lying in their shared bed had been unbearable, and she'd taken to lounging in a chair and reading. These past months, she'd changed the furniture and bedding, enabling her to sleep better, although she still read for as long as the candelabra by her bed would allow, or until she fell asleep with her book on her, whichever came first.

She could not immerse herself in Odysseus's quest tonight, however. Even the calming neutral shades of taupe and white, echoed on the walls, curtains, bed linens and upholstery of the two Chippendale armchairs did not soothe her. William's challenges regarding the tale remained forefront in her mind. Her forearm tingled from the ghost of his touch.

Shifting, she sat with two pillows behind her and legs extended. She tried lying on her side, the book on the bed beside her. Then sat again, legs bent with the book propped on them, then back to her side.

Her nightrail shifted against her skin, chafing her belly and puckering her nipples. Instead of the paper, she felt hair as fine as silk, gold shot with cream, and saw wrists wrapped in snowy linen, with a mouth-watering bulge in the lap below them.

Gah!

She rolled over to her back, abandoning the book. She stared at the canopy of her bed, but still saw William's face. His wide eyes as he stared at her, trying to assimilate why she had tied his wrists. She'd been dying to ask how long he'd taken to extricate himself from the cravat bond.

Her devilish imagination conjured him contorting his fingers to reach the knot, it tightening a hair, and him drawing in a breath of worry. Considering how he would explain it to his friends if he could not undo it. Now his wrists a bit reddened from twisting back and forth to move it closer to his hands. His fingers reaching again, those long, aristocratic, pale fingers with the neatly trimmed nails. How they'd feel inside her.

Stop! He's too young for you. She threw one arm across her eyes as though to block the images.

Has he ever even had sex before? She groaned. That thought definitely did not help. Now she could imagine introducing him to all the joys of sex, that eager gaze absorbing everything.

Not since Charles was alive had her body sung this much. Her rare self-induced orgasms were foothills compared to the mountain of this onslaught of desire. Her body had fully awakened—for a rakelet, no less.

Why this completely unsuitable young man could breach her walls and test her control, she could not fathom. Alone in her room, she was too tired to fight it. She rolled to her stomach then rolled back with a sigh. The best way to alleviate this was self-pleasure. It would not take long tonight, at least.

Sitting, she drew her nightrail up and over her head before lying back. Propping her feet on the bed, she spread them wide.

She pinched her nipple with one hand and slid the other down her belly to pet her nether lips, smoothing over them a few times before parting them to dip in to the wetness created from her daydreams.

Giving in entirely, she pictured William, cravatless, unlacing his shirt to show a firmly muscled chest. Hands still tied, they dropped to the fall of his breeches, peeling them away from his cock as it sprang free, pointing right at her as it dripped with readiness.

Moaning under her breath, she gathered her moisture on a finger and dragged it up to the tight bundle of nerves just above to make slow circles. She arched a bit as pleasure zinged through her. It had been a year since feeling like this. Lord, she missed Charles. Her hand stilled at the thought. But her body was too primed, it needed release.

She rubbed, dipping in to wet her finger every few strokes. Her flesh swelled and heated under her touch, becoming more sensitive. She imagined Charles's face between her thighs, waiting for her permission to lick and suck. When she closed her eyes, though, she gasped. William's face had replaced her husband's in the vision, dark eyes eager as ever. Mouth agape, panting, hot breath against her sensitive flesh.

She conjured his spiced rum deliciousness layered over the thick scent of her arousal. Her eyes slid open, head turning as her hips bucked and her orgasm built beneath her hand. Imagined he was there in the window frame, silhouetted against the darkness, front lit from her candles. His gaze roamed her naked form end to end, silently begging.

She murmured, "Watch and learn, rakelet."

His response was to scramble over the windowsill.

* * * *

What in the world? Conjured images were not that uncoordinated, nor did they make that much noise. He almost fell on his face getting over the casing.

Sitting up, she grabbed one of her many pillows and held it in front of her. Her embarrassment at being caught performing such an act was tempered by her fury at him invading her privacy. This was beyond bold, even for him.

Belle's voice whispered in her head, "You invited him in."

Ignoring it, she focused on the fact that he should never have been at her window to begin with. "Lord Stanton! What do you think you are doing?"

"'Tis William." He grinned at her unapologetically. "I'm obeying your command, Mistress P. Watching and learning. Please proceed."

Oh no. He was not the one who would give orders in this bedroom. Nor would she be swayed by his pretty words like "please" and "obey." He'd climbed the trellis just as Belle had imagined and was in her bedroom! The audacity, the rudeness—he wanted to watch? A lingering spurt of arousal shot through her at the idea.

He continued to stare at her from where he'd frozen a few feet in from the window.

Did he like what he saw?

Focus, Char. You have a strange man in your bedroom.

Yes, but he obeys orders, at least sometimes.

She clicked her teeth together. He needed to obey the rules of civility. She snapped, "Turn around."

He whirled.

Ignoring the skip of her heart at his alacrity in obeying that command, she reached for her nightrail and tugged it over her head.

Gnashing her teeth, she needed to send him away. Her anger ebbed, replaced by mortification. He'd not only seen her near-decade-older body naked, this near-stranger had witnessed her self-pleasure. No matter how satisfied she was with her looks, and how beautiful he said he found her, she looked quite different than girls his age. Grasping at her anger again, she whisper-yelled, "Get out! How dare you climb into my bedroom without permission."

He turned back, his mouth turning down when he saw she was covered. "Mistress. Your statement implied consent, as I was struggling to see enough to learn from there. Would it help if you tied me again, so I do not disobey…?"

Still fighting the burst of pleasure from his inability to look away, she was undone. His words evoked images that shoved the last of her anger and embarrassment aside. Heat flared in her, igniting her sex again, nipples hardening to stiff points.

Oh God, him tied close enough to watch but not allowed to touch.

William must have noticed her reaction, as he stepped forward and asked, "Mistress, pray continue so that I may learn. Please?"

No. 'Twas a terrible idea. She stood, drew her loosely braided hair out of her clothing, and pulled her wrapper around her.

"I think not. Now, tell me what you're doing here—" She held up a hand as he started to speak. "And I do not mean watching and learning. Why did you come here and in such a clandestine manner?"

"I wanted to see you. I could not bear to wait until I happened upon you at another ball. And my circumstances do not allow me much time to make social calls, nor did you permit them."

"Yet you thought I'd permit *this*?" She growled her question in a near-shout as she glared at him.

"I hoped. I beg your pardon, Mistress." His grin tilted further on one side, a sly twinkle entering his gaze. "How may I make it up to you?"

Unh. How had he discovered her weakness so quickly and easily? The rakelet was shrewd as well as brave.

She opened her mouth to command that he leave but could not form the words.

His eyes glinted. "You are gorgeous. Naked or clothed."

She gasped at his continued daring. One did not mention a lady's nudity, no matter what the circumstance, but just like the garden at the ball, his admiration gave her pause.

He seemed to take her silence as encouragement. "I would very much appreciate you continuing to teach me how to behave the way you'd like. Perhaps if you tie me again, then I cannot get myself into more trouble. I would sit quietly. And I could…watch and learn." He bit his lip, his expression shy yet confident.

The tethered lip and image of him tied were her undoing. Her fingers twitched with the urge to grab his wrists. Her nipples pebbled. The idea of educating someone to her tastes was nigh on irresistible. It had been so long. And Charles had already known what he wanted; the education had been hers. This magnificent young man was not even fully aware of what he was asking for.

His gaze flicked down to the hard tips poking through her thin clothing, then back up, tilting his head. "Please, Mistress? It shall be our secret?"

She clenched her fists, fighting her desire. But she'd already primed the pump imagining herself as Calypso holding him captive. Not to mention stroking herself while she imagined his naked form.

He grabbed a chair from the two-person seating area by the fireplace and dragged it around to face the foot of the bed. Sitting, he laid his hands on his knees. "Teach me? I love to learn."

The dratted rakelet had somehow landed on the perfect thing to say. Her conscience was swept away on her next breath. She stood and stepped to her dresser. Wrenching the top drawer open, she pawed through it roughly. Yanking out a colorful scarf, she tossed it on the floor, hopeful. But she did not wear many scarves. She frowned, thinking, then side-stepped to jerk open another drawer, withdrawing gossamer sheer stockings.

Eager to see his reaction, she turned to him with an arched brow. They were going to do this on her terms. She'd use her anger to torment him in punishment for his uninvited visit.

"Mistress?" His throat moved as he gulped.

Good. He was nervous. He should have thought of that before he pushed so hard. She liked keeping a man off-balance.

"Quiet, lordling." Her voice was clipped.

"Right. I can be quiet, I promise. But won't you talk to me, to help me learn, please?"

She bit back a smile at his nervous chatter as she considered his request. "I am angry at myself as well as you, if you must know. You are too young, or I am too old, to be sneaking around for any reason, especially sex."

"Is there a better reason to sneak?" he asked with a

cheeky grin.

"Said with the solitary focus of youth," she muttered under her breath.

He shrugged, his smile unwavering.

"William," she said with a withering glare. "I will gag you if you are not quiet."

His eyebrows rose.

Interesting. His face portrayed curiosity rather than fear. Liquid heat gathered between her thighs at the possibilities open to her.

He pressed his lips together, showing his willingness to follow orders.

She approached him, leaning over to tie one hand to the carved wooden arm of the chair, before moving to the other. Her shyness gone, she embraced the fantasy turned reality. Her pulse pounded in her chest, behind her ears, between her legs. Ah, the pleasure of subduing a partner to have her way with him. There was nothing like it. Wetness seeped down one leg.

She could smell her own arousal—could he? Could he even identify the scent at such a tender age? No, she would not think of that now. He'd pushed her beyond her control, but he was old enough to know better.

As she leaned in, he inhaled. His gaze dropped when the neckline of her nightrail did, and his breath gusted out over the tops of her breasts.

She shivered once, and arched her back to push her breasts toward him before she could stop herself. He glanced up as she licked her lips and mimicked her motion. He was testing her, just as she tested him.

Kneeling to tie his ankles to the front chair legs, she deliberately blew over the bulge between his legs and his hips jerked. His head fell back, eyes dropping closed for a moment before he gathered himself and bent his neck to watch her again.

She considered his ties and the growing bulge in his trousers, then untied his hands from the chair, retying them together in his lap. Standing, she turned away and checked the mirror. She'd been correct. His cock was in an uncomfortable position and he was furtively adjusting himself to get relief in the confines of his clothes.

He glanced up and caught her watching him. He sighed, smiling, and said, "Thank you, Mistress."

She nodded as she removed her wrapper to recline against the pillows on the bed, her legs outstretched.

He opened his mouth to speak.

She frowned at him, wagging a finger to remind him of her threat of a gag.

Subsiding, he licked his lips and leaned forward, looking hopeful.

She drew her nightrail partway up her legs. Her nipples still poked through. He might even be able to see the shadow of rose against cream. Perhaps she should have lit another few candles. For a first lesson, this was enough, she decided, and raised a hand to tweak her nipple.

First *lesson, Char?*

She shook off the thought and slid her other hand under the edge of the nightrail, keeping the bottom hem draped between her thighs, not allowing him to see her womanly folds.

His gaze followed every finger bend, every muscle twitch in her wrist, trying to ascertain her movements. His tongue flicked out to wet his lips again, and she imagined it in lieu of her fingers parting her nether lips. He gave a stifled moan and pressed the heel of one of his bound hands against the iron rod now straight under his clothes.

Knowing he was unbearably aroused at the sight of her touching herself sent a hot lick of fire through Charlotte. Her head arched back and she slowed her circles of her nub to ensure she would not embarrass herself and end this almost before she'd started it.

He moved his hand away, then back.

Her hips bucked without conscious thought.

His eyes glinted with the knowledge that touching his cock affected her, and he focused on her wrist moving in circles with the nightrail caught on it.

She breathed through her nose, trying not to pant, her chest rising and falling against the fingers twisting her nipple.

He licked his lips again and she thought she might go over. Lud, the lordling had not even removed his cravat. She froze, groaning.

He grinned and undid a button on his trousers, his fingers shaking and his breathing erratic.

"No." Her voice was an octave lower, but firm. If he showed her his cock, she might swallow it whole without even asking permission. "You may not touch yourself unless I tell you to. Only over the clothes. And you may not climax."

"Mistress, please. May I at least see you, to better learn what you like?" he dared to ask.

Her hips jerked upward again. He was right. What had brought him into the room were her words, "watch and learn," and his continued requests had ended with him bound at the foot of her bed. Why was she holding back on this last step?

She tugged the nightrail up the last few inches,

showing him her pale hand against a thatch of hair a few shades darker than that on her head, and the swollen, wet folds of her sex, open between her legs.

He stared, leaning back.

Concerned he was uncomfortable at the sight or smell, she observed him. He was uncomfortable, all right—due to the length and hardness of his cock. He clenched his fist around it through his trousers like a club, as though he was going to jerk himself, but instead squeezed hard, cinching his eyes. They flew open instantly, focused on her finger circling her most sensitive flesh.

She dipped her finger inside, then roughened her pace. Almost scrubbing now, sparks igniting from fingertips to toes, she stared at him, almost wishing he was free to see what he'd do, if he knew his way around a woman's body. It had been so long since she climaxed at someone else's hands. But this, this was close enough that she'd take it, use it for weeks after tonight. She imagined his breath on her skin, his hands where hers were, and all her muscles tightened, straining toward the cliff of ecstasy, higher than she'd had in years. She slipped two fingers inside her channel, moving her thumb to press her nub, as her inner muscles rippled with the beginnings of an explosion.

At the sight, he clutched his cock with both hands and shouted, "Mistress…!"

That was the last straw. She curled around her hand, scrunching her stomach muscles. Her swollen flesh pulsed around her fingers and thumb, on and on. Gasping, she kept her eyes trained on him as she thrust her fingers in and out to prolong the pleasure.

He attempted to stand, forgetting he was tied to the

chair, and nearly fell. Another pulse roared through her at the vision of his fall aligning his mouth to her sex to lick her clean. Groaning, she slammed her eyes shut, trying to catch her breath. The last image she saw was him falling back in his chair gripping his cock again.

Chapter Seven

Holy hell, that was the most alluring thing he'd ever seen.

When she'd let him stay, William was beyond excited.

Grateful for his friend's suggestion of trellis climbing, he'd watched the downstairs fall dark, and one room brighten upstairs, and found a conveniently located trellis to just below her window. He'd expected to beg for a future audience if she didn't throw him out. Instead, he'd seen a montage he'd never forget—with his moniker on her lips. Using that to his advantage, he had prodded and perhaps even goaded her into allowing him to stay. He was learning to read her reactions, her eyes blazing when he referenced learning or making amends.

He almost burst his trousers when she tied him to a chair and allowed him to watch as she restarted what she'd been doing when he'd first seen her through the casement. This was beyond all expectations and more fun than he'd ever had in his life. He hoped she'd allow him out a door, as he might break his cock trying to shimmy down the tree.

Then he'd pushed to see more, despite the risk of countering her demand that he not spend. Moisture oozed out of her rosy, glistening folds, and her whole sex was swollen and dark, much as his cock felt. He'd nearly come in his trousers for the first time in his life, only to find that touching himself heightened her pleasure as much as she did for him.

From there, it was a race to the finish. He could not take it all in fast enough.

Her fingers disappearing inside her caused another spurt of pre-ejaculate to seep through his smallclothes, a damp patch forming on the fabric over the head of his frustrated cock.

Gads! Don't come. Don't come. My horse. The family estate. Our finances.

Falling back onto the armchair after watching her convulse around her fingers, he clenched and unclenched his fists, not daring to even squeeze his cock now. It was delicious, inspiring torture to observe and not be allowed to touch.

When her fingers slid out of her channel, wetness seeped out behind them.

He swallowed back the saliva pooling in his mouth from wishing he could taste her wetness. He chanted, "Don't come, don't come," under his breath and waited for her direction with the wild hope that she would not leave him in this torturous state.

Her eyes reopened, and she blinked to focus on him. Her words were slow, but she managed to ask, "Are you all right?"

"Define all right," he gritted out through a clenched jaw.

"Are the bindings too tight? Or did you hurt yourself trying to rise?"

"'Tis the trousers that are too tight. Or my skin. There is only one part of me in pain."

She raised her eyebrows.

He replayed their exchange and corrected himself, adding, "Mistress."

Swinging her legs around, she knelt up on the bed facing him, her nightrail falling back into place.

Interesting. Gone was the angry, embarrassed woman he had negotiated with when he first arrived. He made a mental note that orgasms did wonders for her confidence, as well they should.

"Your self-control was exemplary. You deserve a reward. You may touch yourself now." Her command sounded almost regal.

Ah, gads, she was a scant few inches away now, although not quite within touching distance given his bindings. As he considered her beauty, he wrenched at the buttons of his fall, grunting, and one button pinged across her floor.

"Go slow. I want to see what you have there."

He stifled a groan. Go slow, after that show? Ah, she wanted him to give her a taste of what she'd done for him. She was a master of this. He was learning, all right.

Carefully, he drew his cock out. Afraid his control was at its end and it would explode from a mere touch, he held the base by one finger and thumb as it leaked onto his lap.

She stared, angling her head one way then the other, blinking rapidly.

He daren't ask what she thought, daren't say anything, although if he did it might be to beg permission to put himself out of his misery.

Looking down he tried to see it through her eyes. A dark rose, the crown was swollen into high definition. He was proud of its length, as the boys at boarding school had measured and he often won.

She swallowed and said, "Mmm. You are nicely formed. Your cock is quite handsome. You know, you did not compliment me."

He was indignant, despite his cock pulsing at her reference to it. "That is not fair, Mistress, you said I could not speak!"

She laughed. "Oh, all right, then. If you are going to finally claim obedience."

His lips twisted.

Apparently, someone *is more relaxed now.*

Wanting to ensure she had no reason to reject him, he gasped out, "Mistress, I told you, you are the most beautiful woman I've ever seen. That was reinforced by watching you just now. Thank you for allowing me. For teaching me."

She nodded, her expression unreadable. "You are welcome."

He panted, still holding his pulsing cock, his fingers and lap wet with his pre-ejaculate.

"Right. Now let me see what you want to do next." She sat back on her heels.

He grabbed the base of his cock, the other hand half holding the fall of his trousers open, half cupping his balls. Sliding his fist up to gather more moisture, he turned his wrist at the top, circling the head to spread the liquid and smooth the friction of his hand. His hips surged reflexively, and he gasped. He repeated the motion, gaining speed with each pass.

If she did not allow him to climax soon, it would be out of both of their hands and he'd earn another punishment.

"William, I want to see you come, just as you saw

me. Here, let me help."

Hellfire, if she helps, I might lose consciousness with this orgasm. He gulped.

Charlotte whipped off her nightrail and knelt up, cupping her breasts.

His eyes nearly rolled back as he took in her creamy, rose-tipped breasts and the small mound of her belly above the flare of her hips. Heat shot up his spine and rolled in his bollocks.

He gasped out, "Mistress. Yes. Thank you."

Then she shot him into heaven. Swiping a finger along her wetness, she leaned forward and ran it along his lower lip, saying, "Show me. Can you smell my arousal? Do you want to taste me?"

As she pushed her finger into his mouth and said, "Suck," he came. And came and came.

Thick white liquid spurted up, hitting her breasts, and belly, falling across the bed, the floor and his lap. He was surprised—and relieved—it did not end up in her hair.

His hand had been almost still, his hips thrusting through his fist rather than the other way around. Now, his eyes slid closed as his bottom eased down to the chair. He continued to suckle her finger, not wanting to lose the connection.

She tugged her hand away after a moment, and his eyes opened to catch her licking her lips, nipples hard again.

If he begged, she might let him taste her without the need for fingers. "Mistress, may I—"

He lost his train of thought when she swiped through a dollop of his seed on her breast and brought it to her lips, sucking in that same finger that had been in his mouth.

He gasped and his cock pulsed, when a moment ago he'd have sworn he'd emptied it so completely it would take days to recover.

At his breath, her eyes flew to his then lowered, pink tingeing her cheeks.

"Mistress. Thank you for the lesson. Perhaps I might practice—"

"No." She stood to grab a cloth from the dresser to swipe at herself before drawing her nightrail and wrap as though they were armor. Then she untied him, touching him as little as possible and not leaning as close as when she'd secured his bonds.

Taking a few steps back, she folded her hands across her waist. "Part of me wants to beg your pardon, as I feel I took advantage of your youth. But you were eager enough I won't, especially as I suspect it will offend you. However, you must go. Do not, I pray, come back, via that method or any other."

He'd expected that, but it still hurt to hear. Nevertheless, he had no intention of obeying that particular command. His mind still full of white cotton, a buzzing in his ears—probably from lack of blood— William used the chair arms to stand and righted his clothing as best he could. He could not build a coherent argument to see her again, still recovering from the most intense sexual pleasure of his life. He gave her a wordless bow and slid out the window.

But this was not over.

* * * *

Several days later, William surfaced from trying to make sense of his father's haphazard investments and recordkeeping. Settling into his favorite spot at White's to try to unwind, he waved a lackadaisical hand to one of the servers. Knowing South would find him when he arrived, he sat back and sipped whisky when it was delivered, contemplating the various sides of Charlotte he'd seen to date.

As had happened since his late-night visit to her bedroom, his cock thumped and hardened as he remembered his education at her hands. He had replayed every second, every breath since that night every chance he had, most often while stroking his cock to a climax that was a mere shadow of the original. The memory of her touching herself just out of reach, while he remained tethered, was what took him over the edge, rather than her watching him. Although…she'd *tasted* him.

He had never seen a woman's most private folds up close. Nor had he ever touched himself in front of anyone, and—*unh.* He shifted in his seat, trying to get comfortable and avoid anyone seeing the noticeable bulge in his trousers—certainly never coated a woman's skin with his essence. And her private moisture on her finger was the most delicious honey he'd ever sipped. His eyes threatened to roll back in his head at the memory, there in the crowded club.

South arrived, stopping to greet a group of earls in the middle of the room. "Will, d'you know your father is here?"

"He usually is." He shrugged. He didn't want to think about the older Stanton. This was supposed to be his time, after slogging through his father's mess all day.

"He is with that earl you mentioned."

"The one who hasn't responded to my inquiries about the last investment Father made with him?" He sighed. He could not even enjoy an evening with a friend any longer. He envied South's freedom. All the benefits of being heir to an earldom, none of the responsibilities yet.

"Give me a few minutes to go talk to them, will you?"

South nodded, already ordering a second drink. He wandered over to the group he'd greeted after pointing William to a separate alcove.

"Father."

"William. You remember—" His father's words were slurred.

"I do. My lord. I am glad to run into you here"—*not really*—"as I have not been able to reach you at your residence here in Town. I have not seen a quarterly review of the shipment we invested in.

"We?" The earl chuckled, flicking a speculative glance at his father. "I'm afraid my solicitor handles all that."

"Yes, well, he has not responded, eith—"

"Will, my boy. Gentlemen do not discuss money. 'Tis beneath us." He waved his drink and gestured for a new glass. "Come now, have a drink with us and we'll talk horses and politics like sane men."

William gritted his teeth. His father was quick enough to talk money when friends like this swindler were asking him to invest, no matter what the venue. But all he said was, "Might I call on you tomorrow, then?"

"Of course. Just send a note around, I'm not at all sure when I'll make it home from my mistress's."

The older men chortled, and William gave up, having no authority to force the issue. His hands fisted, he made his way back to their corner seats and waited for South to rejoin him.

After ordering yet another Scotch, South got a glimmer in his eye and asked, "How goes the wooing, my puritanical friend?"

William groaned.

"Any tupping? I haven't caught any rumors of compromising situations. I'm rather disappointed in you." South laughed at his own joke.

"No tupping."

"But wooing?" his friend persisted.

"Mmm. Working on my approach," he demurred. If it had simply been sex, he might have boasted a bit as they had in the past. But her brain, her interest in learning were almost as arousing as her intimate teachings. To find her taking notes at a scientific presentation and pondering investing, after seeing Homer on her bed, were layers he never expected nor searched for in a woman. But until he could work out how to balance that with his responsibilities at home and at Oxford, he did not have words to describe it to anyone.

"And 'tis one of the debs," South pondered, tapping his lips with a finger.

William snorted. "No."

"But you said Ton?"

"Guessing will give you something to do other than those ridiculous bets you get into too often."

South just laughed.

As his friend described some of the wilder bets on the books at his latest favorite gaming hell, William considered the juxtaposition. The silly débutantes from the balls he'd attended were shadows eclipsed by the sun of Mistress P. Not a one cared for anything beyond fripperies and snaring the 'right' husband. He wasn't sure all their brains combined could keep up with Mistress P's.

Or his mother's for that matter. Imagining his mother

and Mistress P conversing, he curved his lips in a wistful smile. *'Twould likely be more informational than a lecture.*

His lips flattened as he considered his mother's reaction to Charlotte being nine years older than him, even if he could overcome Charlotte's reluctance. Nevertheless, one indubitable fact remained. He desired Charlotte, Dowager Countess of Peterborough, and not just for what she could teach him in the bedroom.

He had no delusions that he would get her on his own terms, but how could he make her want him on any terms? There must be a way to create conditions desirable to her. He had a few data points—her wish to learn and her affinity for tying him.

He could work with those. Lifting his arm, he requested a pencil and paper.

Chapter Eight

Charlotte received a note the next morning. Scanning it, she gritted her teeth, frustrated at both him and herself for not expecting this. The scamp managed to ignore her directive not to call, respect her wishes to avoid attention by requesting to call outside visiting hours, pretend he was following up on the salon, yet still offer oblique references to his impertinent bedroom visit. She read it again.

Dear Mistress,
It was lovely to see you at the lecture. I wished to speak with you after to get your thoughts on the steam engine and whether you were considering investing, once you had heard more. But alas, I could not find you in the crowd. You did not even give me the opportunity to serve you a beverage. You know I don't mind being <u>tied down</u> by such service.
Would it be possible to call on you early in the day, perhaps for breakfast, or later in the evening around the time of our last encounter? Same location?
Please, Mistress, allow me to further our acquaintance and learn (about steam engines) before I go. I am begging you here, although I'd much prefer to plead my case in person. What can I

do to earn time with you?
I would like to assure you that I will wait for a reply,
but I confess I am impatient…
Your servant,
William

Charlotte snorted, then shook her head at the brash impulsiveness of youth. She needed to learn his situation to more effectively stop his ill-advised pursuit. *Of course 'tis infatuation, given his age. And not something I should encourage in any way.*

That decided, it was time to visit Isabella for some information. The woman's sources were unparalleled.

A few hours later, she was shown into Belle's parlor. Footsteps pattering down the stairs announced Belle's arrival.

Belle's skirts swished as she quickstepped to hug Charlotte, her custom musky rose perfume cocooning Charlotte in its sweet familiarity.

"Does this mean you've seen Rakelet again?" She should never have told Belle she'd adopted her nickname for William. "Tell me, tell me!"

A servant wheeled in a tray with tea and cakes, and Belle poured them both tea.

Charlotte sipped, before putting it down on the low table by her. Folding her hands in her lap, she took a deep breath. "He attended a salon about steam power and sat next to me."

Belle rolled her eyes at Charlotte's choice of evening pursuits, as she always had. But she quickly moved on. "And?"

"And he asked me about my interest in the subject, and whether I might be investing."

Belle arched a brow, as she too understood the

implications in that. "Quite enlightened of him, don't you think?"

"Yes." Charlotte sighed. "But it can't mean anything. He's a baby."

"Mmm. I'd wait until you see what is in his breeches to decide that." She laughed.

Charlotte's face flamed and she could not meet her friend's gaze.

Belle caught her breath, her laugh stalling, and stared with mouth still open when she saw Charlotte's flaming face.

"What?! When? How? Oh, dee-licious." She rubbed her hands together.

Darn my skin and tendency to blush. There's no avoiding it now. "He-well-I-he—"

"Really…? You don't say…" Belle drawled with a smirk, leaning back.

"If you must know, he crawled into my bedroom the other night."

Belle's eyes widened, her brows close to her hairline. "My word, rather brave for a 'baby,' no? Was this before or after the salon?"

"After."

"Let's see," Belle said, ticking each sentence off a finger as she summarized them. "You meet, whereupon you tie him up. Then you meet again at a lecture and he shows respect for your interest in learning. Then he pays a late-night impromptu visit via the window during which you apparently see his cock, which we'll get to in a minute. Do I have the salient points?"

"Well, yes. And we talked about Homer, and he sent me this letter." She passed it over. "But Belle, he's a puppy!"

The other woman held a finger up, head bent to scan the missive.

"My word. He references the cravat incident? Or did you bind him again in your bedroom?" She glanced up and smirked as Charlotte's face grew hotter.

"Oh, I cannot wait to hear this. But first—" she glanced down at the letter again. "He then asks—nay, begs—to earn time, only to turn around and tell you he's likely to misbehave?" She folded the letter and fanned herself with it. "I want him. If you decide not to keep him, can I have him? Pretty please?"

It was Charlotte's turn to roll her eyes. "Stop it. I am serious. I came because I need help, not to titillate you, for heaven's sake. Give me that!" She snatched the letter back mid-fan.

"Right. Sorry." A dimple flashing belied the apology. "How can I help, dear? Did you need me to loan you some leather restraints? Did you dispose of yours?"

Charlotte never thought she'd laugh at a sentence with those words, but a chuckle escaped her. "No, you ninny. He's a child—of an earl. I shan't corrupt him, and I shan't encourage his infatuation. I need to know how to get rid of him. To do that, it would help to know a bit more about him." She looked askance at the beautiful font of knowledge before her.

"I am happy to share what I know, but I must hear more about this window and cock incident, and there is no way I will encourage you to dismiss him. Aanndd…please do not refer to it as corruption. Expanding his horizons, maybe. Educating him, certainly. There is nothing corrupt between two willing participants."

Charlotte nodded, ceding the point about corruption.

That was something both women and Charles had always agreed on. However, that might not apply. "Since I've never discussed it with him, I'm not sure I can call him willing."

"He visited after you tied him up and then wrote asking for more when you did it again. I think between that and whatever happened with his cock-sighting, we can assume he was." The emphasis on the last few words indicated her friend was impatient with her prudishness.

She conceded that her worries over his age might have clouded her judgment on his willingness. Waving the folded note, she said, "I hope to avoid him until he returns to Oxford."

"But you don't plan to send a reply?"

"No."

"Mmm." Belle sipped her tea.

"What?" Charlotte narrowed her eyes at her friend. Noncommittal answers from Belle were never a good sign.

"Nothing."

"Belle, your 'mmms' are never nothing." She dipped her chin and looked at her friend from under her brows.

"Well, he is no doubt going to climb in your window again or find another way to see you privately if you do not provide a good alternative or order him to cease. As you are not offering either of those responses, I suspect you want to see what he does. Which leads me to ask— what happened in your bedroom?"

Charlotte gaped at her, her thoughts in chaos, rejecting Belle's statement. She wanted him to stop. Gracious, he was still in university. She wanted a partner to spend time with, but not marriage and certainly not pressure to produce children.

Recalling the cravat, the stockings, and his blatant invitation for more in his letter, she reeled.

Spend time tying and controlling, you mean. Perhaps you could do that with him.

Spend time gathering knowledge and learning the world, you mean. Perhaps he would do that with you.

The sinister voice in her head would not stop, and it still sounded like Belle, darn her. But the issue of heirs remained an unsurmountable barrier.

Her friend sipped her tea, sitting back.

Charlotte knew this game. Belle could outwait her. She sighed. Not ready to address the rest of what Belle had raised, she might as well share the humiliating circumstances of his visit.

"He, er, interrupted me."

Two lines appeared between Belle's brows. She tilted her head. "Interrupted you doing what?"

The heat of embarrassment again crept into Charlotte's cheeks. She whispered, "Touching myself."

"Touching—Oh!" Belle's head fell back, peals of laughter ringing as she held a hand to her stomach.

Charlotte glanced nervously at the open door of the parlor.

"Fabulous! I mean, what are the odds?"

"Careful, your penchant for gaming is showing." Charlotte's lips pressed together at her friend's enjoyment of an embarrassing moment.

"Seriously, Char. 'Tis not like you do that every night. Or do you?" Her friend paused her chuckles to peer at her.

Charlotte shook her head. "Of course not." She cocked her head. "Well, except this week."

Belle went off into cackles again.

"Enough, please."

"Only if you tell me the rest. What did you do?"

Charlotte sighed and gave in, outlining how she took control of the situation to bring them both to completion without sullying any purity he might have. "Belle, he hasn't even reached his majority. I could not..."

"You recall I told you the family may be in financial trouble?"

Charlotte considered William's question about her steam engine investment in a new light.

"Here is the best part—" Belle leaned in. "My sources tell me that his mother does much of the work to keep the estate in hand. You can see why he'd be willing to follow a strong woman, even in the bedroom." Her grin threatened to split her face.

Charlotte slumped. This might be harder than she thought.

* * * *

Three days later, Charlotte still had not found the proper words to keep the rakelet away. Each day, she'd sat down with the letter and a piece of foolscap and pen to reply, but ended up staring at the blank page for long minutes before giving up.

She suspected her subconscious was doing exactly what Belle thought it was, but she felt powerless to stop it. However, she kept her window casing closed and her clothes on, and read herself to sleep each night. She'd even begun bringing a glass of sherry up to drink while she read, in hopes it would help her sleep. Nothing worked.

Unlike the previous year, this summer had some warm days and nights. This day was particularly nice and she decided to enjoy the weather. Strolling the back garden, she hoped to find peace in the sun's warmth and the flowers' beauty.

Her book was tucked under one hand, but she was too distracted to read. She was frustrated at herself. Either she did not want him to come, in which case she should be able to write a note to that effect, or she wanted him to come and was upset because he hadn't. Neither scenario pleased her.

After several circles on the garden path, she sat on a stone bench and opened her book, determined not to let William disturb her further.

Only to bounce up when the butler stepped out to announce a visitor—Lord Stanton.

Bowing her head for a moment, she chastised herself. Her stalling had been her way of seeing him without admitting that she wanted to. "Show him out here, please, Austin."

"Good morning, Mistress. You look gorgeous in the sunlight, as you always do."

"William—I mean Lord Stanton."

"I found myself unable to wait for your reply to my note any longer. I do apologize, Mistress, for my lack of patience and for visiting unannounced. I happened to have an hour free and the weather was lovely enough that it was worth a stroll to see if I could catch you at home. How can I make it up to you?"

Her heart pounded at his deliberate insertion of her honorific, then again at his question. That phrase might be the death of her. Every time he said it, she ended up doing something naughty. Worse, she suspected he knew that and used it intentionally.

He did not wait for an answer, instead joining her in front of the bench. He gestured for her to sit.

She did, expecting him to sit by her as he did that first night.

Instead, he went to one knee before her on the stone path. That couldn't be comfortable, but a spurt of warmth flared in her belly at the sight of a young man in his prime on his knees before her.

Imagine what he could reach from there. With his hands…his lips…his tongue.

He brought his arm up and her heart panged. He held two books.

She sighed, refusing to consider whether relief or disappointment prompted her heavy exhale.

William seemed oblivious to her agitation and wild thoughts as he rested the books on his raised thigh.

"I come bearing gifts. I hope these shall help reinstate me in your good graces…?" His gaze beseeched her, all puppy cuteness.

She shifted her gaze to the books, avoiding his pleading look. Staring at them, she didn't see the titles at first. Instead, her brain rioted. Books had been favorite and frequent gifts between her and Charles. William's ability to hone in on her preferences so quickly once again astonished her. Were the books to gratify her? Or did he hope for ties or other discipline for his intrusion? Then an insidious thought.

Do I wish these to please me, or…?

He drew the lower one out—it was more of a handbound pamphlet—and held them side by side. "Have you read either of these?"

His question drew her away from her musings of reward versus punishment. She tilted her head and read the titles. *The Canterbury Tales* was bound in leather, and the pamphlet was *The Heroides (Epistulae*

Heroidum). She had heard of Ovid, but not that work. One of her salon friends, who was more a Bluestocking than she was, had raved about *The Canterbury Tales*, but she had not read either.

Shaking her head, she looked up at him. "No, William, I haven't. I should love to borrow either one, if I may?"

"Absolutely not, Mistress. These are for you to keep. As I said, gifts." He pushed them toward her.

"Oh, no. I couldn't…" She trailed off. Ladies did not accept expensive books from men who were courting, much less younger men they barely knew whom they were trying to discourage. Yet she wanted these desperately. Stroking the gold heart once, she struggled to resist, as she'd never thought to find another man who would give gifts tailored for the intellectual pursuits she loved.

He turned his head to one side then the other, making a show of scanning the garden.

She glanced around, trying to see what he was searching for.

"What society does not know will not hurt society," he said with a grin, laying them on the bench next to her, his arm brushing her skirted leg.

She sucked in a small breath, and he turned from the books to look at her, his face suddenly quite close. She licked dry lips, and his gaze followed the movement, heat flaring in his eyes.

Moving slowly, he pulled his arm away from the bench and books, trailing the back of it along her leg. Her nostrils flared as she sucked air, feeling unexpectedly lightheaded.

His eyelids lowered.

"Now, I shall ask again, Mistress. How else can I make up for my uninvited visit?"

Chapter Nine

William watched her intently, starting to recognize her subtle signs of arousal. He had never cared to learn those about a woman before.

Girls were available and willing, even eager, if he was interested, but his few early encounters had not excited him enough for him to pursue further trysts. He'd had a crush on a house mother once, but she was happily married, and he was rational enough even at fifteen to realize that it was in large part a combination of teenage lust and missing his mother. He had beaten it out of himself with his hand wrapped around his cock as many times as he could get away with in a group home. As had most of the boys, for that matter.

But this creature, this goddess, was a real, full-formed woman whom he could talk to and touch, and he was no longer a lad. He and Charlotte shared a number of interests, from reading everything they could to investing to running complex households and holdings. Their conversations were far more engaging than those with the half-formed simpering misses at balls. He had no idea how he'd find time around his responsibilities and his return to university after Michaelmas, but he yearned to get to know her better. Beyond that, he was wildly attracted to her like no one before, and wanted to learn everything she could teach him in the bedroom.

Now he watched her reaction to his signature question, noting her accelerated breathing, her wide eyes. Dropping his hand to his side, he inched his back knee closer and placed the other on the ground beside it to sit back on his haunches. His fingers rested close to her slipper, and he slid them over to play along the top of her foot.

Gasping, she straightened, her back arching a bit, drawing his gaze to the smooth mounds pushing at the scooped neckline of her periwinkle floral-patterned dress.

Her nipples poked through. They had not been like that when he first entered the garden. "Are you chilled, Mistress?"

"No."

Hmm. He brought up his favorite memory: her spread on the bed. Her nipples had been hard little points then too, making him suspect 'twas excitement rather than cold. He could work with that, especially as she had not yet dismissed him as he'd feared.

He grew bolder, snaking his fingers around her ankle below her skirt. She arched further, which had the added benefit of pushing her breasts at him, whether she was aware of the action or not.

"Mistress…" His voice rumbled out of him, full of gravel. He checked the windows of her home, glad she faced away from them. He would not want to embarrass her in front of her staff. If he had thought about it, he would guess she chose it for the angle of the sun, but he was beyond rational thought. He could only wait on her next move.

"William. You are barely more than half my age."

He scoffed at her blatant exaggeration. She'd have to be nearly forty to be twice as old as him, and he'd bet she wasn't yet close to thirty.

She narrowed her eyes at the sound he made and persisted. "This cannot continue. I very much appreciate your gifts. However, you must return to university. Enjoy your opportunity to learn all the fascinating facts you have access to that not everyone does. Take your time and savor your youth. Then meet a girl your own age, who can give you babies and be your partner."

"Mistress, if I may be so bold, I am not asking you to wed me. I simply want to spend time with you. Clothed or not, preferably both." His response was solemn; he meant every word. She was correct in her statement about Oxford, but he needed more time with her to explore her mind and provide a welcome focus other than his endless responsibilities at home.

Silent, she bit her lip, appearing torn.

"Please. We've only just met, however unconventional the circumstances. I should love to learn about your investments. In return, I could share more of my reading with you, beyond these?" He nodded to the books she pressed under one hand.

"If you only wished to discuss investments, you would not have climbed the trellis to my bedroom."

"I did not say I only wanted that, now, did I?" He smiled. "Let us just say I should love to learn from you, whatever you're willing to teach me."

Her inhale was audible, her nostrils flaring.

He shifted his hand on her ankle and knelt up to give his cock room in his breeches before it strangled itself.

His movement drew her gaze downward, and his cock leaped to be the focus of her attention. Stifling a moan, he reached for words. "Mistress, I am not above begging. Or whatever other appeasement you direct. And I could still use practice at implementing your teachings of the other night."

"Hmph." The sound she made was a cross between a sniff and a grunt.

He smiled.

"'Tis your choice. I am at your service."

She bit her lip.

"Read a bit of Chaucer. I'll return within a few days and we can discuss it. In return, I should like to hear your thoughts and plans on investing in the steam-powered ships, if I may?"

She nodded, as though unwilling to acquiesce vocally.

He'd take it as a win. Bowing over her hand, ungloved at home, he smoothed his thumb over the back of her hand, relishing the softness of her skin.

Brushing it with parted lips, he forced himself not to lick, to taste. Raising his head, he peered up at her, focusing on her lips. "'Twas our first kiss. May it not be our last."

She sucked in another breath as he stood to depart, a promising sign if ever there was one.

* * * *

William arrived at Charlotte's house at the same time two afternoons later, after observing etiquette and sending a note first asking to call.

In a slate-colored dress so dark the folds of her skirt shone navy, she poured tea in the parlor.

He noted the tiniest of tremors as she did and hoped it was a sign of excitement rather than nerves.

He sat back, slinging an ankle across his other knee.

His confidence rose when he caught her glance down to his lap exposed by the wide-legged pose.

"Shall we discuss Chaucer?" Not one to waste an opportunity, he shifted to draw her attention to his body again, then picked an imaginary piece of lint off his breeches, perilously close to his groin. Flicking a glance up at her through his lashes, he verified that she'd followed the motion. Stifling a grin, he kept his face neutral as he raised his head to wait for her answer.

Charlotte sighed. "William, please behave, or this arrangement will end."

"Mistress, if you'd be kind enough as to point out my transgression, I shall remedy it immediately." He could not help provoking her and barely refrained from laughing outright.

She sent him a withering look, pressing her lips together.

He tried another tack. "Perhaps we can focus our discussion of behavior about this summer?" *For now*, his inner voice added, and he jolted, surprised at that thought. "You yourself pointed out that I could learn from you. I would value that very much."

Charlotte froze, not blinking, the ghost of her words to him when she thought him a dream echoing in the silent room.

He chose then to search for another imaginary loose thread. As he was remembering the same thing she was, his breeches were a little tighter as he picked at the fabric, ostensibly flicking off lint.

"William, we cannot. 'Tis not appropriate."

"Mistress, no one need know. Just think about it, please? There are other things we can learn from one another in the meantime. Chaucer and steam engines and the like."

At that she sat back. "I cannot attend lectures with you. I will not be seen being squired about by a youthful future earl. 'Twould not be fair to you."

Hmm. Not fair to me, or she does not want to be seen with me?

The extent of what men could get away with, without harm to their reputation, always amazed him. His father was a prime example.

Negotiating, he countered, "I am amenable to meeting there, just as we did at the last one. I am starved for intelligent conversation about something other than my family's estate management."

He wasn't. His mother could discuss almost any subject, and he'd had to debate Chaucer ad nauseum at Oxford. However, his end goal of getting time with Charlotte justified the exaggeration.

She chewed on her lip, which he was learning was the sign of nerves or, dare he hoped, temptation.

"I confess I am dying to know what you think of the Wife of Bath…" He gave her another nudge.

Her eyes flared.

His hand drifted to her cheek, his thumb tugging on her lower lip again. "As well as who and what you chew on, should the need arise."

Her breath caught, and he swore her tongue flicked the tiniest riff against his thumb.

Chapter Ten

Charlotte craved intellectual conversation more than anything. Well, almost anything.

She had attended several salons even before the Season began, as London remained a haven for intellectual pursuits even in the height of summer and cold of winter. When she'd attended with Charles, they would evaluate the presentations, weighing the pros and cons or facts and theories over sherry before retiring that night. Sometimes that discussion would continue the next day, or prompt them to read more about the topic. She missed her husband in a myriad of ways. His citrus-woodsy scent, his fingers feathering over her arm or through her hair, the rumble of his voice under her cheek as she lay in the curve of his arm. But the partnership of conversation, particularly the encouragement to learn more and ask questions, that was what she missed most.

This student with eager eyes was dangling it before her, as though she was the dog and it was a favored treat, if only she'd roll over. *Or roll him over*, Belle's voice snorted in her head again.

Charlotte closed her eyes. That was a mistake. An image arose of William across from her in the armchairs in her bedroom, books in both their laps, arguing, his tone earnest as he tried to make his point and please her.

Belle's words about enjoying the vigor of youth volleyed with her desire to learn Latin and somehow coalesced. She knew before she opened her eyes that she was going to give in.

Dratted, beautiful, earnest rakelet. "What do you propose then?"

He sat up straighter, his wide grin splitting his face. "Mistress, I thought we might alternate conversations about books with reviews of lecture topics as they arise? I can call upon you most afternoons about this time if your days allow, but only for a short while. I spend my mornings managing estate business, and most evenings at the club for Lords meetings. Or I can come by late at night after the club, and we'd have more time. And 'twould be more private, which you seem to prefer…?"

She flashed him a sideways glance, suspicious of his motives.

His face was again the picture of innocence, puppy eyes unblinking.

Perhaps too innocent, but she was too practical not to see the merit in his second alternative. "Fine, yes. Late night might be best. I may need a bit to adapt as I am rather more a morning person than your average lady of the Ton."

"Certainly, Mistress. You just say the word when you are tired, and I shall be happy to tuck you into bed." The dimple appeared with his sly grin.

"William…" Her voice was a warning. "There will be no such talk, or this arrangement will end, do you understand?"

"My apologies, Mistress. I shall try very hard to behave. Your beauty will make that challenging. Might you punish me instead of ending the arrangement, at least the first time or two…?"

"Stop that." She framed it as an order, leaving off the "please."

"Yes, Mistress. I shall be by tonight, then."

"Right. The household will be ready for you, so please use the front door this time." She sighed, hoping she had the self-control to manage this relationship the way she ought.

She lasted an hour reviewing requests for capital from women trying to establish their own businesses before she gave up and settled into her favorite chair with Chaucer. She grew more and more excited as she made notes about each tale she read. But while her mind might race at the concept of intellectual stimulation, her body warmed with the knowledge that this was the most dangerous kind of foreplay with a young man she was already physically attracted to.

* * * *

Several nights later, they had covered several of Chaucer's characters, the Squire's Tale, the Prioress's Tale, the Knight's Tale, and had moved on to the more sordid characters, the Reeve and the Wife of Bath.

Inevitably, Charlotte had strong opinions about the Wife of Bath and was amused to see William had prepared for them. He posed arguments. Was she amoral, or a product of her time and circumstance? Was her deepest desire to submit, despite dominating her first husbands?

He seemed to enjoy taking whichever side she did not in these discussions, and she used that opportunity to learn how he processed information. Her suspicion was that he intended such, as it mimicked the Socratic method of teaching used at Oxford.

She had to clench her thighs to stop from squirming in her seat during the discussion of submission and domination.

William's reaction did not help matters. He surreptitiously adjusted his trousers when she was rereading a passage, then shifted his feet wider from his seat on his chair to allow more room for his swollen cock and bollocks. His breathing accelerated.

Their setting exacerbated her agitation. Because it was late, and he'd already breached etiquette to go to her room, she'd chosen to have their discussions in the sitting area there. That way, no servants would have to stay up to douse the fire in a downstairs parlor. It was the height of impropriety, but she leaned toward expeditious rather than righteous now she was a widow and therefore less interesting for gossip than a countess.

Her chest rose and fell in time to his, and the muslin of her plain chemise rubbed against her taut nipples. She flicked glances at his lap when she thought he wasn't looking, remembering the shape and size of his member. His words as he bussed her hand echoed in her head, and she licked her lips at the idea of a more passionate kiss.

His chocolate eyes found hers, his expression tight with something that resembled hunger.

Agitated, she shot to her feet and stretched. While it was earlier than prior evenings had ended, he had always taken that gesture as his cue to depart.

When he grumbled a near-silent groan, she glanced over at him. Glad for the layers of her garments that might hide the hard points of her breasts, she stared at him, willing him to leave. She needed him to go, not moan. Every night it was harder to sit across from him and admire his mind and his form while trying not to yield to temptation.

He stood. He'd shed his jacket and cravat earlier and was in shirtsleeves and his waistcoat. He did nothing to conceal the prominent bulge in his trousers. Keeping his hands loose at his sides, he waited.

Charlotte's gaze lingered on his cock for a second too long. Gulping, she turned away, unable to dismiss him. She stroked the pendant at her collarbone, a nervous habit, but even that reminder could not bring forth her voice.

As she'd known he would, William took it as permission to see how far she'd allow him to go. His voice husky, he offered, "Allow me to help you disrobe, Mistress. No need to call your lady's maid when I am here."

He was behind her, panting hard enough that the fallen wisps of hair from her updo gusted on her neck.

She shivered, her nipples hardening further. Her blood thumped in her chest and lower, between her thighs.

He raised his hands slowly to her shoulders. Gliding them across her exposed collarbone, he slid them up over her hair, careful not to catch it.

She sucked in a breath and bowed her head an inch, unable to find the words to stop him.

His fingers made careful forays for hairpins, easing each out as they encountered it. Her hair tumbled to her shoulders, and he leaned in to inhale.

Her heart thundered in her chest. What did she want? Could she find it within her to stop him? Her brain was not sure what she wanted, but her body was certain. Her skin itched for his touch, her fingers curled from the need to stroke him—his chest, his hair, his cock.

He combed his fingers through her hair to check for missed pins before moving to the fastenings at the back of her gown. His swallow was audible as he paused with his hands at her neck. "Mistress, may I?"

Her knees went weak, not because he asked permission, but because he knew enough to do so. Infernal intelligent rakelet.

She bowed her head forward, all the nod her conscience would allow.

She sensed as much as felt his lurch of surprise. His fingers shook as they seized the buttons and fabric and separated them, smoothing down the exposed skin to the next until he met the chemise and stays and she could not feel them against her.

He continued until the dress gaped from her shoulders, then returned to the stays. He seemed to be evaluating them, moving his fingers back and forth.

She pursed her lips. Could this be the first time he'd encountered them? The girls she assumed he'd played with at university or in brothels or the like might not wear them. The thought should give her pause to reflect on his youth. Instead, it thrilled her, more liquid heat shooting through her and pooling in her core.

Gracious, had the other night been the first time he'd seen a woman fully naked?

He'd likely not had a lot of privacy for any sexual play in the past, so clothing might have stayed on. More fire sparked, and she swallowed against the urge to take over.

She waited in silence, not wanting to embarrass him. He'd ask if he needed help.

He smoothed his hands down her sides, fingers wrapping a fraction of an inch below her breasts. Then he planted one hand against her back, and the other tugged on the ribbons. When they came apart after a few jerks, his sigh gusted over the back of her neck.

She grinned even as she shivered from the sensation.

Loosening the stays, he held them in one hand. With the other, he reached through the opening and pulled the gathers of her chemise away from her back, then rubbed where they'd pressed.

The gesture was comforting. Familiar. In a heartbeat Charlotte was in the past, Charles standing behind her, a teeny bit shorter, the angle different, but dropping her dress to the floor, then her stays, then pausing to smooth the creases in her skin from her chemise with tender, loving fingers. Her knees almost buckled beneath her anew as the grief struck.

William brought his hands to her shoulders as she gasped in a breath in an attempt to avoid crying.

Sniffling, she remained with her back to him and tried to compose herself, wiping away an errant tear with shaking fingers, the other clutching her golden heart.

Never mind his firsts. This was her first as well, her first with someone other than her husband, and she was woefully unprepared for the emotions it brought forth.

"Mistress? Please, did I hurt you? What did I do? Why are you crying? Please, please do not cry." Turning her, he placed a gentle finger under her chin to lift her face to his.

This is not fair to William when I've led him to this point, yet he is being so tender.

"How did you—? Charles used to—" She struggled to regain her control. Stifling a sob, she swiped furiously at her cheeks, shaking her head to indicate she did not wish to explain.

He was again annoyingly perceptive, drawing her into his arms.

They stood like that, her gown loose around her, him poking her in the stomach with the persistent erection of a young man not yet twenty. His hand rubbed her back as she sniffled a few times over the memory of another man and the love that accompanied it. Silently, she admitted that she was grateful rather than annoyed at his perception. Many men twice his age were not as discerning or mature in their dealings with their wives.

Her chemise caught in his hand. The heat of his fingers on the bare skin of her back snapped her back to arousal, albeit muted, with an eager, fit puppy wanting to serve her. His height was different, shoulders broader, and his touch was slower, more hesitant.

His spiced rum smell was divine. It had heated her blood on more than one occasion from the chair across from her. With her nose against his throat, it was intoxicating. Sucking in a deep breath, she arched and pressed her breasts into his chest.

Closing her eyes, she whispered into his collarbone, "Thank you."

"Always. I will hold you every time I am allowed," he murmured over her, his end of day stubble catching on her hair as he formed the words.

She lifted her head to attempt to regain the mood, and he bent his head, his lips hovering over hers.

Unable to resist him, fully back in the present, she closed the gap and pressed her lips to his.

Tilting his head, he licked once at the seam of her mouth as though to ask permission to enter.

She parted her lips and his tongue swept in to explore hers. He did not press hard, his mouth gently rubbing hers. It was a whole-mouth caress. Another first for her, but with this, there was no thought of anyone other than the masterfully deferential young man who held her.

Lost in sensation, her blood swimming in her veins, Charlotte pressed her body against his again, only to have him break the kiss.

He stepped back. "Thank you, Mistress. Will you be all right now?"

"Yes, thank you, William. I just needed a minute."

"Right, then. I shall see you tomorrow. Good night."

She raised her brows. *Good night?* Any other man his age would have taken intimacy as far as she'd allow. Testing him, she asked, "What if I invited you to stay?"

He smiled his lopsided grin. "Are you?"

"Not now," she muttered.

The corner of his mouth turned up again. Then he sobered and said, "When—if—you invite me into your bed, I want you to be very sure. And I want to be the only man in your thoughts whilst I'm there."

Chapter Eleven

William spent much of the following day in a fog, struggling to follow his mother's and Percy's discussions around correspondence and various bills in the House of Lords.

He knew he needed to learn these things. If his father passed that day, Percy would still be involved in running the estate until he reached his majority, but ultimately there were dozens of servants and even more tenant farmers relying on his ability to keep the family's holdings secure.

However, all he could focus on were memories of Charlotte's lips, back, the slope of her neck meeting her shoulder, her delicate floral scent. He had not touched anything more than her hand, ankle, shoulders and lips. Yet he wanted her with every fiber of his being—his mind as much as his cock.

Already his two relatively tame intimate encounters with her excited him more than any sexual opportunities he'd had in the past. He'd read Ovid's *Ars amatoria* for university and unconsciously followed the poet's advice, finding what Charlotte liked and meeting her on that plane, then last night stepping back to allow her to miss him. He hoped it was the right balance. Hmm. He might be able to apply a few more ideas from the ancient

Roman text.

After a long day, he dressed to meet Charlotte at the salon scheduled that evening. The topic was a more detailed discussion of steam engines, this talk about applying their use than the invention itself. Charlotte seemed most interested in the applications, in order to direct her financial interests.

As this paralleled his reason for attending such discussions, he hoped they could share knowledge—his more on the scientific side and hers on how best to manage the financial risk and return. He'd already followed her guidance in convincing his mother to invest in the further development of steam locomotive rail lines.

Back in her library, he asked, "What were your thoughts on this evening's topic, Mistress?"

"I'd already read quite a bit about the use of steam power. The steam locomotive has proven successful in its first year, albeit expanding more slowly than I would have liked. But the ironworks are key for more than the railway tracks. The demand for iron seems to be growing as steamboats get larger, with longer range."

"Steam-powered *ships*? Are they fast?"

"Combined with sails to supplement, apparently they are. Which mitigates the risk of loss to investors. They are also larger and thus can carry more cargo or passengers."

"Have you decided to invest?"

"Not yet. If you'd like, you may read the correspondence and a few newspaper articles I've saved, William. I'd be interested in your thoughts on the matter. Then if we both decide to invest, I can introduce you to my man of affairs."

"Really?" He was surprised she valued his opinion on this. Poetry, even Applied Maths, certainly. But he was a university student and still learning to manage the small world he'd inherit. This was her area of expertise, and he was happy to follow her lead. "Thank you. I look forward to reporting back to you. However, you should know that I prefer to defer to you on investments. You have more experience with them, whilst I am still learning my way."

She whipped her head around, her mouth agape, and stared at him.

"What?" he asked.

"You are willing to take my advice on financial matters? A woman? Someone without a degree?"

"What does gender have to do with it? As for a degree, other than the language barrier, you have studied far more than me or most of my peers, in addition to having real world knowledge."

"William…" her voice caught and she turned her head away.

Realizing her emotions had gotten the best of her, he wished to help her regain her equilibrium. Despite his anger at their society that made his deference surprising, he teased, "Mistress, I am always prepared to follow your lead. If I might demonstrate in the bedroom?"

She twisted around to give him a quelling look.

He winked at her, and her lips quirked in a small smile. His mother being a strong role model made him more receptive to the type of relationship he was trying to forge with Charlotte. But she might not know his family's situation.

"You know about my father's preference for drink over responsibility. Percy helps whilst I am away at university, but my mother has taken over much of Father's duties."

"Ah. I see," she said, nodding.

"Father dabbles in investing. Frankly, Mama and I would rather he did not and try to stop it whenever possible, as his judgment is impaired. Mama hasn't the time or opportunity to learn about investing. So much of that is learned through casual conversation at the clubs."

"Ah, yes, men and their clubs, where most important conversation is held, ensuring women are excluded."

"I hadn't thought of it like that. But you are right, I can imagine it is frustrating."

"I am resigned to it, although the attitude of superiority is annoying. The intellectual salons help, and Charles and I made our decisions together, so I never felt like I was missing out." She turned the subject back to his family. "Does your mother mind having to juggle all of that?"

He cocked his head. "Honestly, I do not know. She takes it all in stride, although she is grateful to have me home for the summer to help."

"Hmm…I suspect her happiness is not simply about you helping with the accounts." Charlotte smiled.

He was still frowning, his thoughts on his parents. Grinding his teeth, he banked the anger that surged whenever he considered his father's irresponsible behavior. His tone reflecting his frustration, he said, "I cannot fathom how it all came to be. She never angers, even when he is at his worst. At least as much as I can see."

"William, do you remember happier times? Is there something that caused the change in your father's behavior?"

"I've thought and thought. I was too young to know, perhaps. I remember the first few years after Emily was born were happy, or I thought they were." The most time he'd spent with his father had been learning to ride, which the earl suddenly abandoned around the time he started drinking.

"How much younger than you is she?"

"Three years."

"Hmm. They never wanted to try for another son?" Common practice among royalty and the aristocracy was to produce an heir and a spare.

"I don't know. 'Tis not something I've asked."

"Fair enough. So, you'd have been six or seven when things changed?"

"I guess so. I suspect mama tried to hide it for a time." He stood and paced the length of the room, flinging out a hand. Sometimes he hated his father, as much as that sentiment felt disloyal. He could have had a much harder life, as Folly reminded him on occasion. But it was hard to watch his mother struggle as his father ignored his duties. "I don't understand why she puts up with it. Couldn't she get rid of all the spirits in the house? Keep the family sequestered in the country?"

"William, you know better than that. Women do not have many choices. If she hid the whisky, he'd just go to his club more, which would cost more and possibly be more embarrassing. If she tried to retire to the country, he could simply decline and stay here, and it would be harder for her to manage the estate without the solicitor nearby and your father to sign things."

Her words took the edge off his fury. He was again impressed with her ability to evaluate a situation thoroughly. Intelligence layered with maturity was more than alluring, it was downright seductive.

He loathed his family's circumstances. More, he disliked having to admit the sordid details to his Mistress, who was the epitome of competence. Perhaps most, he abhorred them limiting his time with her. However, this time was a welcome escape. Here, she took the lead, allowing him to drop the mantle of familial obligations that threatened to overwhelm him.

* * * *

The next morning, he ransacked his room looking for the items he needed. He would go to a bookstore for them if he needed to, but he'd prefer his gift be more personal. Nor did he relish having to explain to his mother why he wanted to visit a bookstore or even spend funds on something unnecessary.

He was tired of being accountable to his mother, and his months away at university these past two years had given him a taste of freedom. He'd already begun mentally mapping out his Grand Tour, then arrived home to a near-financial-crisis. He still was not certain they could dig their way out of it, and that concern weighed heavily in his thoughts.

Shaking his head to bring himself back to the more pleasurable task at hand, he stared at the tomes he held. Perfect.

He'd cast about in his memory for works in Latin that might lure her into a response. Recalling a reference that had arisen in their studies of influences on Virgil's writing, he chose a book of Catullus's poems. They had not been covered in classes, due to their risqué nature, but several students had read them outside of class and talked about them in the pub.

Pouring over them, he marked several before

selecting carmen thirty-two as a starting place, grabbed his notebook to find a blank page, and began translating…

List, I charge you, my gentle Ipsithilla,
Lovely ravisher and my dainty mistress,
Say we'll linger a lazy noon together.
Suits my company? Lend a farther hearing:
See no jealousy make the gate against me,
See no fantasy lead you out a-roaming.
Keep close chamber; anon in all profusion
Count me kisses again again returning.
Bides thy will? With a sudden haste command me;
Full and wistful, at ease reclined, a lover
Here I languish alone, supinely dreaming.

Staring at it, he debated leading with this. It was arguably to a courtesan, and could well be considered presumptuous or worse, directed toward a noblewoman. However, he was confident she'd appreciate the reference to commanding him and her quest for knowledge would smooth the way for more teachings—by both of them. A pulse of heat went through him as he pictured himself supine and at her command, ready to learn.

Putting aside his translated poem and the second book he'd found for that night, he abandoned the chaos of his room to continue digging through the mess his father had gotten the family into.

An eternity later, his struggles were done for the day, the family had supped together, and the night was his.

Tucking the book and paper under his arm, he jogged to Charlotte's, eager to see her reaction to his new proposal to trade educations.

Chapter Twelve

Distracted by all the ways William tempted her, Charlotte sent a note around for Belle requesting a visit.

Posing as a baker delivering goods, Belle brought a delicious apple cake with her. Charlotte's cook was never able to replicate that particular recipe as well as Belle's source, which Belle refused to share, and she looked forward to this particular disguise every time.

Her friend sat forward, chin on hand, tea and cake forgotten beside her elbow on the table as Charlotte recounted the undressing, her momentary breakdown, the kiss, his graciousness.

"My word, Char. What an incredible balance of obedience and maturity, and at that age. He's a gem." She fanned herself with her napkin.

"I hate to admit it, but you're right. I was in shock when he did not defer to my wishes, but it was admirable. But Belle, we've been over this. He's under twenty. And inheriting an earldom and in need of heirs."

"Char, we've been over this." Belle mimicked her words back at her, wagging her head with a grin. "This needn't be a forever thing. Why can't a widow have a lovely summer fling with her university rakelet? And besides, as I've been telling you for years, we shall never know if the lack of children was because of you or

Charles…well, unless you marry again. In the meantime, you need some happiness in your life, and some physical gratification by someone other than yourself. Who better than a man who clearly has a *tendre* for you, who is open to whatever games you want, and who admires your brain? I do not understand why you are fighting this."

Charlotte shook her head. Belle knew she and Charles had wanted children, not simply as heirs but to love and nurture. She'd been heartbroken when years passed without success. Both a physician and a midwife said that it was likely due to her menses being irregular. Her *fault*. The guilt still plagued her, although widowhood with a child or more would have been that much more difficult. Belle had told her countless times that no one was at fault for physical limitations.

Having no desire to rekindle that argument, she focused on the difference in age. "Belle, I do not want to hurt a young man who deserves someone his own age. Not that he'll necessarily fall in love with me, but you must see that someone that age is impressionable. What if he expects women after me to tie him up?"

"What if he does? You're not thinking you'll 'ruin' William for 'normal' sex, are you? We had that conversation when I first started training you. First, 'tis—"

"—not ruining,"—they spoke together, Belle having long ago drummed this recitation into Charlotte—"and second, he would not do it if it didn't appeal to him."

Charlotte added, "I know. I know. I regressed for a moment. If the desire is not in someone, it would not arouse them, no matter the influence. If 'tis, then it is as normal as any other intimacy. Honestly, more than anything, I do not want to risk our conversations about his studies."

"Why limit yourself? You can make your own rules, Char."

"How? He cannot call on me without gossip. 'Tisn't as though we can slip away at every ball to discuss poetry and philosophy. I can just imagine the talk if we attended an intellectual salon together." She sighed.

"First, William seems to have been inventive enough to date, so I am quite sure there is a way. And second, society be damned. You are a widow, you have a bit more leeway now, and no one seems to care what men do. Hell, his friends would toast him if they thought he was tupping an attractive, *slightly* older woman."

Charlotte pursed her lips. She'd called William's interest an infatuation, but what of hers? She did not want either of them to be hurt by a short-term affair that had no possibility of being anything more. And she was starting to worry about her own heart as much as his.

"Char, please think about it at least." Belle pleaded. "You've already negotiated the intellectual side. You might similarly barter the sexual side as well. Given that he has repeatedly expressed interest in that, you'll need a stronger argument than you have now, because even I am not buying it, and I don't want you like he does, much as I love you." She winked and smiled.

Charlotte could not stop her laugh.

"Besides," Belle continued. "I think that taking control in a short-term relationship with a like-minded gentleman could do your confidence a world of good, and set you up to then search for your happily-ever-after with whatever age limits and other prerequisites you want to place on that role. Either way, you owe me my winnings from our wager at the start of the summer."

* * * *

That evening, Austin ushered a still-panting William into the parlor. She hadn't trusted herself with upstairs, or releasing the servants.

She took a moment to compose herself. It would not do for William to see her agitation. Given his missives, she suspected he'd use it to his advantage.

And yours.

Shushing the devilish, Belle-like voice in her head, she rose to greet him and paused, her knees unable to sustain the motion of walking for a moment. Lud, he was delicious, all golden hues and plain dark clothes, hair parenthetically framing his forehead.

Her knees. Had. Gone. Weak. *Really, Charlotte?* They hadn't done that since Charles had first called on her, too many years to think about now. *When you were his age.*

She willed strength back into her limbs and continued toward him. His scent wafted to her.

Cloves, that is it. Spiced rum and cloves.

She took a long sniff, as his eyes trailed over her heaving bosom, bright with excitement.

When she reached him, he bowed low and reached for her hand, ungloved in the privacy of her home. He kissed it, lingering. "Mistress."

Ignoring the pulse of heat low in her belly, she tugged on her hand. "Did you run here?"

His breath sniffed in before he released it and straightened. He was blushing, and his free hand held what appeared to be a book.

She peered at it as she sat, choosing her preferred rosewood armchair. He chose the settee, and she tried to ignore him tucking the item half under his leg.

"I, ah, might have hurried. I brought you something."

Ack. How did he manage to be sweet, sinfully beautiful, *and* possibly submissive? She slid her gaze to the sofa beside him, but she stayed silent, attempting not to appear too eager. Internally, she berated herself. She should not covet his gifts, even if they were books. 'Twould only encourage him.

He slid his hand into his jacket and produced a piece of paper, passing it to her.

Opening it, she read the line at the top noting its source, then the poem. She pressed her lips together at the last few lines in an effort not to grin, feeling his eyes on her. How on earth he kept finding new tokens perfectly suited to her, she had no idea. Once again, his choice was spot on.

"Thank you, William. I confess, I am not familiar with Catullus. This is lovely."

He grinned. "There is a whole book of his poems. They were passed around at university, as they are too racy to be taught in our classes."

"Yes, I can see why the administration might have decided that."

"Sadly, I've only seen copies in Latin. Which led me to think…" His hand dropped to the tome and drew it out an inch at a time.

She followed his hand's path without blinking.

He held it out, face up. A Latin primer.

She gasped. This was better than any poetry, any science that led to better investing. This was a door to a whole universe she wasn't privy to.

"I dug this out of a crate from secondary school."

She glanced up at him, then back to stare at the book he held, still silent. Her lust for knowledge—which would be far more available by learning Latin—might equal her lust for this magnificent specimen of a male in his prime. She flicked her gaze up again. *No, probably not, but it is a…close?…second.*

"Ahem." He cleared his throat, then swallowed, glancing from her to the book then back. "I thought you might like it, and I could help you with it as you wish whilst I am here…?"

She wanted to snatch the book to her, to ensure he could not change his mind. But as the mature adult here—her imagined snort sounded a lot like Belle again—she would mind her manners.

"What a thoughtful gift, William."

Drat! Her voice caught. Indeed, it was the most thoughtful gift she could have imagined, and she suspected no other man, of any age, would have thought of it. She pressed her lips together, biting her tongue to try to avoid crying. She daren't weep in front of him a second time or he'd never kiss her again. Wait, she should not want that. Heavens, her emotions and thoughts were in turmoil with this lovely but oh-so-young man.

Her eyes slid shut to hide from him, but one tear escaped, rolling down her face. Embarrassed, she whirled away and sniffed.

William set the book down on the table in front of them and leaned in to offer his handkerchief, questioning, "Mistress? Did I upset you? I beg your pardon. I will take it away, 'twas clearly a mistake."

"No!" She turned back and slapped her hand down on the book, her voice and arm like whips.

His back jolted straight, although he continued to hold the linen out. "Oh. Of course not, 'tis yours to do with as you wish. Er…if not the book, then may I ask what made you cry?"

She drew the book into her lap greedily before accepting the handkerchief to dab at her face. "I was not crying. I simply got something in my eye."

"Oh. Right, then. I am glad. Uh, not that you got something in your eye, but that I didn't upset you…" He blushed.

It was just what she needed. She giggled a bit at his clear discomfiture, and, when he gaped at her abrupt turnabout in emotions, giggled again.

"Does that mean you do like the book? I can help you with it. It was ever so hard at first. There are many interpretations for each word." Gone was the reserved knight of the evening before. The eager puppy was back.

Yum.

Alarmed at the thought, she shoved it away for later, her worry turning to lust-tinged panic at her ability to resist him when she heard his next thoughts.

"Mistress, I've made it quite clear that I wish to learn from you. I believe you wish to teach me as well. I—you…"

He blushes beautifully. She sat back, interested to see where he would go with this line of thought, content to let him stammer, while she attempted to keep her libido from finding the nearest set of restraints—those curtain ties would work—and having her way with him.

He arched a brow at her recline, realizing her intent. "You know of what I speak, Mistress. I was thinking that for every five words I teach you in Latin, you could teach me something. It would not be possible to learn the whole language this summer, but I think at that rate you'd make significant progress."

She was impressed that he'd already planned his approach and was ready to barter. However, she thrived on dickering and refused to make this easy. "And, just to be clear, what would I teach you?"

"Mistress." He sighed out, sounding exasperated.

"William, if you cannot say it, then I daresay you are not ready to learn it." She grinned.

In for a penny, in for a pound. Although that is quite dear. Belle would be proud. She stifled an inappropriate giggle.

"You are right, Mistress." He took a breath. Still blushing, he nonetheless held her gaze as he finished, "You could teach me…more ways to serve you…in bed."

She acquiesced without a fight. After Belle's pushing that afternoon, her conscience had been attempting to wrestle her craving for this gorgeous, fervent young man back into submission. But when he presented his personal Latin primer as a gift, her desire slipped its lead and was running amok. The only thing she could control was the end date. "First, William. Let us set a time period for this arrangement. You refer only to this summer, do you not?"

He blinked and swallowed. His gaze flickered away. "I suppose I hadn't thought that far."

She suspected he was lying, but she'd take his statement as agreement. "I have. Whatever we decide on here, I am stipulating that it ends when you leave for university."

He frowned before smoothing his expression and nodding.

"If you are in my bed, I expect you not to be in any others. Is that understood?"

"Absolutely, Mistress." He sat forward, his smile eager.

"And I will offer you the same courtesy."

His eyes narrowed.

She smirked. She would have not have done such a thing, but it was all part of the negotiations. William had not considered that side of it. He needed to feel that she was giving something up. "Lastly, absolutely no attachment. You do not fall in love, you do not fall in lust, and you do not write to me when you return to Oxford."

"Hmm. I am not entirely sure I can control all that, Mistress, but you have my word that I will do my best."

She considered for a minute. 'Twas not like she could hold him to any of that, anyway.

He'd also proven that he'd do what he wanted whenever he could get away with it.

She nodded. "Fine. Then for every 50 words of Latin, one night in my bedroom, although not necessarily in my bed." She smirked.

He leaned in. "No."

"I beg your pardon." She arched her brows, pretending hauteur to hide her glee at his willingness to haggle. He had no idea of the extent of her skill with money and investing, the best form of bargaining in her opinion. How entertaining.

"Mistress, I wish more than anything to pursue this arrangement with you, but fifty words is too much." He continued, "I said five because for every Latin word there are a myriad of ways to translate based on context, when it was written, and frankly, the individual reader. It's a language that cannot be rushed to be appreciated, and I cannot wait for fifty words to touch you again."

She loved the enthusiasm, but he should be sure about what he was signing up for. "You might be waiting longer to touch me if you do not behave, puppy. I can tie your hands each and every time and torture you to my heart's content."

His eyes flared at her moniker, a smile teasing one side of his mouth even as he groaned and sat back, his hand in his lap surreptitiously plucking at his trousers to offer relief for his strangled cock.

After a moment of enjoying the view, she offered, "Twenty-five."

"Ten. Mistress, please. I beg you, ten." His mouth begged, but his eyes said he knew what that word did to her.

Naughty rakelet. Well, never let it be said that I do not reward good behavior. He did use one of my favorite words, even if he knew it would help his case. "Done. We shall work in the library tonight."

He jumped to his feet and bounced once more in ill-concealed excitement before following her to her desk in the other room.

She hoped her own pleasure was less obvious. Her blood felt thick and hot in her veins as she sat in one of the two guest chairs at her desk. She swallowed against his scent and her core thrummed in anticipation. He'd better be a good teacher as she needed to master those first ten words quickly.

She groaned when he placed the naughty poem next to the primer and said, "We shall use this to learn a few verbs."

* * * *

A sennight later, Charlotte had a better appreciation for William's characterization of Latin. Groaning, she threw her pen down, spattering ink across her notes. She had been rushing to get through her second set of ten words.

She'd learned the first set easily, although she suspected he'd chosen very basic words.

Afterwards, she had requested another kiss, and indeed, he'd been the only man in her thoughts from the first step into her bedroom. She'd then allowed him to touch her everywhere while bound to the chair but for one hand, after which she had returned the favor—with him still tied, of course.

She was dying to taste other parts of him, but this second set was making her brain hurt. She looked back at him where he hovered standing next to her desk chair, having only arrived a few minutes before. "William, please. Give me an easy one. A pronoun, a number, anything."

"Pronouns are not always—" he gulped.

Her gaze had strayed down to the bulge between his legs.

"Sex," he said, panting.

"Yes, please." She stood.

"No." He shook his head. "I won't have you say I cheated our bargain. Sex is six. Six is sex. In fact, here's another: that is decem. Decem is ten."

"Sex and decem. Done. Thank you. Now lead the way to the bedroom. I enjoy the rear view as much as the front." She grinned at him, hoping he was as primed as she was for the rest of their evening.

Upstairs, he undressed her, again rubbing her back free of chemise creases, this time without tears.

Turning, she slid one foot forward to press her hip against his groin.

He stopped circling his hand on her back, pressing into her now to hold her in place and humming low in his throat but waiting for her instruction.

Mine to teach, to taste. She shifted her hip fractionally left then right. He gasped, surging into her microscopically, as though trying to remain still and failing.

"Mistress?"

Always the polite puppy, checking for her permission. Gracious, he could be addictive if she let him. She was past politeness, though. More than a year without intimacy made her hungry, and William himself turned her ravenous. She slid her hands to his chest and gave a small push.

He stepped back and his calf caught against the bed, sending him sprawling. He stared up at her, his hands having landed up and out from his body, elbows bent, creating a supplicant pose.

Charlotte shrugged, and her dress dropped forward, catching on her hips, her stays loose over her breasts. A shimmy sent the dress to pool around her, and a second one dropped the stays onto the dress.

William stared, unblinking. One arm slid along the counterpane, edging toward his cock.

"Stay still, William."

"Yes, Mistress." His voice was guttural, almost unrecognizable.

Heat flared anew in her. She wanted this, she was ready. And, she took a moment to reflect, Charles would want her to have this, just as she would have for him, and if their situations were reversed, the young lady with him might easily be twenty. With that, she banished William's age from her mind.

Her breasts strained against her chemise, wanting to feel his muscles and smattering of chest hair against them. First, though, there was torturing to be done. Leaning over him, she unfastened his waistcoat first, spreading it. Then came his cravat, unwound after being untied. She straightened, running the cravat through her hands.

"Remove your shirt and shoes. You may sit up to do so, then remain sitting."

He scrambled, grabbing the dress shirt below the collar and yanking before realizing he needed to unbutton the collar to avoid choking himself.

Charlotte watched, keeping her expression neutral. Inside, she was panting like a bitch in heat. Her control was ready to snap, but having this gorgeous young man under her power was intoxicating. She strolled around the side of the bed. When he turned to keep her in sight, she admonished him with a tsking sound, and he stared forward again, his arms shaking.

She could feel the barely-leashed lust in every shake. As he couldn't see her, she allowed herself a small smile of pleasure before swallowing it and her own eagerness down. She knelt on the mattress, and tugged one of his hands as she directed him. "Lie up on the bed, head on the pillows."

As he swung his legs up and around to lie, she carried the wrist she held and wrapped the cravat around it, then around a carved wooden bed post. A wave of nostalgia washed over her as she did so, and she smiled, excited she'd found a worthy playmate.

Not ready to use leather cuffs and risk frightening a novice, she used his shirt for the other wrist. Crumpling it beyond repair, she secured his second hand then slid a finger between his skin and the fabric to ensure his hands would not go numb.

Scooting back, she stood at the foot of the bed and scanned his length. He was delicious. Reminding herself that this was a summer fling, she basked in the moment. This rakelet wanted her. Oh, she knew she was attractive enough. But he could have anyone, a different girl in his bed every night. Yet, he'd chosen her. Her ego preened for a moment before she reined it in. He was not hers to keep, only to enjoy for a short time.

So enjoy, she would. Legs sprawled haphazardly framed a mouth-watering bulge she was salivating to see again. Candlelight flickered over the planes and ridges of his lean torso. A hint of rib under pads of muscle led to puckered nipples begging to be pinched. A trace of hair led from each tiny bud, narrowing to a single line that disappeared into his waistband. His throat bobbed as he watched her, his biceps still twitching as though testing his bonds. The lily white underside of his upper arms invited a feathery tickling touch to make him squirm.

Her mouth watered, wanting to skate over each inch, tasting and savoring. Her fingers would lead the way or follow. Her breasts grew heavier, and she was tempted to cup them, or feed them to him. The sensitive folds between her legs pulsed and throbbed, ready for more.

But, oh, where to start?

Chapter Thirteen

William closed his eyes to attempt to regain some control. He would be mortified if he came in his trousers simply from Mistress positioning and observing him. He opened them a heartbeat later, not willing to miss a second of this.

She stood in chemise and petticoat, and he remembered what was beneath. The firelight flares allowed him to see the dusky shadow of one nipple behind her chemise, now hard and poking the fabric.

He arched his back a bit, testing the give in his bonds. Being tied, basically helpless, amplified his desire, his cock pulsing and leaking its eagerness through his trousers. He might be daft for doing this. A sane man would be nervous should a woman they'd met a handful of times restrain them and stare at them with such hunger, wouldn't they? Instead, he was eager to please, ready to follow whatever commands she wished to give.

I want whatever my Mistress wishes to do with me or to me. He stopped tugging as the phrase "my Mistress" reverberated in his head. This was his place. It felt right. More than that, not having to make any decisions was freeing. He was forced to lie still and learn.

He relaxed to indicate his subservience. Then surged against his bonds once again when she ran her palms up his legs, kneeling between his thighs.

She skipped his torso to whisper her fingers over the insides of his arms, raising gooseflesh and causing an all-over shiver of sensitivity. Moving to his nipples, she pinched.

"Ah! Blazes," he gasped. Realizing how close her knees were to his heavy sac, he shook his head to clear it so he could appreciate all the sensations as she surrounded him.

Raising his head, he dared, "Mistress, I want to touch you. Please, may I touch you, kiss you?"

"No. Now lay back. And no more talk."

Feeling daring, he started to ask about repercussions.

She forestalled him by saying, "Or you shall not get the reward I have in mind for you."

For heaven's sake, that reward better include relief for his cock soon or he *would* embarrass himself. Throwing his head back on the bed, he concentrated on not thrusting up to seek friction for his cock.

Charlotte drew patterns on his chest and stomach with her fingernails. "You appear to have a secret desire to submit, William. The gentleman doth protest too much about the Wife of Bath's Tale, methinks."

He squirmed, barely following her mixed Shakespearean and Chaucer references. Uncertain if he was allowed to answer, he hoped it would further his cause. His voice gruff behind a clenched jaw, he ventured, "Not so secret," and licked her finger when she laid it across his lips.

"Hmm…useful." She circled the wet tip around one of his nipples, and the cool air and hot finger hardened it further.

He thrashed his head from side to side, gritting his

teeth and squeezing his eyes shut as he concentrated on controlling his cock's reaction. Her hands on the fall of his trousers shot his eyes open, and he curled his head up to watch, unable to conjure chagrin at the wet spot there.

She unbuttoned him, the back of her hand brushing his rod.

"Unh." Lava surged in his bollocks, her fingers branding his shaft, claiming him as hers. He flinched and gulped, pleading with all the deities he could think of to not spurt as soon as the air wafted over his sensitive flesh.

Watching her, he found her focus both admirable and infuriating. He needed to touch her, to be touched. Saliva pooled in his mouth with the desire to taste any part of her, if she'd just get close enough. This slow, methodical unveiling was killing him. His teeth would be ground to nubs by the end of the night.

Cataloging the silk of her skin and fullness of her lips in the candlelight did not help his trouser predicament. However, he had no idea if he'd be granted this experience again. Thus, it was important to commit everything to memory.

She seemed to know how close he was, carefully peeling back his trousers then tugging the fabric below his hips to free him.

His cock bounced out to thump against his stomach, and they both gasped.

His eyes flew to hers. Her expression was finally less calm, her gaze hot as she licked her lips at the view of his naked flesh. Knowing she was hungry for this ramped his own arousal higher and he resisted the desire to squirm.

The trousers bunched below his hips shackled his

legs close together.

Charlotte moved to straddle him, her petticoat obscuring his garments and framing his cock like pretty flower petals around a stamen.

Blazes. He leaned his head back and squeezed his eyes shut yet again, unable to bear the sight without exploding all over that pristine undergarment. His chest heaved in air as though he'd been underwater for minutes.

MistressMistressMistress.

"Yes, William? Shall I tell you how you can serve me?" He hadn't realized he was whispering the chant behind his teeth until her question came.

"Yyss plllss." There were no vowel sounds in his hissed response as he met her gaze. This exceeded all expectations. He had dreamed of many things these past weeks: silly boy that he now knew he was, he had only pictured scenarios with his hands free to serve her, to touch or taste her, despite the evidence of their first two encounters. Sure, some of those visions began with bindings, of his hands or his cock. But as they progressed, his imagination and experience were too limited to get to this. His few fumbled encounters at boarding school and Oxford had not prepared him for the sensations evoked simply from lying here under Charlotte's regard.

Their conversations, lessons, the whole mating dance had all been driving toward this. The ultimate vulnerability and closeness from submitting to her command, from giving her his willing surrender. His heart pounded with more than excitement. *This*, this was what he'd always found missing in those furtive bumbling incidents: this incredible closeness and partnership. He hoped she felt the same.

The bed shifted then, and he lost the ability to think at all.

Her hair trailed over his exposed thigh.

Agh! Don't spend, don't spend!

He needed to *see*. He bent his neck to witness her honey locks pool on his hips. His cock pulsed with the warm tickle of her exhale, knocking into her lower lip. Then leaped again at the feel of that cushiony softness giving way under it, her teeth a hard barrier behind it.

For heaven's sake, he'd heard about this from school mates, but nothing could have prepared him for the ecstasy of that simple touch. More liquid beaded at his slit, and slid along his length. Sucking in a breath, he clenched his abdominal muscles and awaited her command.

Charlotte did not move her head away, just glanced up at him and grinned, tucking her hair behind one ear. "Eager puppy, aren't you?"

Her breath gusted over him with each word, that alone edging him closer to what would be an excruciatingly embarrassing explosion with her face right there. Uncertain whether she was addressing him or only his cock and unwilling to forego what he prayed to the heavens was his reward, he bit his lip and stayed silent.

She did not seem to require a response. "Such a handsome toy. A big, firm, silky toy. And I remember how tasty you are."

Another bead of moisture, another involuntary pulse toward those soft lips.

"I think I need a sip. Do not spend."

He nodded, gaze riveted on her, every muscle in his

body tensed.

"You may enjoy your release when—or if—I tap your hip, puppy. Whether I tap it depends on how well you behave. Nod if you understand."

He dropped his head back and nodded frantically, hair slipping on the bed, hoping he could keep his word.

"Hmm…." She licked up his shaft.

"Aaahhhhh." Heaven. A hot, wet, touch of heaven. His hips canted, out of his control. His shoulders raised off the bed as he curled every part of him toward her, clenching his hands around their ties to pull him up. Blood surged through him, all centering where her lips lingered over the crown of his near-painfully-hard member.

"Pleasepleaseplease." He was whispering under his breath again, through gritted teeth.

Still humming, she glanced up at him to evaluate his state. His muscles loosened and he settled back against the pillows.

Her lips slid down, and she swallowed him.

The vibrations of her continued purr tested his control to the point of breaking. His jaw set, his whole being went rigid as he attempted to enjoy these new sensations without ending them. Her mouth was wet and hot, but any similarity to sexual interludes from his past ended there. It was a different shape, looser until she swallowed or sucked, narrowing when she took him to her throat. The sharp edges of her teeth were cushioned but present, framing her movements against him. He suspected that if she bared them, he'd like that bite of roughness as much as he did the softness of her tongue and lips. And she was sucking his essence down as it leaked from him. The sheer eroticism of that thought nearly undid him.

She placed a hand on his stomach.

Was she releasing him? No, it was not a tap and not his hip. *Blazes.* He needed to move, but the realization that snapping his hips up might choke her helped him find calm. He'd never do anything to harm his Mistress. Instead, he writhed, twisting his arms and shoulders and pulling against the bedframe, needing friction, motion.

She waited him out, breathing through her nose, the puffs of air moving the curls at his groin.

Finally, panting, he unclenched his fists and lay back.

She promptly slid up his length, and, holding the tip in her mouth, swirled her tongue around the hard ridge forming the head.

"Mistress!" he yelled. Fire swirled at the base of his spine, his bollocks drawing up and his buttocks and stomach tightening to stop himself from exploding.

She ignored him and sucked him all the way in again, her lips hitting her hand still holding the stem. Twice more she glided him in and out at a snail's pace with him groaning and grunting, and engaging every thought and muscle and trick he could fathom to avoid spilling without permission.

Then she sped up.

"Nonononono…"

What felt like a year after her lips had first touched him, fingers tapped his hip thrice. Exulting, he allowed his hips to make miniature thrusts at a gallop, shuddering.

Her lips stayed firm around him mid-shaft, hitting her hand at the base on each thrust, her tongue flicking his frenulum in a masterfully choreographed dance.

"Mistre—" Meaning to warn her, he lost control of

his body when his mind refocused to form words, and he spurted, twisting his hips up now, seeking the continued warmth of her mouth. Blazes, was that allowed, or considered impolite? He stopped worrying about it and reveled, knowing that she was untied and could retreat at any time. The wet heat of her mouth was better than anything he'd experienced, anything he could have dreamed. His cock pulsed against her, sending jet after jet into that sweet tunnel.

Charlotte stayed with him through it all, sucking him in, swallowing.

Her throat closing about his tip to ingest his seed made him spurt more, his hands cramping around their ties in sensual agony.

After long minutes, he sagged, dropping his hips and opening fists. His stomach muscles unclenched, and he dropped his head against the pillows.

She gentled her mouth, swiping up and down once to clean him, before raising her head, lips shiny with both of their liquids.

William's blinks grew longer and longer, his energy sapped. After all that time with muscles tensed, mind centered on following orders and not pre-empting them, he was exhausted. He'd offer to return the favor in a moment, he just needed a second or two to recover.

He panted out a heartfelt, "Thank you, oh thank you, Mistress."

Her satisfied smirk the last thing he saw as his eyes fluttered closed.

* * * *

Pushing back from the desk, William swore and ran his hands through his hair.

He'd barely had two hours to savor Charlotte's

ministrations of the prior evening before the latest disaster in his father's mismanagement had plunged him back into despair. Funds he'd hoped to access to cover much-needed roof repairs for their stables at the country house had been redirected to invest in a high-risk venture led by one of the earl's cronies.

Heaven save me from the drunken aristocracy.

Speaking of which, he hadn't seen South in several days and his friend's drinking had been accelerating since Easter term at university. Yet another person he felt responsible for, as South's family lived up near the Scottish border and hated London life. He knew South struggled more than he did at Oxford, and was at loose ends much of the summer. William had often wished he could switch roles with South. Even loneliness might be better than the weight of the people depending on the earldom. However, as he spent more time with Charlotte, his wishes had changed.

Jotting a note to have a servant send around to South, he added a note to Charlotte. He owed her an apology, a punishment, or an orgasm for leaving without ensuring her satisfaction, but she'd bustled him out of the house after giving him an hour nap. And now, he'd be unable to make it up to her for another day or two.

"Mama, have you seen this particular debacle of an investment?" He carried over the document he'd found.

"Another one?" she asked with a sigh.

"I'm afraid so. And it appears it will be at least a year and a half before we know if we'll even get our initial investment back. It's another shipping venture."

"Which means all or nothing. If they load those ships too heavy to try to cut costs like they did last time, we might lose it all."

"Could we ask the tenant farmers to make a temporary roof repair and offer to take a lower percentage of their yield next season?" A shudder went through him at the alternative, which was turning people out of work. He stifled a sigh and a wish for a stiff drink. That was the last thing Mama needed—another man relying on drink to allay his nerves. But he felt woefully unprepared to make these decisions.

His mother stared at the fire, tapping her finger on her chin, which he knew meant she was considering all the possibilities.

"'Twould have to be this harvest, not next year. Their time would otherwise be spent on their crops. And the repair would have to be done after Michaelmas, but that might also help it last through the winter." She was nodding by the time she finished. "'Tis an excellent idea, William. Please write to the steward there and propose it, and ask him to expedite his response so we know whether we need to find another solution."

Chapter Fourteen

Charlotte had ignored all correspondence from her solicitor to learn the next ten Latin words. She hadn't minded William falling asleep in her bed, taking it as a compliment to her skills. But self-satisfaction to the memory only worked as a temporary salve after having her rakelet tied to her bed. There was much more she wanted to do with him.

Mimicking his expedience, she learned the rest of the numbers from one to ten, hence ensuring she had a start on the next set of words and thus the next interlude. They were running out of summer, after all.

Having mastered those and reviewed the poems, she was able to refocus on the quarterly reports on her investments after two days. In the late afternoon, Leah Godwin and Beth Orford arrived to discuss further opportunities to help working class women establish their own businesses. These were not investments, they were gifts and guidance to help direct them toward success. The two ladies had extensive networks—Beth had a knack for matching people in need with those having the skillset needed due to her gregarious nature and her position on the edge of the Ton as wife to an earl's second son. Leah was an investor in a London theatre and mother hen to her flock of courtesans.

Between the two, they had an unending list of women in need of assistance. The trio met most months to evaluate and prioritize whose needs were the most urgent, as well as who seemed most prepared to manage an enterprise.

The meeting had run long and she'd called for a second round of tea with cheese and bread, which would serve as her supper.

As the ladies wrapped up, Austin announced another visitor.

"At this time of night?" Beth wiggled her eyebrows. Her observance and ability to ferret out gossip was as key to her successful networking skills as her affability.

Charlotte groaned. She knew the young woman was a vault, but she was also close friends with Charles's brother and new wife, and Charlotte was not ready for even family to hear of her escapades with someone younger than any of them. If she hadn't set an end date with William, she might feel differently. But he needed heirs, and she had a long marriage and a decade of living, which made her too high a risk.

Leah smiled. "Beth, 'tis none of our concern. Do you not have a new husband waiting for you?"

"He's probably busy with Folly or with his leatherwork. I'll bet he hasn't even eaten supper."

"Which means if you leave now, you can eat with him. Come along," Leah answered.

Charlotte mouthed "thank you" to Leah behind Beth's back, and after a surreptitious check that the hall was clear, walked them toward the door.

"Thank you both for coming. I am excited by the progress we've made on our list and the success of those whose establishments are underway."

As soon as the front door closed, she stepped into the

parlor.

William lounged on the settee, bouncing to his feet when she entered. "Mistress. You look lovely as always."

"William." Coming forward she kissed him on each cheek. "Tea? Port? Whisky?"

"You are all the nourishment I need, Mistress."

She rolled her eyes. "Too much poetry at university, puppy."

He just grinned. Sobering, he asked, "May I inquire what your meeting was about?"

"I provide the initial capital for women who want to start their own business, to help them get started."

He stared.

"What is amiss?"

"You *give* money away?"

"Well, yes. We also offer counsel if they want it. Cheltie does the same." Charlotte had thought William had heard of her wealth, given how fast gossip in the Ton circled. Now, she was starting to think he hadn't, or at least was unaware of the extent of it. She watched his expressions, unsure how much she wanted him to know. Men were too often uncomfortable with a woman being wealthier, smarter, or even simply more independent than them.

"Yes, but…Cheltie…"

She raised a brow. "Cheltie what?"

"By all accounts is one of the richest men in the country."

"Hmm, yes. Suffice it to say that I have more than I need and this is something I choose to do. Other women knit bonnets for foundling babies or volunteer their time to teach at schools. I teach and contribute in my own way, using my strengths."

"Yet another layer of you I uncover—an impressive one." His eyes were wide.

She gave a small smile, ducking her head. "Yes, well, no one would want to wear anything I knitted, I am certain."

He laughed.

"Mistress, I confess to jealousy as well as awe. I am so far removed from your position, I cannot even fathom what that would be like. I am honored you allow me to serve you."

The darned puppy was being cheeky again. She shook her head at him.

"Speaking of gifts"—he began, and for a second she worried he might ask her for money and she wasn't quite sure how she'd react—"you gave me a gift the other night, and I have not yet had the chance to offer you anything in return. How is your Latin progressing?"

"Come. I will show you." Charlotte breathed a sigh of relief at the subject of money being dropped and led him back to the library.

Sitting in her desk chair, she drew the primer and her notes toward her. Struggling to resist the urge to squirm in her chair, she forced her thoughts away from what she wanted later that night—his cock inside her. The scent of spiced rum set sparks of pleasure off and her eyes drifted shut, her mouth flooding with his remembered taste.

Opening her eyes, she showed him her list of English words matched to Latin. As he reviewed it, her gaze ran over him, itemizing all the parts she wanted to lick, perhaps to bite.

Raising his head, he caught her look and sucked in a breath. "Thank heavens. Now, how may I serve you?"

"We shall see. 'Tis my turn to teach you, young William, but never fear, I shall endeavor to serve myself whilst I do so."

"Oh, thank you, Mistress." His response was a thread of sound drifting back to her as he preceded her up the stairs. She could not get enough of this view, the reason she'd established such an unusual protocol.

In her bedroom, she turned and issued her first command. "First, undo my gown. Then, clothes off. And get on the bed."

Once she was unlaced, she spun to face him and allowed the gown to drop. Reaching around, she pulled at the bow at the bottom of her stays, loosening the laces, dropping those then untying her petticoat to add it to the growing pile of feminine fabrics.

William rushed to rip off his cravat, waistcoat, collar, shirt, shoes, trousers, and socks. All landed in a haphazard heap on the floor, shoes on top of the white of his shirt, unnoticed.

Her greedy gaze ate up the planes and valleys of his muscled form—her playground, her about-to-be lover. She tossed her chemise away and stepped forward, her eyes hot as they ran over him from head to toe. That iron shaft, deliciously swollen and weeping, was going to be hers tonight. Her inner walls contracted at the mere thought of possessing it.

He sat on the bed. At her shooing motion, he scooted back to lay in the center, head on one of the pillows.

She grabbed leather cuffs, attached to the headboard in readiness, and made quick work of fastening a wrist in each. Then two more fetters from the corners of the bottom of the bed were used to stretch apart his legs. He was at her mercy.

He watched her with narrowed eyes.

Did he suspect that she had choreographed this or wonder about the origins of the leather cuffs? In the end, she'd decided to get new ones for him. Every man should have his own. She giggled internally at the thought. She might be a little drunk on the idea of having relations again after so long, especially with this tasty morsel.

He did not speak, which was good as he'd already earned a punishment.

She needed to finish that and get to the good part, where she got to sit on his cock and ride to her heart's content.

He tugged on the cuffs one by one, finding he could move them a few inches. He swallowed when he found he could not close his legs.

Yes, my beauty. All *of you is available to me.*

His cock bobbed once and she basked in the knowledge that his captivity heightened his pleasure as well as hers.

She placed her foot on the end of the bed between his, and rolled down a stocking before switching legs to remove the last of her clothing.

"Mistress?" The puppy had found his voice. "You make it hard for me to serve you with this position."

"Do you think so?" He had much to learn. She smiled at her wicked thoughts.

His cock bobbed again. "Right." He gulped. "How may I serve you, Mistress?"

"'Tis funny you should ask, William. I might simply stand here and serve myself with you as entertainment." She lifted one foot to the bed between his legs again. With one hand, she pinched her nipple, as she drifted the other between her legs. Gathering wetness on her finger, she drew it up and circled her nub, her hips pitching forward in reaction. Teasing both of them, she repeated the circle. While it wasn't what she wanted for the night, her favorite foreplay was teasing William, whether touching him or remaining just out of reach and reminding him who was in control.

The tendons in William's neck stood out as he tensed his entire body. "Please, please may I help?"

"Do you think I need help, puppy?"

"No, Mistress, but I need to help."

Dratted rakelet always had good answers. She climbed onto the bed and knelt between his legs. Running a finger up one inner thigh, circling around his groin without touching it, she then traced across his belly and down to the other thigh. Dipping deep between his legs, she grazed his perineum, watching him for a reaction.

She wasn't disappointed.

He gasped, rearing up, caught between alarm and pleasure.

His acquiescence pleased her. He was responsive without letting his fear of the unknown halt her explorations. She cupped his sac then ran that one finger up the throbbing vein on his cock to circle the head.

He closed his eyes and sucked in an audible breath, his biceps bulging. His hips strained forward a fraction of an inch and held there. He'd be sore if she allowed him to remain like that for long.

Sliding up his body, she straddled his hips.

His eyes flew open at the bounces on the bed as she changed position, and he watched her without blinking.

She smelled her arousal and his perfuming the air and groaned. Her heart pounded and she clenched her teeth to maintain her control. Moisture slid down her leg.

When it hit his hip, he gulped and begged, "Uh…help…Mistress?"

Although it was not clear whether he was asking *for* help or *to* help, she responded with her own question. "Yes, puppy, you may help. With your lips or your cock, which will it be?"

His cock bucked, hitting her folds hovering above him, and both of them gasped.

Before he could answer, she added, "But you may not spend until I say, either way."

"Yes, Mistress, cock, please, no wait, whatever your pleasure…Please? Cock?" His eyes continued to beg up at her as he fell silent, awaiting her decision.

He was attempting to be good and offer her the choice, but his eagerness could not be contained. It was just as well. That was also her choice. "Right, then. No spending."

"No spending, Mistr—" His words were strangled as she brought the tip of him to her hot, wet entrance. His eyes rolled back in his head, and she swore she heard him muttering the conjugation of random Latin verbs.

"Please—I need—" he gasped as she slid down him. "—a minute. Mistress."

"Certainly." She'd been so wet, there hadn't been even the slightest resistance, despite his size. Now fully seated, she was content to sit still and enjoy the sensation. Closing her eyes, she reveled in the fullness, the connection. She'd only ever had one other man inside her and she'd been the pupil until he'd asked her to take command. It had also been more than a year, and she'd forgotten the emotional intimacy that came with being physically connected, penetrated by someone with whom attraction had been building for weeks. Feelings she was not ready to address swirled in her head and her chest, spreading warmth that intensified the swirling physical rapture emanating from where their bodies were fused.

The burning rod in her pulsed, which she took to indicate he wasn't ready for her to move. Her walls contracted around him in response, and his hips twisted incrementally. Her moisture wet the wiry nest at the base of his shaft and dripped down to his bollocks.

He lunged, hips pushing up, a wordless shout echoing in the room. His bonds snapped him back against the bed, and he ground his head into the pillow beneath it, gritting his teeth. "Argh, Mistress, I can't…"

"Ah, William, the joys and hindrance of youth." She tsked, feigning amusement when she was so enraptured by his reaction she thought she might need only a few strokes to go over herself. "Right, then, puppy. I am going to ride you until I have *my* pleasure. Do what you will."

She began posting, smiling as she found her rhythm. The tethers, the position, the angle all added a mental layer to the sensations coursing through her. Riding him gave her the control she yearned for. His eager submission was better than any sweetly loving intimate moment. Yet it wasn't his surrender, or his youth, or his fervor that made this special. It was all of it and more; William made her feel this way. What they had was special, even if it could not be forever.

Shaking her head, she pushed the thought of the future aside and added a forward roll of her hips.

William bucked under her, and his eyes rolled back in his head. The cords in his neck stood out as he tipped his head back, likely to help him continue to stave off his release for her sake.

His visible struggle as well as the friction of his damp curls against her sensitive nub sent her over. She keened through her teeth as her internal muscles contracted around him, pulsing waves of pleasure through her as the ever-tightening ball of sensation exploded. Zips of sensitivity sparked through her limbs, over and over. Ah, gads, she'd forgotten how fantastic orgasms with a partner were. She tightened her hold on his sides, digging into his skin and muscle to hold on.

His cock kicked inside her and shot hot spurts of liquid into her, extending her pleasure as his hips managed small thrusts. His muscles went taut, then slack in the aftermath.

They both stilled, her hands on his chest as she wilted over him.

He watched her with an unsettling amount of warmth in his gaze. Different than the sexual heat, it made her nervous. She'd made him swear to avoid emotions.

You did not swear off them yourself, though, did you?

Ignoring her Belle-voiced inner conflict, she untied him.

He gathered her into his arms, and tugged her over to his side, settling her in the crook of his arm.

Although she knew better, she snuggled into him, enjoying the warmth and lassitude of post-coital hugs. She feared the fall and winter would feel even colder than her first without Charles, after this. Despite her vow to him and herself, William's departure for school would hurt, and not just because she'd be without a sexual partner again. Her first intimate interaction with him had shattered her illusion of being able to maintain distance between them.

His hand stroked her hair, relaxing her even further.

When she woke in the morning, she startled awake and patted the bed, worried they'd be discovered if he had fallen asleep with her. Finding herself alone, she replayed the night. She vaguely remembered his arm sliding out from under her, a kiss on the head and a whispered, "Thank you, Mistress."

Chapter Fifteen

William floated through the next two days until he could rejoin Charlotte. It helped that he discovered no more hidden investment commitments and received a positive reply from the steward at the Harrington estate in Northamptonshire regarding the roof repairs.

He flew to her house after supper the second day, skipping pudding. He'd managed to procure a second copy of Catullus, and held that and a transcribed poem as his latest offerings to please his Mistress.

"Another book! Thank you, William." Her eyes glowed.

"Here is a translation of one of the poems in there. I know you haven't learned all the words, but I think you've learned enough that you can match it. See what you think."

If, Juventius, I the grace win ever
Still on beauteous honied eyes to kiss you,
I would kiss them a million, yet a million.
Yea, nor count me to win the full attainment,
Not, tho' heavier e'en than ears at harvest,
Fall my kisses, a wealthy crop delightful.

Her head bowed, and his gaze traced the curve of her

neck, the weight of her hair up in a knot on her head. He swallowed to resist the temptation to put his lips to that bare nape. His cock stirred in his trousers, and he hoped he'd end the evening naked and serving her pleasure again.

Side by side at her desk, they labored over the poem and primer for an hour. As most of Catullus's poems did, the theme kept them focused on the activities following their studies.

Finally, she raised her head to meet his gaze and licked her lips.

The poem forgotten, he leaned forward and offered, "*iube*."

"*Iube?*"

He grunted. "A command, or bid."

She smiled. "Ah, I shall remember that one."

"*Sinu tenere.*"

"*Sinu tenere*? What is that?"

"Taken separately, they can be used in different ways. Together…" He reached out and traced the valley of her cleavage with a finger.

"Ah, now, puppy. We have talked about you touching without invitation. It seems you need a reminder lesson." Gesturing for him to follow, she swept from the room.

Thank heavens. He found her waiting at the stairs and led the way up to her room. He suspected that her preference for him leading was not just to ogle his bottom as she'd said, but also a way of ensuring he accepted his role. She directed, but he had to ascend of his own volition. Either way, the thought of directing his own submission while she watched him made him ache and need to adjust his cock in his trousers to manage the last few stairs.

In her bedroom, she began with her usual commands to undress her then himself. Then she proceeded to show him exactly how to use his mouth on her, before allowing him to find his own pleasure.

* * * *

As Folly's birthday was in August, the boys and William's mama had established a tradition of dinner at the Stanton residence followed by a night on the town for the three friends. It was one of the few times Folly was happy to venture into Mayfair.

"Sir, Mr. Follett has arrived. I've shown him to the drawing room to keep Mr. Lynwood company." The butler bowed from the library doorway.

William piled the never-ending paperwork to one side of his desk and rose, looking over at the servant. "Thank you. I'll be right in."

Hearing a clatter in the hall, he frowned. A second later, Emily went flying by behind the butler.

When he entered the drawing room, Emily had Folly's hands clasped in hers and was talking a mile a minute, while South lolled against the fireplace with a whisky in hand.

"I see I don't need to offer drinks," William said with a momentary frown.

South raised his glass, nodding and smiling. It was always an easy way to judge what number drink he was on by how well he contained the beverage in his glass when he made these grand gestures. Still only his first or second.

"Emily, what has you so animated?" he asked his sister. He'd always included her in any outings that were appropriate for a young lady, thus she was quite familiar with Folly and South. He'd been close with his sister all his life, at least in part to protect her from seeing more of their father's drunkenness than necessary. But he'd never seen her so focused on a private conversation with Folly.

"Last year, Folly declined to allow me to join you on your outing, saying I might this year."

"It would not be Folly's decision." William raised his brows, baffled as to why she'd have asked his friend rather than him.

"But it is his birthday, and that might give him sway with your decision."

"Might being the operative word, doll. You're still too young." Folly's baritone interrupted, carrying a thread of steel.

She stamped her slippered foot. On the rug, it was silent, which made all three men snicker. "I am seven-and-ten now. Do you not recall what you three got up to when you were my age? I seem to recall notes from the headmaster, William…"

"Emily—" William began.

"Give us a minute, Will?" Folly spoke over him.

Confused, he nodded. If Folly wanted to wrestle with Emily's waywardness, it was his birthday. William would just as soon not fight with his sister. Especially as it seemed he needed to keep an eye on his other friend.

Folly led her over to a corner of the room, out of earshot but still within sight, where they whispered furiously for long minutes.

William poured himself a cup of tea and watched South refill his whisky. "Pace yourself, South, you know this is destined to be a long night. And Mama will have your head if you are soused at the dinner table."

"Yes, yes." South's tone was impatient, the swing of

his glass a little more expansive, the slosh a little higher. "I have found a new gaming hell I am dying to show the both of you. Folly at least cannot bow out tonight."

They covered the cost of his birthday outing each year, but William was concerned at the frequency of South finding "new" gaming hells. For him to be playing dice and cards that often was bad. The fact that he kept bouncing from place to place was worse.

"How fares the lovely widow? Is she the reason you've been quitting White's early? You know, I'm not certain I understand the appeal. I suppose with age comes experience. What has she been teaching you?"

William growled at his friend.

South's head shot back and he blinked, then drawled, "Really? 'Tis like that then? You do recall you have another year of university. And you leave for Harrington in a sennight."

"I know. But she's different. Girls our age are just that—girls. I swear she is smarter than I am."

Folly rejoined them then. "Who is? Emily?"

William shot him a quick look, then glanced around for his sister. She'd left the room, presumably to see where their mother was and check on dinner.

"Will's widow." South wiggled his eyebrows.

"Oh." Folly cocked his head, perusing William's face. "What are you going to do when you return to Oxford?"

William's lips twisted. "I haven't worked that out yet. She wants to end it."

South hooted. "Oh, she's just using your young nubile body for a summer fling? Drat it all, why couldn't she have picked me?"

Ignoring him, Folly said in a gentle voice, "Perhaps

that would be best. You have enough to juggle. If 'tis real, then you can renew your acquaintance next summer."

"What about all the men who have more to offer her? More life experience? Less…" he lowered his voice, his eyes sliding sideways to check the doorway for family members, "…baggage? They'll be here all those months and I will not." He wanted to wring his hands and weep just thinking about it. Some more polished suitor would sweep in and woo her and he could not even use the tools he had to fight from Oxford. Or could he…? He was suddenly grateful he'd gotten her a second copy of Catullus's work. There might be a way to press his suit from afar.

"If 'tis real, that won't matter." Out of the three of them, Folly was the philosopher. That fact always amazed William, but it also helped ground him in how important his worries were in the grand scheme of things. After all, Folly had already conquered challenges that William was still learning, like feeding, clothing and housing himself.

Changing the subject, he asked, "What were you and Emily discussing over there?"

Folly gave him a lopsided smile. "I was convincing her that she, too, could wait another year to celebrate my aging."

"Without a tantrum? Well done." He turned to South, but found his friend's back retreating toward the whisky decanter again. William frowned, opening his mouth to say something when his mother swept into the room to greet his friends and announce dinner. It promised to be a long night of corralling South again, after long days of cleaning up his father's messes.

Chapter Sixteen

Charlotte dawdled in bed, something she almost never did, enjoying William's spiced rum scent on her sheets underlying the woody, slightly bitter aroma of her tea. Intimacy with William the past weeks had been sensational, beyond her expectations. A small part of her wondered if some part of the splendor might be due to the novelty, learning each other, or her abstinence in the prior months. But her heart told her it was William himself and the way they fit together in all aspects of life.

Not all. This had to end in a matter of days, she reminded herself. She could pine all she wanted, but she needed to release him to wed someone appropriate, who could bear children.

If the issue had only been the difference in their ages, she might be convinced to deal with the gossip. But the larger issue was her inability to provide heirs for the earldom.

Of course, there was always the risk some debutante that William picked—her heart twisted in pain—was also barren, but the odds against Charlotte were higher after a decade of trying. And any shrewd investor would not recommend against those odds, particularly when the future of an earldom was at stake.

Hearing Belle's voice downstairs, she scrambled into

a day gown and pulled her hair back from her face with combs at her temples.

"Ah, there you are. Did I disturb anything?" Belle stood in the dining room doorway, her gaze sliding past Charlotte to the stairs.

"No."

"Late night with the young stud then? How much longer do you get him for?"

"Only a few days," Charlotte muttered. She already missed him and they'd only parted six hours ago.

"We shall find something—or someone—to distract you when he leaves." Belle wiggled her brows.

Much to her embarrassment, her eyes welled with tears.

"Oh no," Belle exclaimed. She hugged Charlotte and led her to a chair, pouring tea before sitting next to her. "We can't have this. Your heart got 'short-term' confused with 'happily-ever-after,' didn't it?"

Charlotte nodded, sniffling.

The courtesan considered. Tilting her head, she said, "I still think that is doable—"

"No. I am too high a risk. He needs heirs."

"We don't know—"

"No, we don't. However, we know it's less likely than the average young miss who has just come out and is a decade younger, besides." When Belle took a breath to retort, Charlotte added. "Please, Belle. Not now, I can't bear it. Perhaps I'll have a better perspective after he's gone. In the meantime, I wanted to talk to you about something more tangible."

"What is it?"

"You mentioned that William's family is struggling financially. I wonder if I could—or should—help them in some way."

"You mean a loan?"

Charlotte shrugged.

"A gift?" Belle's voice rose on the word. "How do you think that would make him feel? I am quite sure he's not ready to call off the earldom and enter my line of work."

Charlotte gasped. "It wouldn't be like that."

"It would likely feel as though it were, don't you see?"

"Ugh. I hadn't thought of that. Regardless, gift, loan, is there a way to help them without hurting his pride?"

"Have you spoken to him about this?" Belle asked, frowning.

"No, I wanted to think it through with you first—and given your reaction, that was the right thing to do."

"Right, then. Let's consider. I suppose it would depend on how much they needed, who would control it, and how long they needed it for, assuming it would be a loan."

"Why?"

"Because if his father is going to drink it all away or whatever he's doing, then you're throwing good money after bad, aren't you? And I don't know that you want to mix business and pleasure. I mean—" she grinned. "—I'm fine doing so, but when the lines are blurred, 'tis not such a good idea."

Charlotte giggled. "More good points."

"I think you'd need to know more about the specific needs to figure out how to circumvent his father. But first and foremost, you need to discuss it with him. If this is really ending within days, it is best to wait and think more about it when your mind is not clouded with lust or misery."

"You are right. If you hear anything about the situation becoming more dire, though, please let me know."

* * * *

With the family's removal to Harrington rapidly approaching, William had managed to sneak out a few times during the day.

The afternoon was warm, and Charlotte had brought him to the garden to study.

However, her rakelet was agitated, pacing the path in front of the bench on which she'd settled.

He turned on a heel and in a fast flurry asked, "May I invite you to visit Oxford in a fortnight, Mistress?"

Her heart broke a little more. Apparently, she'd hurt both of them by allowing this to go too far, and emotions were involved on both sides. "William, we discussed this. This ends when you leave London. You need to focus on your studies, then find a suitable girl to marry."

"But, Mistress, what of your studies?"

"I shall muddle along just fine. Or I'll pay a tutor, if need be." She waved a deceptively casual hand, ensuring it did not shake.

He growled.

She raised her brows. "I beg your pardon?"

"I want to help you."

"Now you sound like a petulant child," she admonished him, despite wishing the same.

He hung his head. After a moment of silence, he raised it, his eyes bright. "May I have a token to remember you by? Please, Mistress?"

"Like what?"

"Like a lady would give a handkerchief or something

for a knight to remember her when he rode into battle."

"I dearly hope Oxford is nothing like battle." Her tone was dry.

He grinned. "No, but I shall be fighting the constant desire to return to you."

"William, you know how important I find education. Don't you dare waste your opportunity." She was frowning.

"A token would help." The puppy eyes were back.

She shook her head and sighed. What would it hurt to give him something to remember her by? Perhaps something that would fade with time, as his memories of her should. Resolved, she said, "Come and kneel down and unbutton your trousers."

"Holy hell," he whispered, dropping to his knees.

Her teeth set at the imagined feel of his poor knees hitting the stone walkway, but he did not seem to notice.

Wrenching at the fall of his trousers, he had them undone in a moment, his cock bouncing out.

She took a moment to admire the delicious sight, enjoying once again the joys of being with a man barely twenty. His young cock hardened with a few words. "Pull your shirt out of the way."

One eager hand held his shirt, the other the flap of his trousers.

Not wanting to abuse his trust, she doublechecked that he was out of view of the house, blocked by her and a bush offset behind the bench. He hadn't bothered, remaining riveted on her. An arrow of pleasure shot through her. If she never found that singular focus again, she vowed to be content with this second chance at such a unique version of happiness.

His cock bobbed, and her breath caught, heat

gathering at the juncture of her legs.

She took her time raising her arms, enjoying the movement of her breasts within her garments.

His gaze dropped for a moment.

She smiled as her fingers caught her hair ribbon and tugged. Her hair fell around her face, and he looked at the ribbon as she carried it forward.

He smiled. "A tie. How perfect, Mistress."

She reached for his cock and he made a strangled noise.

"Yes, William?"

"Nothing, Mistress. Please proceed."

His heat seared her even before her fingers touched the silk-over-steel shaft. She wrapped them around him, sliding down the length.

He moaned under his breath but otherwise knew to remain silent after their weeks together.

She squeezed once—just to torture him a little more—then slid the ribbon around the base of him, pushing the wiry golden curls out of the way. He surged in her grasp and she tightened her grip.

"Mistress," came a whisper of sound.

"You didn't really expect a handkerchief, did you?"

He gave a strangled chuckle and shook his head.

"Then hold still." She wrapped the length around him a second time, then tugged the ends a teeny bit. Ignoring his breathed curse, she then tied a knot, tight enough that it would keep him hard longer, but still stay on when he softened. Sitting back, she admired the contrast of the ecru satin against the dusky red of his shaft, the creamy satin giving way to silky skin. The sight made her salivate.

She made him wear it all afternoon before finally

leading him to the bedroom and fulfilling her wish to suck the length of him down until her lips met that ribbon. He only lasted a few minutes before begging to be allowed to pleasure her.

* * * *

As the following afternoon was just as nice, Charlotte had William shown to the garden again. He immediately tried to convince her to take a stroll with him.

"No, William, just no."

"Mistress, 'tis but one outing. Please. We've met out at two salons, and I've been visiting in the dark of night for weeks. I am asking for one joint outing for an ice, as the weather has been beautiful."

She folded her arms and shook her head at him. She hated the dual standards of society at the best of times, but had always managed to avoid being the topic of gossip. Rumors, she could handle, however. Acquaintances seeing them together and then asking her about him in a month might destroy her, as the anticipated pain of losing him was already crippling.

"I shall pay whatever penalty you deem fit. Whatever punishment you can concoct." His young, clean-shaven face was earnest, his eyes pleading as much as his words.

Her blood fired, a spark of heat shooting low through her belly. Damned rakelet. How did someone that young know her so well, so quickly? Scenarios with him on his knees, or supine and tied, begging for her touch, raced through her mind before she could stop them. Closing her eyes in a slow blink, she tried to regain control, but she knew her flush was visible.

He pressed further. "One. I have less than a sennight and am running out of late-night hours to spend with you."

She did not care to dwell on that fact, she preferred to focus on enjoying the precious hours they had. Even before Belle asked, she'd worried she'd allowed him into her heart as well as her body. His departure would leave her bereft, no matter how temporary and ill-advised this dalliance was.

William tried a new tactic, sliding to his knees at her feet. "Please, Mistress. See, I beg you on my knees. How can I make it up to you?"

She gasped, staring at him open-mouthed. Such entreaty was a level of power play she had not experienced or even desired, at least until her vision of a few minutes ago. But the thrill that shot through her now, pointing her nipples and wetting her core, made her wonder why she hadn't put him there sooner.

The puppy dared to slide his hand under her skirt, to skim it up her leg.

She stepped back, frowning. "I beg your pardon. What is the golden rule?"

His hand dropped to his lap and his smile fell. He bent his head to stare at it and muttered, "My apologies, Mistress. No touching without permission."

"I should deny you all requests after that. I'm very disappointed in you, puppy." But then she heard herself continue, "But as it happens, I find the day quite hot, and am in need of an ice."

His head snapped up, his brows high in hope. "Truly, Mistress?"

She sighed. This was a bad idea, but she could not regret it when seeing his reaction. Ah well, there would be time for kneeling later.

"Truly. But do not think to avoid punishment for that

transgression."

He leaped to his feet in one smooth bounce. "I know just the place. 'Tis out of the way, you shan't be too uncomfortable. Come, let us go now, please, Mistress!"

And so they went. He held the door for her, then they perused the list of choices side by side.

The shop assistant strolled over to hover in front of the attractive lordling puppy. Simpering, she leaned forward and asked, "My lord, what can I get you?"

"Please serve the lady first."

"Oh!" Her glance flicked between them several times. Her voice conveyed confusion when she continued. "I did not realize you came together."

Stricken, Charlotte considered their appearance. She'd replenished only part of her wardrobe after deciding to socialize again as a widow, and her clothing and bonnet were conservative. She also hadn't anticipated an outing; her day dress was on the plain side. His clean-shaven face made him appear even younger than his years, and his enthusiasm added to his youthful mien.

Unable to answer, she took a hasty step back when William reached for her. Turning blindly, she somehow found the door, the step, and even a hackney cab.

William followed, talking in a low voice, apologizing.

Her jaw was locked to keep from screaming, crying, shouting. Anger roiled in her, wanting to erupt. Not at him, but at herself. Just as she'd thought she'd been ready for balls after mourning Charles, she'd believed she was prepared for the gossip. But the stab of pain she'd felt at the stranger's reaction told her just how far she'd fallen in love with her rakelet. She'd just wanted to please him in return for his well-thought-out gifts throughout the summer.

Still silent, she climbed in the hack, barring his way when he moved to follow her. Her pulse pounded in her temples. The chit likely thought she was a spinster aunt he was being kind to. At least the girl would not spread gossip; she'd avoid painful questions. Gracious, *she'd* judged him when he'd first approached her, knowing it was inappropriate even as she fought her attraction to him. Above all, she might have been able to get past all that, if not for his need of heirs. The whole escapade made her feel woefully inadequate and despondent.

Biting her lip to avoid crying in public, she told herself that it would have been over in a matter of days anyway. With this, at least he understood why she'd resisted and would not contact her. He'd get on with university, find someone his age, and enjoy his life. If she'd taught him a technique or two that he enjoyed in the future, perhaps he'd remember her fondly, as she would him.

Stumbling out of the conveyance, she made it inside and told her staff to lock all doors and windows. Their concerned looks changed to sympathy when she added that she was not at home to visitors, even Belle and most certainly Lord Stanton.

Unable to deal with their pity, she took to her bed for the day, pulling the covers over her and clutching the heart pendant around her neck. Like losing Charles, the abrupt, unexpected loss left her reeling. The worst part was that this one could have been avoided. She'd known better.

Despite her wishes, the girl's questioning look played on repeat in her head, bringing tears anew every time. She knew the next day and the day after that, and all the days following would be forever marred by his absence.

158

Chapter Seventeen

Every day until his family retired to the country, William attempted to see Charlotte, trying every avenue he could think of.

He did not care about what a silly shop assistant had to say. He…cared about her. He hadn't dared tell her, then that foolish girl had to be, well, foolish.

Frantic and furious—at the shop worker, at himself, at the unfairness of society's rules—he checked the front door, the back gate, her window, everything. He sent gifts daily—books, flowers, even chocolates, which he'd never seen her eat. In one wild moment, he contemplated asking Folly if she was a client to see if Folly could fake a delivery. But he would never betray his Mistress's confidence, nor would he want to place Folly in a position that could jeopardize his income.

He returned home and stewed, his anger overriding his frustration. *Stupid, immature puppy, I had to try for a public outing.* He'd wanted to show her off out of pride that she chose to be with him. And with the clarity of hindsight, he saw his goal had been to prove to her that they might continue their relationship after the summer. Instead, he'd reinforced her beliefs.

As his days in London dwindled, desolation at the loss of those last evenings with his Mistress plagued him most of all.

Time ran out, and he was forced to pack and leave for the estate without having any chance to apologize or make it up to her, or even attempt to negotiate the idea he'd had fermenting—encouraging her to continue her Latin studies with his help from university via correspondence, another idea he'd borrowed from Ovid's *Ars amatoria*. He packed the books, gave the chocolates to his sister, and began crafting letters to her in his head during the carriage ride.

Once in the country, he was too busy for much of anything except handling estate business: resolving conflicts, managing the books, and writing correspondence until he left and his mother and cousin had to take over.

A month flew by, his yearning for Charlotte increasing rather than fading. Back at Oxford after Michaelmas, he sat with his books at his elbow on the desk, unable to concentrate on his courses. His longing may have increased, but he feared she might not feel the same.

Despite her mandate of no correspondence, it was worth trying. He grabbed paper and pen. At least through the post, the letter would not be returned. Whether or not she would read it was another matter.

My dearest Mistress,
I have arrived back at Oxford. I have thought of you every day. I beg your forgiveness for my poor choice in ice shops, indeed for the arrogance of my impertinence. My fervent hope is that you realize it stemmed from a desire to spend more time with you. My greatest wish is that I could beg in person, which

might prove more successful.

I hate that a shop worker had the power to hurt you. I confess I also had not anticipated that you were vulnerable to that. I see your strength, but I should have recognized that everyone's armor has a weak point which can be pierced.

Please accept the enclosed memento as a small part of my apology.

Your copy of The Odyssey was translated by Alexander Pope. Whilst that is the most widely available, I thought you might be interested in learning that George Chapman's earlier translation was so transformational that Keats wrote a sonnet about it.

The short poem was published two years back in the paper. I found a copy and have transcribed it here for you. I was also able to locate a copy of Chapman's translation in a bookstore here at Oxford that I am sending with this missive.

Your silence is the worst punishment you've ever devised. I'd beg you to write to me, but I feel it necessary to do more to earn your response after being irresponsible. However, you have my solemn promise that I will do so only after my studies are complete each week-end.

He reread the note, his pen hovering as he considered whether to expand on the idea of punishment. Deciding against it, he hesitated over his closing salutation. "Your loving servant" was too strong and would tip his hand. He knew his mistress. And for that matter, his mother. Until his majority, he needed to step carefully. Neither would react well to a declaration of his love before then.

"Your caring servant" sounded wishy-washy. In the end, he opted for "faithful" and signed it with a flourish.

Your faithful servant,
William

The following weekend, caught up on his reading, he again addressed the desolation that had swirled in his stomach since their outing.

If he could entice her to read his letters through the fall and spring, his schedule would become more flexible after graduation. He could manage estate matters from London more of the year than not. He cast about in his memory for works in Latin that might lure her into a response. Recalling the book of poetry by Catullus, he debated whether skipping from deference to naughty boldness would work. He shrugged. He had several months; he could attempt various sallies and see if any provoked a response. If nothing else, they would keep him forefront in her mind and perhaps even wondering which direction his next letter would take.

Mistress,
How is your Latin progressing? In a further attempt to edge back into your good graces, I thought to offer another poem from Catullus. I've included the reference here so you can identify words.
I miss your wit, your intellect, your humor, as well as your touch.

This carmen (#96 in your book) speaks to the depth of my sorrow…
If to the silent dead aught sweet or tender ariseth,
Calvus, of our dim grief's common humanity born;
When to a love long cold some pensive pity recalls us,

*When for a friend long lost wakes some unhappy
regret;*
Not so deeply, be sure, Quintilia's early departing
Grieves her, as in thy love dureth a plenary joy.

*It was written by Catullus to a friend mourning the
loss of a loved one. I would never equate my misery
with yours upon the passing of your husband—
indeed, no two griefs will ever feel the same, don't
you think? Mine, though, has the added torture of
being my own fault.*
*I read this again and try to imagine how it would feel
to lose you forever. I cannot. The pain is too much to
bear. Please, you must forgive me. I beg you again.*
Your suffering servant,
William

His next letter took one more step toward boldness,
including two poems.

Mistress,
*I count the days until my graduation. Much as I
should do so in thanks for my mother's
resourcefulness in ensuring I got this far, and for the
freedom and autonomy formal adulthood—my
'majority'—brings, those are not my reasons. As you
know, I much prefer the bindings, cuffs, or ribbons
you offer to any freedom.*
*You can likely tell from the bent of this opening how
much I miss you and in how many ways…*
*How is your autumn faring? Do you miss me as I
miss you? I thought to challenge you, thus I am not
including the poem number for this translation. Can*

you find it?

After flipping through the book of poetry once more, he added another reference below the first translated poem.

I hope this next one makes you laugh. You shan't find this particular carmen translated anywhere in a bookstore...

O ridiculous thing, Cato, and absurd,
Worthy of your hearing, and of your sneering.
Laugh, Cato, as you love Catullus;
The thing is ridiculous, nay, too absurd.
I just came upon a lad who on a girl
Was thrusting and, if it pleases the mother of Venus,
I pierced him with the stiffest staff of mine.

Your beribboned servant,
William

* * * *

Staring around the dim pub, packed with drunken Oxford students, William swore again. He and South shared one class, but he had not seen his friend in over a week. Even when he had, it had not been in the classroom.

Wading his way through the crowd, he headed for the back corner South preferred, watching for a swinging tankard. Finding a mutual acquaintance, he leaned in to shout, "Where's South?"

"Haven't seen him."

"Today?"

"For a few days." The student shrugged and turned

back to the conversation at the table.

William swore again and turned to stomp out.

A barmaid tugged his sleeve. "Milord?"

"Pardon me, I need to—" he edged away.

"Your friend was in most days last week but was gone by the time the other upperclassmen arrived. He came in today to give me a bit of coin in thanks and said he was returning to London."

"London?" He was aghast. "'Tis the middle of the semester."

She shrugged. "I was just trying to help you."

"Thank you, miss. I do appreciate it. I did not mean to yell at you."

He rushed to South's rooms.

His friend was packing books in crates, his clothing already in trunks.

"What're you doing?" William hovered in the doorway, hands on the doorframe.

"I'm heading back to London. Oxford and I don't mix."

William noted the flask on the empty desk.

South followed his gaze, and grimaced. "No lectures, please. At some point I'll have to face my father, and I may never hear the end of it then."

"But I can help you—"

"You've *been* helping me. Last year, getting me home a few times this summer from various spots when I wasn't fit to walk. I still manage to fail—classes, bets, life."

"South, no. Please don't throw this opportunity away. I'll do more, help more. 'Tis only a few more months." William wasn't sure how, but he could not bear to see his friend leave. More, he worried what South would do alone in London with no one to carry him home. He was ready to not sleep for the rest of university if it meant stopping his friend from becoming like his father.

South stopped packing and stared at him. "Will, I appreciate the kind offer. I know it is well meant. So please do not take this the wrong way." He sucked in a breath. "I don't want you to."

William's shoulders dropped. He nodded, stepping in to hug South and pat him on the back. "I'll write, and be down to see you as soon as I can. Please don't be a stranger to Folly."

South returned the hug without responding.

Chapter Eighteen

Charlotte's autumn had been troughs of wallowing in misery, occasionally interrupted by posts from William.

She paced the library. She was beyond being calmed by the warm floral tones and fluffy throw pillows. "Dratted puppy!"

Belle lounged sideways in her chair at the tea table in the corner, one arm slung carelessly over the back of the intricately carved chairback, legs crossed and the top one swinging. She watched like the soliloquy was Shakespearean theatre, a half-smirk betraying her amusement.

"What am I to do with this?" Charlotte shook the latest letter full of cramped handwriting and the two poems at her friend. The book lay where she had tossed it on the table.

"Frame it?"

"Belle. I'm serious."

"You're also being silly. You needn't *do* anything with that. Respond if you like, ignore it if not. You ignored his last letter."

"But, but…"

"Exactly. You cannot, because he knows you, perhaps better than anyone."

Charlotte flashed her a look, uncertain if Belle was

comparing the rakelet to her husband. Belle's face was expressionless, eyes following her as she roamed the room.

Belle continued, "I told you, he is a great match for you in spirit, intelligence, and in bed. I understand why you think you need to, but I maintain that you should stop fighting this and enjoy finding such a partner. This proves my point yet again. He knew just how to engage you, even if you don't respond."

Charlotte threw herself down across from Belle and poured more tea. "You were the one who suggested it as a fling, a-a- *practice*!"

"That would have worked, too, had you not fallen for the puppy. When you did, I adjusted my advice accordingly."

"Convenient." Charlotte pressed her lips together, irritated more at herself than Belle for allowing William to continue to affect her this much. "Belle, I cannot. That girl meant no harm, but we must have an end date given my barrenness. And I was devastated. I have no desire to go through another loss—worse, one of my own doing."

Belle arched a brow, recognizing what Charlotte knew. Her reaction at the end of summer said she already had.

"I understand your concern, dearest," Belle said, patting her hand. "But you've said yourself, you wish to wed again, you want to find someone to spend your life with and enjoy intellectual pursuits with. Why not him? The rakelet has made you cry and laugh just through letters. There aren't many aristocrats out there who would spend that amount of time or effort."

Charlotte recalled his letter with the poem on grief. She'd been sniffling by the end of it, silent tears streaming down her cheeks as she reread his words about losing her forever. A small, mean part of her was a tiny bit glad he was as miserable as she was. But more, the maturity to read that and empathize with her loss impressed her. He was so often lighthearted and playful but then surprised her with his thoughtfulness and perception.

Then the more recent letter with overt references to a threesome. He was outrageous and funny and caring and…kept giving her cause to fall further in love with him even from a distance. Dratted, beloved puppy.

* * * *

Charlotte spent Christmas in Peterborough at the family estate, with her brother-in-law Edward and his lovely wife, Sophia, but kept her trip short.

While the house held no painful holiday memories for her, as she and Charles had spent most of the year in London for the sake of salons and museums, the couple were still newlyweds and she suspected they valued their remoteness from society, including her.

Sophia was about William's age, while Edward was a year or two behind Charlotte. Despite the similar age gap, she did her best not to think about William, knowing that society viewed their age difference quite differently and his need for heirs was a bigger issue.

Back in London, Belle dragged her to a demi-monde party celebrating the New Year, but she warned her coachman to stay close and managed to escape after the midnight toast, returning to her quiet home as she preferred. Pretending not to wonder if William was back in Town on Christmas break was exhausting.

Strolling into the library for the decanters on the sideboard, she spied the books he'd given her on the corner of her desk. She poured herself a port to take upstairs but then plopped down at her desk to snick open her drawer, pull his letters out, and read them for the umpteenth time, admitting to a teeny bit of surprise at not having heard from him again.

Melancholy welled in her at this time of year, just as it had the year prior. The holidays were particularly lonely. She and Charles had had such an active social life that included many holiday fêtes, then they'd hole up in this house for the days after Christmas to spend private time together. They gave half their servants Christmas and the first half of the week off, and then the rest the second half and New Year's. They'd often lock the library door, build a fire, and partake in fireside intimacies at her direction.

She'd redone this room a few months ago. She'd spent several months after his passing to alternate between wallowing and basking in memories of their time there. Then she'd taken herself in hand and repainted their bedroom, replacing the chairs by the window and the bedding. Then the dining room. Then just the two armchairs in the parlor as the one had been her "throne" of sorts and they were a matched pair. Finally, she'd felt ready to make the library into her own sanctuary, rather than the remains of theirs. The room was now her favorite room in the house, and its floral tones of yellows and oranges with spots of green almost always soothed her.

Looking at the colorful printed pillows, she imagined reclining on them with William. The reds and golds of the flames in the fireplace reflected the tints of his hair. What gift would he have given her for Christmas? His gift-giving skills were masterful. And she might have gotten him something from Folly's and the Orfords's latest catalogue of leather restraints. Or a Christmas-colored ribbon.

Shaking her head, she returned her gaze to the poems he'd challenged her to identify. The holiday was the reason for her weakness. This would not do. She was too strong a woman to indulge in this over a mere boy. Grabbing her port, she went to bed.

* * * *

Still set on ignoring him and his tempting correspondence, she put them away and continued her efforts at Latin, but she struggled with the number of ways many words were used. It was contextual, which meant learning a list of words was not as helpful as say…reading poems.

She held out for another week, although his letters re-emerged from the drawer and the paper grew soft and worn from handling.

Then, one night as she lingered over a second glass of wine, she wandered in to stare at his signature. Unable to resist any longer, she sat and pulled her Latin primer and the Catullus book toward her on the desk, to study them.

Damned rakelet.

She was more drawn to the first poem than the second, despite the earthiness of the threesome depicted.

She needed a diversion. At the bookstore, Charlotte perused the books of Latin phrases. Her preferred bookseller did not have these in stock, and rather than make her wait for him to get one in, he had kindly directed her here. The new store's owner had been eyeing her suspiciously since she walked in, his lips pursed at her position in front of the boys' education shelf.

Deciding on one that seemed to be for beginners, she made her way to his counter. As she did, the shop door snicked open behind her and skirts rustled.

She handed the book over. The man's eyebrows lowered, and he stared at her. "Madame, would you like this wrapped? I presume 'tis a gift?"

Old misogynistic goat. I should dearly love to tell him that I shall be using it, but with my luck he'll not sell it to me. Shouldn't a shop owner be happy for any sales? She sighed. 'Twould be easier to go along and get the book then never return. "Pick your battles, Charlotte," her husband always used to say.

"No thank you. 'Tis for my son."

A gasp sounded behind her, and she whirled, a hand to her chest.

"Oh, Sophia, Lady Pe—er—'tis lovely to see you, of course. Ah…" Charlotte trailed off and gaped at her sister-in-law, who knew very well she did not have a son. If she had, Edward would never have become the Earl of Peterborough.

Charlotte turned back to the shopkeeper, with her most imperious look—one William had never caused her to use, even at his boldest. "Please hold that for me. I shall return within the hour." She nodded at him, and turned to Sophia. "Lady Peterborough, I did not realize you were here in Town. Would you be so kind as to walk with me for a spell?"

Sophia smiled and leaned in to kiss her cheek. "Of course. We are in for the opening of Parliament. 'Tis lovely to see you, too. And remember, we are family. 'Tis Sophia, always, please."

The two Countesses of Peterborough, past and

present, linked arms and set off to meander along the London street, busy as Spring reigned and the Season neared.

"I beg your pardon for that small untruth, Sophia. My preferred bookstore is a few blocks away, but Mr. Choplin did not have what I was looking for and referred me here. That old curmudgeon was sure I could not be learning Latin. I debated arguing with him, but I doubt it would help"—the women exchanged resigned grimaces—"so I made that up to expedite the sale."

"Ah. I hope you will give me your preferred bookseller then. I only came because Edward wanted something very specific and he's found it at this bookstore in the past. I shall advise him not to use this particular shop again, however."

Charlotte smiled at her, appreciative that Edward was willing to take advice from his wife. The brothers were very different in many other ways. For instance, she knew that Edward preferred a role more like hers in the bedroom and in fact had at one time belonged to a spanking club. It probably was unfair that she knew more about Sophia's sex life than Sophia did of hers.

"You're learning Latin?" Sophia asked, sounding impressed. "What prompted that?"

Without thinking it through, Charlotte asked, "Do you know Lord William Stanton?"

He was, after all, close to Sophia's age. Charlotte ignored Belle's voice snickering in her head about that fact.

"Hmm." Sophia's brow furrowed. "The name rings a bell. Who are his parents?"

"The Earl and Countess of Harrington. And his cousin is Percy Stanton."

"Oh! Of course. Lady Harrington. Lovely woman. I'm surprised you don't know her, actually. She is very well-spoken, and always reading something new. Much like you."

Charlotte frowned, quickly turning away from Sophia, sorry she'd raised the subject. Now how would she explain her question? Caught between embarrassment and anger at society's double standard, she flushed.

"Charlotte? Are you quite all right? Why do you ask about Ruth's—er, Lady Harrington's—son?"

"Never mind. I met him at a few lectures." She waved her hand to dismiss her question as a passing interest.

Sophia watched her. "He is close to his mother, for reasons I shan't gossip about. And to his cousin. They are, all of them, lovely."

Charlotte noticed she did not say a lovely family. Apparently, William's father's drinking was common knowledge.

"Yes. Well. I have only met William."

"You must come to Roslynn's salon. Ruth attends when she has time. I don't know why I didn't think of it before. Likely because I am horse-obsessed like Edward and don't attend enough myself." Sophia rolled her eyes at herself, smiling. "And in London about as often as you are not. How fortuitous that we met like this. Why, then, did you ask about Lord Stanton? And how does your learning Latin relate to him?"

"'Tis not important." Charlotte's hand was beginning to flap wildly in a poor semblance of not caring. She turned from Sophia to continue walking, hoping her blush was not noticeable.

Sophia was quiet for a moment, as they turned to stroll back along the other side of the street, staying in sight of their coachmen. She stopped before the entrance to the bookstore.

Charlotte reluctantly halted and turned to face her.

"We are here for a sennight. I should like to have you 'round for dinner and see how you have been these past few months. Seeing you now and hearing about lectures gives me hope that you are starting to get past the worst of your grief. I think, from what Edward tells me of him, Charles would have wanted that for you." Sophia hesitated. Then, cocking her head, she said slowly, "You know, just as you mentioned that William is my age, I believe Edward is your age…"

Charlotte bit her lip, stunned at how perceptive this young person was, like William.

Sophia continued after a beat, "If you and he are…friends…perhaps we can meet him sometime. I'd like to think that we would all have much to talk about. Edward and I are very happy, and we'd like to share that with family."

As Sophia kissed her farewell and departed, Charlotte pictured Belle and Sophia meeting. Belle might be less subtle, but they were both strong-willed women who spoke their minds. Such an encounter wasn't likely, but she smiled at the thought of how well they'd get along.

Dratted women friends, all shoving me toward William. One thinks I am sex-starved, the other seems to worry about me being lonely.

They had a point. She missed far more than sex with William. The lack of someone to share the little day-to-day things created a loneliness that was crippling some days. Sophia had noted her recovery from losing Charles, but she was still mired in misery from losing William.

Sophia had easily accepted the idea of a relationship between Charlotte and William. However, as the current Countess of Peterborough, Sophia should be well-versed in the expectations of her role. Charlotte was surprised at her unquestioning support.

Belle's voice rang in her ears. "…open to being tied, willing to call you Mistress, bold enough to pursue to a point, and has an innate understanding that you need to take it from there. How is that not everything you want? You were a mere year older than him when you married Charles…you should stop fighting this and enjoy…"

Based on the prior year, William would be home in two months. She had time to consider taking her friends' pep talks to heart, and to identify the poems with her new Latin dictionaries.

Chapter Nineteen

William gripped his desk when his housemate delivered the note, afraid of embarrassing himself by either falling in a faint or launching himself at the missive. Wanting to relish the moment, he pulled the ribbon from his pocket and gripped it in his left hand as he clumsily broke the seal on the letter one-handed.

His eyes skipped to the signature, and he bit back a shout. 'Twas from her!

Scanning it, he began to grin.

Dear William,
Carmen 56, I believe. I do not yet have enough words in my vocabulary to be sure of the first, but with your tip, my guess is 51.
Best of luck in your final term at Oxford.
Sincerely,
Mistress Charlotte

He read it a second time. Then he did launch himself, grabbing his thick cloak and flying down the stairs to stalk up and down the High Street, sucking in deep breaths of the frigid air to calm himself.

As brief as it was, her underlying message was clear. She was keeping the door open to their relationship, despite how the previous summer had ended. He'd never expected her to write to him, he'd written simply to have a fighting chance of rekindling their romance when he returned. Unable to take it in, he kept staring at the letter, almost turning his ankle on the cobblestones.

He wanted to leap for joy, skip along the road, he wanted to grab a horse and ride through the night to her, studies be damned. He wanted to use reams of paper to scribble all of his thoughts and feelings to her.

However, he needed to be strategic. To do so, he'd have to find his composure and contemplate his approach with care. His fingers were still shaking when he composed his reply, but his mind was serene. Their correspondence was like a cricket match, it would not be won in a day. This was an inning; the rest of the match would be played—and won—when he returned to London.

Dear Mistress,
Why is it that the pleasure you bestow is most sweet after a punishment? Never mind, I do not need the reason. I shall bask in your attention either way.
The brevity of your reply tells me you have not fully forgiven me. I shan't push (see, I can be trained), but here is another passage for your Latin lessons—an excerpt. Can you fill in the next line or two before I arrive?
Dear one, a kiss I stole, while you did wanton a-playing,
Sweet ambrosia, love, never as honily sweet.
Dearly the deed I paid for; an hour's long misery waning
Your obedient servant,

William

Blazes, he wished he could see her expression as she read this apology. By the time it got to her, she would not have time to write back, as he'd be on his way back to London.

In the meantime, he needed to find patience and focus on graduating. He had done everything he could think of for now. Once he was home, he would have easier ways to regain his spot in her affections. He refused to entertain the possibility of failure. His heart might shrivel in his chest if he had to live without her much longer, to say nothing of other parts shriveling, as no other women interested him.

* * * *

William had been home a mere day, most of which he slept after a week of writing his final exams, packing his room at Oxford, and traveling to London.

Exhausted, he still hoped to sneak over to Charlotte's house to start the process of regaining her good graces.

Instead, he was summoned to the parlor by Emily, where Folly waited.

Confused as to the reason for his summoning and Folly's presence, he asked, "What is this?"

Folly responded, "A graduation celebration. 'Tis not every day nor every working class lobcock who has two friends complete their university studies."

"Ah, when was the last time you spoke to South?"

Folly thought for a minute. "My birthday last summer."

"What?" William paced. "He left Oxford in October."

Folly's eyes widened.

"He said he felt…lost. I told him to come by and let you know he was back so he'd have a voice of reason." William's vision of having one night free of responsibilities in Charlotte's arms went up in smoke. As did any likelihood of celebrating his own matriculation. They needed to find South.

"Let's go."

Emily stepped forward.

William frowned. "Where do you think you're going, squirt?"

"With you. I'm already in my first Season, and I'm eight-and-ten now. There is no reason I cannot join you."

"There is if I do not agree."

Folly cleared his throat.

William glanced at him, still frowning.

"I sort of promised her she could come, at least for part of the evening."

William's brows shot toward his hairline.

"What? Why? How?"

"'Tis something of a long story. I'm happy to discuss it some other time than lingering in your front hall," his friend said sheepishly. "Obviously, 'tis a moot point now, as we need to find South."

"What? No. I can help," Emily pleaded, her focus on Folly.

"No." Both men spoke at the same time.

Folly added, "If we find him quickly, we'll come back here. But if we're not back in an hour, we aren't coming." He turned to William. "Does that sound fair?"

"Depends on what state we find South in," he muttered.

They left Emily pouting. South was not at his family's London residence, nor was he at the first four gaming hells they tried. After trying his haunts in St. James and Soho, they edged their way into the seedier parts of London. They now tread closer and closer to the Limehouse canal, its odor intensifying as they neared.

Folly asked, "Could South return to Oxford to finish his studies?"

"I don't know for sure. I suspect within a reasonable amount of time, as an earl's son he could manage it. But he always needed my help with classwork. I know he didn't enjoy his time there, but he was almost finished. I just don't understand."

"What do you think put him over the top?"

"I don't know. I'd been frustrated with his drinking, and his behavior was similar enough to my father's, that I did what I do with my father—I distanced myself. As his friend, I should have at least stepped in and offered to listen, to support him." William was chastising himself with every minute they couldn't find South.

At the last venue, they'd discovered South's London friends called him by a different moniker. Spinning off his last name of Lynwood, they'd dubbed him "Lyon." Thus, William and Folly would need to double back and ask for Lyon at a few places. William suspected his friend was at a less clean, less honest joint, though. He'd hoped South would take some time at home to regroup and find his path, but the unkempt, thinly-staffed townhouse had appeared as though he'd continued on with self-destruction.

Finally, at two o-clock in the morning, they found him sagging in the corner of a gaming hell, propped there by a member of the staff until he slept it off. Piling him into a hack cab, they took him home, dropping Folly at his forge on the way, as his workday started earlier than

William's.

* * * *

The morning after his friends surprised him, his mother informed him they were attending a ball that evening.

Already impatient to see his Mistress, he ground his teeth. He scribbled a note to Charlotte asking if she planned to attend and requesting permission to call on her after. Then he went to change, starting with a frayed ribbon, faded from being washed this past year.

He stood with Percy as usual, as his cousin and cronies exchanged stories. Percy was a listener much more than a contributor these days, and their plan was for him to attend a few balls to smooth the transition to William as the family representative to their allies in Parliament. William was glad that he had spent the time learning how to navigate balls last summer, no matter how boring he found them. At least now he knew how long he needed to stay, and for the most part, who he needed to visit with. Besides, he could not hate them entirely.

If not for these blasted balls, I might not have met my Mistress.

The mere thought tightened the ribbon he wore under his trousers. He'd tried wearing it at university, but the friction was too distracting. Washing also dulled the sheen which he wanted to preserve. Instead, he kept the folded length of ivory in his pocket and took it out to run through his fingers as he studied. Holding the satin, he could still remember the hot silken glide of her grip around him before she tied it. Tonight, hoping to see her at the ball, he had chosen to wear it with a plan to tell her or even show her.

He glanced around, hoping to spot her. He had not received a reply to his note, but hadn't expected to, so had no way of knowing if she had a prior engagement or, worse, a new suitor. Pain stabbed him in the chest as he considered the idea of her being wooed by someone else.

No. She had written to him less than two months prior. He was relatively sure that she would not have sent him any response if she had moved on. Of course, he still needed to convince her of that fact.

There was no forced end date for a dalliance now, and no reason they had to hide, at least to his thinking. His father was fifty, he had plenty of time to woo Charlotte, wed her, and finish mastering the nuances of the earldom. For the most part, he was ready to don the mantle of the earl's responsibilities aside from the title and give Percy and his mother a bit more sleep once he'd caught up on this year's Parliamentary issues, negotiations, and alliances. His mother might balk at his choice of Charlotte, but they had time to overcome that, too. For the first time since putting the pencil down after his last exam, he was excited. He had his whole life ahead of him, and a plan for it.

Convincing Charlotte would be tricky. Despite the fact that he'd reached his majority, he had no doubt she was still preoccupied with the age difference. He hadn't figured out a plan to change her mind yet, but he would persist, as *Ars amatoria* recommended. He smiled to himself. It had worked thus far, in multiple ways—letter writing, sex games. It would work for this. It had to.

He did not see her. Turning back, his mother caught his eye as she conversed with a younger matron.

Wait.

His head snapped back. Honey and gold hair coiled

on her head, ramrod spine, a deep teal dress, with teal organza cap sleeves that played peek-a-boo with her upper arms and the edge of her shoulders.

My Mistress—with my mother.

Unsure what to make of that, he cocked his head watching them.

They spoke animatedly, their hands making small but forceful gestures.

How did they meet? What are they discussing?

Watching them, the similarities leaped out at him again. Both women could speak on a myriad of topics, and often had a strong opinion about them. Both managed their own money, and both knew how to navigate the Ton and their relationships with a private strength and public unity that he respected and admired.

He thought of his friends at university warning him, "Always look at her mother. That is what you'll be tied to in twenty years." Not him. In his case, he needed to look at his own mother. He had modeled what he valued in a wife on his mother's strengths, based on his high regard for her.

The certainty of his future settled into his heart and mind. He had wanted to marry Charlotte eventually, in the abstract. Watching his two favorite women together, his heart beat with love for each. For his mother, it had the confused edge of wondering why a strong woman dealt with a weak man, something he'd never quite dared ask her. For Charlotte, while he hated that she'd been hurt by a stranger's judgment, there were no questions. He was completely, irrevocably in love with her. If he thought she'd allow it, he'd whisk her out to the garden and go to a knee that very moment. But with his Mistress, he had to handle things differently. And he found he loved that too.

I must find a way to gain permission to propose.

He strode over to the women with new determination.

Chapter Twenty

Sophia had invited Charlotte to the ladies' salon she'd mentioned, and introduced her to Ruth Stanton, Countess of Harrington and William's mother. Charlotte was nervous to the point of wringing her hands before she caught herself, but thankfully no one seemed to notice. And since Ruth was unaware of Charlotte's liaison with her son, the awkwardness was one-sided and dissipated as they became better acquainted at the salon's meetings.

As Ruth's warmth and intelligence were unveiled through her comments on the topics raised by the group, the similarities between them became clear to Charlotte. William's dismissal of their ages and his ready acceptance of her as a decision-maker made sense. Charlotte had planned to attend this ball anyway, but when William's note arrived, she found herself questioning her choice of gown, hairstyle, and even gloves.

She forced herself to stay with the gown she had planned, then dawdled deliberately so she would not be among the first to arrive in her eagerness to see him.

Upon her arrival, she spied Ruth and forged a path to greet her new friend. She was eager to discuss an article in the paper that day about child labor in factories, a topic that had arisen over Sophia's tea.

Mid-discussion, the back of her neck warmed. The air shifted, and the fine hairs on her arms lifted even as she breathed in spiced rum and…William. She hoped rakelet's mother would not notice her nipples standing at attention all at once.

His arm brushed hers as he came to stand facing them both from the side. She shivered once before tamping it down and straightening another fraction.

"William. Excellent. Countess, allow me to introduce you to my son, Lord Stanton. William, this is the Dowager Countess of Peterborough. We met a month ago at the Earl of Peterborough's home. She is an excellent conversational partner, I am pleased to say."

Charlotte flushed, embarrassed at the effusiveness of the praise. She raised her chin and regarded her puppy.

He waited expectantly.

Oops. Etiquette required she recognize him first. She nodded and offered her hand to him. "Lord Stanton."

He bowed over it and rose with a wide grin. "Now, now, Lady Peterborough, do not pretend we do not know each other. Why, we met last year at a similar ball, and I've seen you at a number of scientific lectures. I should be crushed if you did not remember me." His easy smile lingered as he squeezed her hand before releasing it.

"Of course, I do. And I am flattered that you recall a widow such as myself."

Ruth chimed in. "William just completed his studies at Oxford, and was kind enough to forego a Grand Tour to step in and assist his father and I at home." She glossed over the details. "William, we were discussing the article in the Times about the possibility of factory reform laws getting through Parliament finally. Do you have any thoughts on that?"

"Yes, Mama, but I decline to discuss them when there is a beautiful woman, no matter how intelligent, with whom I might dance. Char—er, Lady Peterborough? May I have this dance?" He bowed.

"Ah well, find me later, dear, if the gentlemen allow you a rest between dances. Enjoy, you two." Ruth ceded her to William's care before Charlotte could find an excuse.

The tongues would wag over this, even a single dance. She'd only danced with long-time friends until now. Her body did not care, however. Every inch of skin strained to close the gap between them, to search out his skin, the pads of muscle underneath, the rod of steel she knew awaited. It was all she could do to remember that a ball was the worst place for such thoughts.

They needed to talk before any clothes were removed, anyway. While she found she could not resist the lure of spending time with him again, she needed to ensure he understood her rules and timeline. They still had an end date, as he needed to marry someone who could give him children.

The puppy grinned at her the whole time, and not-so-subtly steered them toward the doors to the terrace. He kept hold of her hand as the dance ended, threaded it into the crook of his elbow, and clamped his other hand down on it, all but dragging her.

"William!" She hissed at him, glancing around for observers. No one seemed to be paying attention to them.

"Stroll with me, please, Mistress?"

"No." She planted her feet, but saw an opportunity—he needed a reminder of her rules. "Did you forget what happens when you touch without permission?"

"Fine." Heaving a huge sigh to indicate his suffering, William acquiesced quickly, making her narrow her eyes at him. "We shall do it your way for now, my lady. I shall see you at your home in a couple of hours then. I do hope you enjoy your time here. I know you shall enjoy your time later." This last was said in a low tone to ensure it was not overheard.

Charlotte blushed, but as always with him, arguing was futile.

* * * *

Charlotte sipped sherry in her bedroom, not daring to change out of her ballgown for fear she'd leap on William as he came through the door.

She was debating a second sherry to calm her nerves and temper her lust when he burst into the room.

He was in full puppy mode, eyes eager, panting, his hand wrenching at his cravat before he dashed over to scoop her into a hug.

"Mistress," came out as a sigh against her hair.

"William. If I had any doubt after your letters that you missed me, this would dispel it. I missed you as well."

"Good. I mean—" he gulped.

She laughed "I understand. But we do need to talk. Come sit." She led him over to the seating area. "Sherry? Something stronger?"

He waved it off, and plopped down as soon as she sat.

"What are your plans now you're home?"

"To continue managing things in my father's shadow, to alleviate some of the burden on my mother, and to woo you."

She sighed. She'd been afraid of that.

"William, we discussed this before we started. This was supposed to end last summer."

He sat forward, taking a breath to respond.

She held a hand up, and he closed his mouth, waiting to hear more.

"Your letters made it obvious that you were not planning to comply with that. And—" she heaved a breath "—as I said a minute ago, I missed you too. I have a new proposal."

He straightened in his chair and grinned. "I'm all ears."

"I hope not *all* ears, puppy," she said with a glance down at his lap.

He choked on a laugh.

"I am willing to have the same arrangement as last summer. But we need to set an end date. At some point you need to find a more suitable girl to marry. I know you have many responsibilities already heaped on you, but heirs are important. You'll need to consider them soon."

"I want to consider them with you."

"I can't."

"Don't you mean 'shan't'?"

"No. I mean I cannot. William, do you know how long I was married?" She raised her hand to caress the heart pendant that hung on a chain around her neck.

"Uh, I believe it was close to ten years?"

"Yes. And what is the next thing anyone says about my marriage, when you hear others talk about it?"

He thought. She could see when it registered.

"Mistress." He leaned toward to her, arms out to hold her, but she held an arm out.

"William, I'll say it if you will not. I cannot have

children. I assumed you'd realized that when we did not use protection against pregnancy. And you need heirs." She turned away, walking to sit on the edge of her bed, face averted, hand now clutching the necklace. Every time she had to admit that fact hurt, but they both needed brutal honesty to reach an agreement.

Kneeling before her, he put a hand over hers in her lap and laid his forehead on their joined hands.

She dropped her other hand from her throat to his hair.

He grabbed it and kissed it before putting all of their hands on her thighs and holding her gaze. "Mistress, I am sorry. What end date did you have in mind?"

Here was the catch. She hadn't been able to make herself set one. "Michaelmas?"

Gracious, she had not meant to frame it as a question. Where were her negotiating skills?

"Next Season."

"No. Christmas."

"Next Season."

She smothered a grin. "Ah, perhaps they did not teach bartering skills at Oxford. The goal is to find a compromise."

He arched a brow. "Apparently you did not understand my starting point. Forever. Next Season is as far as I'm willing to compromise."

Mischievous, unrepentant puppy. She could also see he had no intention of holding to that date. She'd regret this, but Belle and Sophia and even Ruth, as well as her own longing for him, weakened her will. She answered, "Fine. For now. I reserve the right—"

He'd slid out of the chair to his knees before her. "Yes, Mistress. No, Mistress. Oh yes, Mistress."

She swore if he had a tail, it would be thumping the floor.

Running her fingers through his hair, she firmed her expression. "Now, there is the matter of you writing to me when you were meant to be studying, in addition to touching me without permission earlier."

He was still grinning like a loon.

She shook her head at him, holding her pose for a moment before standing. "Remove your clothing and get on the bed. Oh, and unlace me please. I dismissed the servants for the night."

He bounced up and followed her toward the bed, tugging at her laces hard enough she feared he'd break one. In no time, her gown and stays were loosened and his clothing was flying off.

"Kneel here, please." She pointed to a spot on the bottom half of the bed, facing the headboard. After removing everything except her chemise, she checked on him.

His focus was on her face, as though awaiting commands. Hers, however, roamed his length, settling on the bobbing erection between his splayed knees. It bounced with each pulse, liquid beading at the tip then tracking in hot tears along the shaft to wet…her ribbon.

Ignoring the thump her heart made at that, she licked her lips. But no, this was a punishment, and while it would eventually be fun for him, he needed to work for his pleasure. She stepped back to her dresser and drew out two pair of leather cuffs attached by leather straps. Like the first set she'd used with him, these were new. She'd bought them for him after sending her letter to Oxford, knowing it would come to this.

They'd arrived a week ago, and she'd slept with them

the first night after an amazing bout of self-pleasure completed while envisioning how she'd use them on him. Now reality and memories coalesced, and she squeezed her thighs together at the spurt of wet heat between them.

Approaching him, she pulled her chemise off. Naked, she shortened the straps to place the cuff at each end a few inches apart from its mate.

He clenched his muscles and his cock thumped against his stomach.

She allowed the hint of a smile to play on her lips before containing it. "Widen your knees and hold your ankles."

He shifted so his bollocks hung in the space between his legs, his bottom still on his heels. His arms went straight down along his sides, long fingers wrapped around ankle bones. A cuff went around his wrist, the other around the ankle. She slid her fingers between the fabric and skin to check the fit before she climbed onto the bed on his other side to tether his right wrist and ankle.

She knelt there next to him, just behind his shoulder, trying to corral her thoughts. Half her brain was setting up a torturous path to bliss for them both. The other half was running around tearing at her hair, caught between fear and elation. She'd been fighting being in love with him since last summer, but gracious, he was tempting.

He knelt before her, wrists holding ankles in a grip tight enough she wasn't sure she needed cuffs. He had no idea of the extent of his allure. If he knew she'd fallen in love with him, almost ready to forget society's rules in order to keep him, he'd never give up. But her fight was for his sake and his family's. She also hated the idea that he'd be hurt as much as she would be if this didn't work.

"Thank you for wearing this." She stroked the ribbon with one fingernail, careful not to touch the skin of his cock, even when it bucked under her caress. Tugging on an end, she slid it free and placed it on the table next to her bed.

A stifled moan came from his throat.

"Look straight ahead, William." The involuntary gruffness of her voice betrayed her arousal. He was gorgeous. She wanted to stare all night, but also touch and lick all night.

He gulped and lowered his chin.

Rewarding his patience and submission, she brought her palm to his shoulder and stroked along his spine, one word echoing through her thoughts. *Mine.* How she wished she could keep him and not worry.

Forcing her concerns away, she pinched his muscled buttocks because he was too cute not to. And because she could. Then she grabbed pillows and lay them in a long column straight out from the space in front of his spread knees.

She knelt on the closest pillow, being careful not to touch his lower half. Tipping his chin up with one hand, she slanted her mouth across his, licking into him and reveling in his taste. She swore his flavor was eagerness salted with servitude. Whatever it was, it was delicious, and she lingered.

I could kiss him for days.

She hadn't given him license to come visit by day, though.

She dropped another degree into her Mistress headspace, noting his lean toward her, his nipples and cock pointing at her, his hands clutching his ankles. It was time to teach the puppy new tricks. He was ready to follow any command to please her. More than that, she wanted to spend every night showing him new heights of pleasure, new ways that two compatible souls could connect.

Startled at that thought, she drew back. Shaking her head to clear it, she lay on her back on the pillows. Her essence was already leaking from her folds, her face and chest warm with a flush of anticipation. Placing her bottom about two feet away from him, she spread her legs over his, her head on the farthest pillow. It was as though she surrounded him. Her blood pulsed in her veins.

She skimmed her hands up her legs, over her belly, tweaking her nipples.

He gasped.

When he remained still and silent, she bestowed a small smile upon him. "You may touch me now, however you can manage."

He instinctively tugged at his bonds, thinking to touch with his hands. Then he looked at their positions for a moment and his lips curled up. "However, Mistress?"

Ah, the rakelet understands the challenge.

"However." She nodded.

He shuffled his knees forward a few inches, groaning as his bollocks skimmed the first pillow she'd placed in front of him. Then he leaned forward, his stomach muscles, thighs, and upper arms tightening to maintain his balance.

She licked her lips at the sight. Ah, the joy of having William back in her bed, following her commands. It was more than that, though. A tightness had loosened in her chest as soon as she'd received his note before the ball. She'd missed him more than she'd realized. Just as his shoulders dropped after a few minutes in a room with her, so did her loneliness dissipate in his presence. She only wished she could keep him. That longing magnified when he was naked and cuffed between her knees.

His lips found the tight bud of her nipple, a lock of hair falling onto the sensitive skin of her breast.

She gasped, abandoning the future to the present, and arched up to aid his reach. Holding his shoulders, she gave him the added support he needed to shift, without restricting his movements.

He moved to the other breast, lapping at it before sucking it between his tongue and the roof of his mouth, as he knew she loved.

She twisted, her need for him rising. Her pulse was urgent, beating in her throat, in her chest, at the apex of her thighs. This gorgeous man—for he was a man now, legally as well as physically—was hers, at least for the time being. She wasn't sure she had the patience for this lesson, wanting to tip him over and ride him to oblivion. But knowing she always ended up enjoying the control as much as the sex, she forced herself to maintain the pace she'd set.

He closed his teeth on the tip he'd been sucking and she writhed again, drawing his attention down her body.

His shaft thumped against her knee as he stared at her swollen, wet center.

He dipped his head, his cock dragging a hot, damp trail lower on her leg as he shuffled back to get the right angle without toppling.

His shoulders rested on her thighs as most of his

chest settled onto his upper legs. He met her gaze for a moment, his enthusiastic smile wresting a grin from her.

She needed someone to paint him smiling like that so she could look at it every day. Shoving concerns of the future aside again, she arched a brow expectantly.

His gaze lowered, and she felt his tongue swipe as his nose hit her sensitive nub. Gripping each lip in his mouth, he sucked and tugged on them in turn to open her more. Then his warm, wet tongue flattened below her folds and swept upward with the most delicious firm pressure.

She bit her lip to keep from crying out, wanting him to work a little harder. This was, after all, meant to be punishment.

He swiped again before nuzzling her raised bud of pleasure with his nose, his tongue flicking at her entrance.

Her hips flexed without her permission, pushing at him to seek more.

"Ah, Mistress," he groaned, shifting against the bed. She pictured his sac brushing the counterpane, and perhaps the tip of his cock. But with his heels stacked under his bottom, he would not get the friction he needed. He'd have to earn that.

"You've found my magic spot with your fingers and your tongue. Let's see if you remember." She reached down to hold her lips spread.

He nuzzled her again, breathing her in, then traced her folds, his gaze locked on her face to watch her reactions.

Shifting up a fraction, he delved under the protective hood to circle her most sensitive flesh.

"Ahh, ahh." The student had been paying attention in

class. His intelligence was part of his infinite appeal.

Her eyelids dropped, shuttering her view of his servitude. She dropped her head back and braced her arms on the bed to get the exact pressure she wanted.

Heat swirled in her core, from his breath on her and from the blaze he'd ignited in her. Elbows still braced, she pinched her nipples.

He must have been watching because he hummed against her.

She twisted her head, careful not to lose contact with that delicious pressure. "Ah, yes."

She actually felt him smile, but he did not remove his tongue, continuing to circle, tap, and lick.

Her voice was a rasp. "Yes, please, there, William. Ah, there!" She abandoned her breast play to grab his head and hold him against her. Her favorite way to orgasm was from external stimulation. The internal ecstasy was heightened by the sensation of her muscles and flesh throbbing against her partner and seeing that pleasure reflected in his eyes.

The first flutters of her pinnacle started, gaining strength as his tongue pressed harder, pulsing. Convulsing, she moaned, raising her head to watch. She wrapped her heels around his lower back and clutched fistfuls of his hair.

He rubbed his whole face up and down her, tongue flat, catching every drop of her essence, every heartbeat in her hard nub, delighting in her response.

When her hands loosened and hips dropped, he softened his tongue. Finding she was too sensitive for even that, she dropped her feet and pushed at his head.

With one long, gentle lick, he sat up, the lower half of his face shiny with her juices.

"Thank you, Mistress. You taste divine." He waited, looking hopeful.

Hmm. He used to beg, now he thinks he does not need to.

But she wanted it as much as he did. His punishment was over, although she declined to inform him of that fact.

Scooting the pillows and her hips closer, she pressed her core against the hot stalk between his legs. He raised his eyebrows at her. "Mistress? Will you untie me now?"

"I'll untie you when I am quite ready. Now hush or you won't get your reward."

He snapped his mouth closed.

She grabbed his cock, and it jerked at her touch. *Mine.* The silk-over-iron shape in her hand felt like coming home. Familiar, comforting, but also full of well-known pleasures.

He grunted but cut it off, biting his lip.

Tugging it downward, she ran it up and down her folds once, flinching at how sensitive she still was. Holding him in position, she inched her hips forward. The head of his shaft slipped into her swollen channel.

They both moaned.

Pushing herself up, she placed one hand behind her, leaning back in a half-sit. She loved this angle. When his cock was fully embedded, the thrusts would rub a spot on her front wall as sensitive as the one he'd already found.

Without waiting for her command, he drove his hips forward, shoving in further. The student had indeed graduated.

Someone grunted. Stuffed full and super sensitive, she belatedly realized the grunt had been her, not him.

She swore she could feel him up to her belly button.

His hips pistoned in and out, in and out.

She had no words, and rested back on her elbows, legs curled around his hips, and rode him.

"Ah, ah, Mistress."

Finding coherence, she retook control. "Wait for me, William. You've broken enough rules for one day."

"Always, Mistress."

Her gaze flew up from where she'd been watching his cock plunge.

His hands were fisted next to his ankles, and his expression was serious. "I will wait for you forever if need be, Mistress."

Her throat constricted at the realization he was not just talking about intimacy. Then the words and his shortened thrusts right against that tender spot inside erased her worries with pleasure. Ecstasy poured through her, everything contracted, and she was thrown into a shockingly sudden explosion.

"Oh!" Her shout became a groan as her inner muscles squeezed him rhythmically.

Registering his expression of shared agony and ecstasy through slitted eyes, she belatedly released him. "You may come, William."

When she snaked a hand between their hips to graze his bollocks, he yelled and exploded, his hips losing their rhythm and doubling their pace.

Hot spurts of liquid filled her, causing echoing bursts of pleasure. Regret that they needn't worry about pregnancy flashed through her thoughts, but she rejected it. She loved having him come inside her, it was another part of how she claimed him.

She fell back against the pillows to catch her breath.

Gathering herself, she sat up to unfasten his cuffs.

When she started to stand to put them away, he gripped her wrist. Tugging them out of her hand, he dropped them and threw the pillows back toward the top of the bed. Then, still kneeling, he dragged her onto his lap. Holding her close, he buried his face in her hair. As always, he gave her, "Thank you, Mistress."

She tucked her head into his neck, curling her legs with her knees along his hip and her feet next to his thigh, glad he could not see her face. She'd missed this as much as sexual intimacy. Clenching her jaw to avoid crying, she pushed away her dread of how it would feel to end this, allowing herself to enjoy this first night back together. The future would come, whether she wanted it to or not.

Chapter Twenty-One

William had told Charlotte about South dropping out of Oxford and his penchant for dice and cards.

She commiserated, although she did not see a way for William to help. His concern was exaggerated by his experience having to cover for his father's behavior, but she wished he would not try to take responsibility for things outside his control. But William was a caretaker, something he'd proven all too often with her.

In addition, she suspected she was a part of the reason he felt obligated to his friend. He often excused himself from White's early to come to her house, which was when South headed to the gaming hells.

They attempted to find a balance. William's need to meet with his mother each morning, South's worrisome behavior, Emily's desire to see and do everything *now*, with their desire to spend every moment together they could.

She allowed him to spend the night when he could, based on his meetings and family, even though he had to depart at dawn. She too had responsibilities, but she'd missed having a man in her bed, and the puppy was a particularly good snuggler.

Even better, William's family had recently departed for their estate. He had more latitude in not accompanying them now that he had established an effective routine for managing the family's interests.

One night, he surprised her by appearing with South hanging off one shoulder, his friend's arm draped around his neck to remain upright.

"Mistress, I beg your pardon. This is the friend I told you about. His family is in Town this week of all weeks when everyone else has gone, so I cannot dump him in his own bed to sleep it off. Our families are friends, and the servants talk; I cannot take him to my house. I wasn't sure what to do."

She wondered how big a gossip his friend was, especially when in his cups, but she could not refuse them, knowing it would add to William's stress. "Bring him in. Can you get him up the stairs, or do I need to call Austin?"

"I can manage. I do most nights I let him drag me out."

"I had not realized it was that bad. I am sorry, William." She followed him upstairs and folded back the bed in a guest room.

William shucked his friend's shoes and left him there, arrowing straight for her room. Sitting on the bed, he put his elbows on his knees and hung his head.

Charlotte stepped between his feet to rest her hands on his shoulders, and his hands came around her waist. As he buried his head in her stomach, she combed through his silky hair, a new habit they were both coming to enjoy.

"Mistress, I need you." He gazed up at her, his chin digging into her stomach.

She nodded. "I understand. No games tonight, puppy. You are free to do as you wish."

At that, he proceeded to make passionate love to her, murmured endearments and encouragements replacing commands and begging. While she had always preferred control, she was not averse to giving it up occasionally to relax and enjoy intimacy without thinking or planning her next step. William's unfettered eagerness was delicious in its own right, too.

In the morning, she woke before him and descended to the dining room to request breakfast, knowing he'd awaken as the bed grew cold.

Isabella arrived within minutes.

Of all mornings. Given her two male guests, Charlotte quickly debated the odds of getting rid of her friend and decided that Belle knew her too well. If she attempted to plead an appointment, her hair being down and casual day dress would give her away. Then Belle would dig in. Instead, she hoped Belle's commitments would keep the visit short.

Ten minutes later, her hope was dashed when William swung through the doorway. He was shoeless in stockings and trousers. His shirt was unbuttoned, no cravat, waistcoat, or jacket in evidence. Even if he'd been fully dressed, the hour and Belle's knowledge of him would have given away his identity.

When he caught sight of her visitor, his brows twitched at a woman in servant's garb sitting with her, but he did not miss a beat. Bowing shallowly, he said, "I beg your pardon."

Charlotte shook her head and gestured to one of the other place settings, but as she opened her mouth to invite him in, she was overridden.

Belle turned at his voice and grinned so widely, Charlotte thought she might count all her teeth.

Charlotte rolled her eyes. There'd be no peace now.

"Puppy? Puppy!" Belle bounced once. "Ooh, Char…he's delicious! How could you not have mentioned he was here?"

Charlotte shook her head. "Because I knew you'd react like this. Behave, please, Belle."

Belle pouted. "You know you can't make me, right? I'm not as trainable as some…" Her gaze slid sideways.

He blushed.

"Aw, how adorable." Belle clapped once.

"Stop it. Mind your manners." Charlotte slapped her friend's wrist lightly before gesturing. "William, may I introduce my friend, Isabella Rossi? Isabella, Lord Stanton."

"Madame." He nodded at Belle, then turned to Charlotte. "Lady Peterborough, would you prefer to have a ladies-only breakfast? I can make myself scarce. We can, uh, have that Latin lesson another time."

A snort of laughter came from Belle. Dripping sarcasm, she drawled, "Is that what we're calling it these days? Latin lessons? How quaint."

He flushed again.

Belle snickered.

"Thank you, William, but no. There is no avoiding Belle; she is a force. And I should like for you to meet my closest friend, although I should have warned you about her atrocious manners." She glared at her friend again.

As always, Belle ignored her. "So, Lord Stanton, tell me. How do you find wooing our Charlotte?" She leaned forward, head on chin, elbow on the table, eyes sparkling mischievously.

William faltered, looking from one to the other. "As

always, I find Mistr-- Lady P the most scintillating of companions. My time with her is always educational."

Belle laughed outright.

Charlotte tried to stifle her grin, but Belle did not need her reaction to read between the lines given their history. She really ought to have warned William.

His brows rose as he put Isabella's greeting of "Puppy" together with her chortle.

Charlotte watched him, relieved and a tad surprised when his shoulders dropped and he grinned at Belle. Dropping into his chair, he leaned over to kiss Charlotte's cheek.

Belle watched avidly.

He winked at his new audience and said, "For all that she has trouble with some of the Latin words, I find it immensely satisfying to get my tongue around certain English…words."

It was Charlotte's turn to blush. She frowned at his boldness.

Belle watched them like a tennis match at Hampton Court Palace, a permanent grin on her face, breakfast forgotten.

Charlotte busied herself pouring him tea and offering him some of the cake on the table. He took an extra-large slice as it was a ginger cake she'd brought home from a shop she'd invested in. It was owned by, of all people, an earl's wife who had been his courtesan before they made waves in the Ton by marrying.

He cocked his head, asking, "How did you two meet?"

Feeling awkward, Charlotte would not meet his eyes, suddenly very occupied with her cup and saucer. She should have given him more information about Belle.

Regardless of her habit of dropping by unannounced, the woman was her best friend and she had nothing to hide. Knowing William, he'd be grateful for Belle's tutelage.

Belle arched a brow. "She hasn't told you? Not much time for talking in this house, eh? Or are there not Latin words for it, Char?" She snickered. "By the way, you still owe me my winnings from our wager. We met through Charlotte's husband about a year into their marriage, and have been close friends ever since. Closer than Charles and I ever were."

Charlotte's eyes flashed up at her in surprise, then softened. What a lovely thing to say.

"Rossi. I don't know that name. Did you grow up here in London?"

"Yes, but you wouldn't have heard the name. I suspect you're trying to understand how your Mistress and a person dressed like a delivery person know each other. I shall tell you. I grew up working class. However, I dress like this as a disguise and use Char's back door to protect her reputation. I am a courtesan, and quite a good one, shall we say. Besides which, she's helped me invest. I likely have nigh as much money as she does."

Huh. Apparently, she needn't have said anything. Belle had summed it all up quite well.

"Ah." William was wide-eyed trying to assimilate it all.

"So, you ask," Belle continued. "Is that how Charlotte came by her delicious directorial skills? Why yes, yes it is. I take full credit."

Charlotte sniffed, frowning at her friend. She'd gone too far.

Belle ignored her, off again laughing so hard she almost fell out of her seat.

"Oh! Well in that case…" William grabbed one of Belle's hands, bringing her to an abrupt stillness.

Both women stared at him, wondering where he was going with this.

"Madame, you have my most heartfelt thanks. That thing she did with the chair? Magnificent."

Belle gawked at him.

He winked.

"Oh, good boy!" She snorted and slapped his hand gently, laughing her head off again.

Charlotte rolled her eyes at both of them. Perhaps it was better that they had not met until now. They encouraged each other's bad behavior, and she could only punish one.

There was a clatter in the hall, and a man's voice grumbling.

Belle's eyes went wide. "I taught you well, my friend."

Charlotte hissed at her. "William's friend had overindulged and he brought him here to sleep it off. In a guest room."

South rounded the corner, and drew up short. "Ah, William. I wondered where I ended up and as there was no wench—"

William cleared his throat loudly.

South blinked and looked around, saying, "This is not your house." His gaze kept sliding to Belle.

"No." William's voice was grim. "'Tis the Countess of Peterborough's. Charlotte, allow me to introduce my clodpate of a friend, Luke Lynwood."

"Lord Lynwood." She raised her chin, declining to rise after his lead-in.

"I beg your pardon." He bowed, then glanced at Belle

out of the corner of his eye again.

"And Isabella Rossi," William added, gesturing between her and South. "Luke Lynwood."

"I prefer clodpate," Belle said with a raised brow.

South stared for a long moment. He swallowed before bowing and repeating, "I beg your pardon."

"Oh, no. That is not begging. You'll need to do better."

He cast a wary glance at her before telling William, "Thank you for waking me. I am going to get a hack home."

"I am leaving now, too. We shall share a hack and I can start teaching you how to beg." Belle rose, dropping her serviette by her plate.

South acquiesced, amusing Charlotte and William to no end.

* * * *

Fall arrived, the days growing shorter and colder.

Charlotte had fallen as well, deeper and deeper in love with William. She'd fought it. Although she had not raised the issue of heirs again, it nagged at her always. However, she could not fathom letting William go.

He was beginning to press for public outings again, as well.

She had allowed him to escort her to a few salons, introducing him to friends he had not yet met, the men closer to Charles's age than hers or William's. Given how frequently he spent the night with her, she'd also encouraged him to tell his mother, despite the risk to Charlotte's friendship with the woman. If an emergency arose at home, they needed to be able to find him, as the acting head of household. Besides, it felt duplicitous to attend the ladies' group and converse with Ruth with that secret between them.

They walked into the latest presentation, a discussion of new uses for rubber.

Ruth Stanton stood across the room speaking with the host.

Before Charlotte could react or even contemplate disengaging her hand from William's arm, her gaze caught Ruth's.

The older woman smiled, drifted to William beside her, and then down to their linked arms. Her head tilted, brows drawing together.

Charlotte leaned in to William. "Does your mother know yet?"

"I have not yet had a chance to discuss it with her. Why?"

"Because she is here." Charlotte nodded in Ruth's direction. "And I do not think she liked seeing us walk in together."

She could imagine Ruth's reaction. After Charlotte's decade of marriage without producing an heir, the countess would have legitimate concerns about their courtship. And that was without the age difference.

Her stomach churned and she worried she might lose her supper. The room swam around her, and she swayed, breaking out in a cold sweat.

She recalled Charles's suit, the first dance, the betrothal, all the social events. Never had there been this intense fear of loss should something go awry. She had loved him, certainly. But it had been a young girl's love. Not like this all-encompassing need for William, this innate knowledge that they were perfect together. This was a mature, well-rounded, learned love.

Her hand tightened on William's sleeve as she

reeled.

When Ruth started across the room to them, she shivered, fearing the coming confrontation.

I cannot lose him yet. Please, just a little more time.

Chapter Twenty-Two

When Charlotte gripped his arm like a vice, William glanced down.

She was white as a sheet.

"Mistress? Are you unwell?"

"You should have told her," Charlotte managed through clenched teeth.

"And I will." He shrugged.

"William!"

"Really, Mistress?" He frowned but kept his voice to a whisper to avoid anyone overhearing. Knowing his Mistress was sensitive to public opinion made him regret not finding the time, but reporting on his private life to his mother stank of childhood and he'd put it off. Being chastised for it also smarted. "I am one-and-twenty, and I'm handling more of the estate than she or my father at this point. I don't feel the need to report to my mama."

She frowned back, then smoothed her face as Ruth reached them.

"Lady Harrington, 'tis lovely to see you again." Charlotte's smile was lopsided.

William bit his lip. She was really worried. He put his free hand over hers to squeeze it before releasing her to his mother.

"I seem to recall that we were Charlotte and Ruth to

each other." The countess clasped Charlotte's fingers and leaned in to buss her cheek.

"I beg your pardon, Ruth."

"William." She kissed his cheek in turn. "How do you come to be here? And with Lady Peterborough?"

"Well, Mama, you see I took the curricle, and drove to her house, and brought her here," he teased her in an attempt to diffuse the tension.

His mother arched a brow, and stared him down.

Damnation. He tried another tack. "Mama, I did not realize you were interested in the rubber industry."

The brow and stare remained fixed.

He sighed and glanced at Charlotte. She pressed her lips together in a message of, *I told you that you should have said something.*

Squaring his shoulders, he got it over with. "Mama, I have been courting Charlotte. We get along famously, and she knows more about half these subjects than I do." He gestured toward the seating area set up for the presentation.

His mother's brows rose at his first statement, and remained there.

Charlotte's hand clenched and unclenched along his leg, her knuckles grazing him each time. He wanted to squeeze it and soothe her, but his mother's stare stopped him.

"I see." Ruth turned to Charlotte. "My dear Charlotte, would you be so kind as to give me a moment alone with my son, please?"

"Certainly. I shall find us seats." Charlotte's voice remained calm, but she continued to fist her hands. "Ruth, will you be joining us?"

The countess shook her head. "No, thank you."

Charlotte nodded and lowered her head, moving away.

When he paused to watch her progress, his mother grabbed his sleeve and tugged him around to face her. "William, what are you doing?"

He was not having this conversation with his mother in public. She had no say in who he spent time with, but he recognized her concern came from love. While he would not be able to avoid discussing Charlotte at home, he refused to be scolded at a salon with the woman he loved barely out of hearing.

Raising a brow, he answered in a mild voice, "I believe we already covered that, Mama."

"What on earth would make you think the Dowager Countess of Peterborough is an acceptable match?"

"Because she is a stunning, single, available lady with whom I have much in common." When his mother opened her mouth to retort, William held up a hand. "This is neither the time nor the place, Mama."

"William—"

"No." His voice was hard. "I would argue that there is no time or place for you to question me on this, given my age and our circumstances. However, I respect and admire your leadership of our family to date, and understand it may be difficult to relinquish. Therefore, I shall revisit this with you tomorrow. Now, if you'll excuse me."

"William—"

He bowed and pivoted on his heel to find his Mistress. Fighting anger, he took a moment to catch his breath and unfurl his hands. Charlotte needed his support and he needed to appear mature and in control to both of the women he loved.

Charlotte sat in a back row off to the side, with all the seats around her vacant. Her head was bent over her lap, and she picked at beading on her reticule. Her breathing had a catch to it, as though she was fighting tears.

When he lowered himself to the chair next to her, she did not lift her head. He reached for her hand, tugging it away from the beads to cradle it in both of his.

"Mistress."

She dragged her gaze to his, trepidation in her eyes, her lips quivering.

"I am sorry about that. Would you like some air?"

"Are you—are you staying, then?" she managed.

He frowned. She thought he might leave? Did she not see him as an adult either? This night was becoming more frustrating by the minute. He began to see why she had dreaded outings, but he refused to give in to stupid rules that did not make sense.

She was watching him.

"I am doing whatever my Mistress wants, as I always try to do." He gave her a gentle smile.

"William." Her breath whooshed out. Her shoulders sagging, she grabbed his arm again. "Yes, please. I'm sorry, but could we just go?"

"Of course. Come, then." His hand under her elbow, he hauled her upright. Tucking her hand around his arm, he cinched it between his bicep and his ribcage and directed them back out the way they had come.

Neither of them looked around for his mother.

* * * *

Fury and fear fought within William. He peered at Charlotte in the dark carriage, trying to read her expression in the flickering light of the street lamps.

She petted her heart pendant once before letting her hand drop to her lap.

Being chastised by his mother like a schoolboy was frustrating enough, but seeing its effect on Charlotte took his anger to a new level. He had planned to ignore his mother and ensure Charlotte had an enjoyable evening, but altered that plan when he found her pale and upset. Had she heard what his mother had said? Or was she envisioning the worst-case scenario?

His mistress needed reassurance, and that was hard to give in the confines of a carriage. He settled for holding her hand until they arrived back at her townhouse.

As he handed her out, she turned to him. "You should go, William. Will your mama not expect you home?"

He growled, trepidation morphing into irritation. "Why do you both think that I am answerable to my mother?"

She shook her head wordlessly.

He stalked up the front steps to where the butler held the door. "Mistress? Am I invited in?" Teeth gritted, he all but snarled the words at her.

"Yes, of course, William." Her voice sounded tired, sluggish.

Turning, she aimed for the library, but William did his best talking in her bedroom. It accented the power dynamic between them, keeping him in the mindset of pleasing her while making his own wishes known. The downstairs was for visitors, for learning Latin. The bedroom was for relationship dialogues.

He caught her arm and gently redirected her. It was a testament of her ennui that she allowed him to turn her even before he whispered, "Please, Mistress, upstairs."

In her room, he led her to her chaise longue, a piece of furniture he'd never seen her use. It seemed too passive for her forceful nature most days, but suited the moment now. Laying her back, he stepped over to the bed, turning down the covers. He poured them each a sherry from a decanter on a side table and returned, perching on the edge of the couch by her knee to hand her a glass.

She took it without comment but did not raise it to her lips.

"Do you feel better now? You were quite pale."

"I am fine, William, thank you." Her fingers touched her pendant then dropped away.

"You seem to take solace from that necklace." He had wondered about her habit.

She started and blushed. "I am sorry. I suppose I should remove it. 'Tis from Charles." She did not reach up to unclasp the chain, though.

They had already discussed her loss, her grief, thus he had some understanding of how that might be soothing, especially as his own relationship with Charlotte was complicated.

William shook his head. "I see no reason to remove it, Mistress. He was an important part of your life. While I hope you will find solace with me as well, we have not been together as long, and I am not always available. I am glad you have something that reminds you of that love."

She cocked her head, blinking as though fighting tears. "That is a beautiful and incredibly mature thing to say. Thank you."

He nodded, his expression solemn. "You are welcome. Now, I should like to give you solace, as 'twas my mother who upset you, I suspect. How may I serve you?"

She lifted a hand to cup his cheek. "I am not fit for service tonight, I am afraid."

He covered her hand with his own. "Hmm. I disagree. Tonight, of all nights, you need service more than ever. But you are not of a mind to direct me, mmm? I shall take care of you. You can redirect me if I do something wrong, but I feel sure I can manage without much instruction."

"Puppy…"

When she did not continue, he took hope from her use of her pet name for him. She'd called him "William" only moments earlier.

"Trust me, please." Standing, he put his sherry aside, and removed his coat, cravat, waistcoat, and shoes.

She took a first sip of sherry and watched his movements.

Shirt loose at his throat, he leaned over her. "Roll to your side for me."

Without the "please," it bordered on being a command, and her eyes flared, but she rolled over without a word.

He ran a hand down her back from shoulder to hip, soothing her before he undid her gown. Spreading the edges, he reached through to also unlace her stays. Next, he reached up and fished for pins in her hair, combing through it with his fingers.

Grasping her shoulder, he rolled her back to face him, and pulled her dress down to her lap, then her stays, then had her raise her hips to pull them past, then off.

Handing her back her abandoned sherry, he waited for her to take a sip.

"Hold tight." He lifted her in his arms, and carried her across to the bed. Putting her drink on the table, he tugged her to face away from him on her side, keeping her hair out from under her.

She lay still, eyes closed.

He grabbed her hairbrush from her dressing table and went around to sit cross-legged in the middle of the bed facing her. Running the brush through her hair, he considered her emotional state. He did not want to disturb her, but some things needed to be said.

"Mistress, you do know that I realize not all service is sexual in nature? Teaching you Latin, taking care of you when you're unwell, even something as simple as fetching you tea. I enjoy all of it. For you, and for myself."

She blinked at him, her mouth still downturned.

"It has been drilled into me from a young age that I will inherit the title of Earl of Harrington, and all the responsibilities and commitments that come with it. As soon as I finished university—even before that, as you saw—my parents needed my help. Now, at the age of one-and-twenty, I resolve disputes for the estates, manage our money, and try to influence Parliamentary decisions that affect the British people and the future of our great nation."

She was watching him more alertly, up on an elbow, and he paused in his brushing.

"Whilst it may appear that my submission to you benefits you more than me—"

She gave a small snort.

He slanted her an acknowledging grin before continuing. "—you are my salvation. I come here, and I can…not forget, but put aside…all the decisions I must make daily. You take the reins, and I do what you need, what you want, what you *decide*. I adore serving you, and it keeps me balanced. But it is far more than that. I've told you since the beginning, but it bears repeating tonight. You are an impressive, intelligent, breathtakingly beautiful woman, and I am lucky you allow me to love you."

Her eyes filled with tears.

He belatedly realized this was the first time he'd told her he loved her. He'd worry about the fact that she cried in response another time. "Mistress, no. Please, whatever it is, 'tis clear you do not want to discuss it tonight, but please let me reassure you. 'Twill be all right. I will do everything in my power to make it so. Come, let me hold you, please."

He gathered her in his arms, and pulled the covers over them, loosening her petticoats under the quilt where she would stay warm. Then, still in shirt and trousers, he pulled her into him and held her, running his hand from her head to her hip, slowly, until her breathing deepened and slowed. Only then did he close his eyes and allow sleep to take him.

* * * *

The next morning, he found his mother in her usual position in the study, head bowed over the ledgers.

He had made two stops on his way home. Approaching the guest side of the big desk, he dangled a cloth bag over the blotter.

Ruth sniffed, and her head snapped up. "Scones? Are they cheese? Please tell me they are cheese."

"They are indeed." He set them on the desk. "I called for tea and plates."

"You are a love. Thank you."

He came around and bussed her cheek. "Come, Mama, take a break to eat."

As they sat at the small round table, he hoped that the scones and the second item he had brought would smooth this morning's conversation about Charlotte.

"You asked me to come talk to you first thing this morning. Before we talk, allow me to present you with this. 'Tis something I ordered for you as soon as I returned from Oxford, and it just now was finished." He slid a small brown leather pouch across the table.

Ruth pulled the drawstring open, glancing from it to him. "William, dear, what is this for? I fear *I* should have had a gift for *you* for graduation."

"Mama, if 'twasn't for you shouldering all this these past years, I would not have graduated. 'Tis a thank you for hiding and hoarding and scrimping and saving to ensure I had that time."

She blinked at him.

He could not remember seeing his mother cry. He supposed she had been hardened by the constant sorrow his father brought her. But now her eyes shimmered, even as she continued to blink.

Drat, this was the second woman in a matter of hours who he'd brought to tears when he'd meant to be supportive. He might be going about this wrong. "Mama, please. This was meant to bring you happiness, not sadness. And you have yet to even open it."

"Oh, my dear sweet boy—" Ruth broke off with a gasp as the onyx starling brooch fell into her palm. "William! No. We do not have the funds for this." She stood, folding her arms with a small frown.

"'Tis fine, mama. Sit down, please, do not hover over me and berate me for your gift." He grabbed her hand, tugging.

She reluctantly resumed her seat, her back ramrod stiff, her gaze on him wary.

He sighed. "Mama, do you not trust me? I have been handling our investments for over a year now, and the returns have been splendid. You spent far more on my education. And, if you'll pardon me for saying it, father's monthly club bills are more than this. I chose to do this. It was commissioned, so whether you like it or not, you are stuck with it." His jaw set. This was not going as he'd hoped.

"Really? We can afford fripperies?" She gestured.

"'Tis not a frippery, 'tis a gift for my mother," he gritted out.

Her back relaxed a bit. "I beg your pardon, William. I do trust you, and I love you very much. You make me happy and proud. I do not need gifts, but"—she added quickly when he glared at her—"every woman enjoys receiving them. 'Tis lovely and I shall cherish it."

Leaning in, she kissed him.

He braced himself. They needed to finish their discussion of the night before. Gifts might smooth her ruffled feathers, but they would not make her forget.

Just as he suspected, his mother set her shoulders. Placing the brooch to the side of her plate, she took a breath and said, "We must discuss the Countess of Peterborough. She is simply not acceptable for you, William. To begin, she must be a decade older than you."

"She is not. Anyway, what is the age difference between you and father?" He knew it was more than a dozen years. "Charlotte mentioned that her husband was a decade older than her." He shrugged. "It seems quite acceptable, from what I can see."

"William, please do not be obtuse. What can she possibly see in you, a youth just out of school?"

He tried to rein in his anger. Striving for patience, he took a breath and said, "Hopefully the same thing you see in me. A well-educated *man*, doing most of the work to manage his legacy without the authority he'd normally have to do so. A responsible adult who shares a number of interests with her. By the way, that"—he gestured at the brooch with his chin—"would not have been possible without her guidance on investments."

She scoffed. "Even so, her inappropriateness for you goes beyond the age difference. Not only do women need more childbearing years, but they need the ability to bear children. She was married for more than eight years without any children."

"That is true. But she has plenty of years left. Who is to say whether that was her or her husband's fault?"

"You cannot afford to risk it. You are the only son of an earl!"

"She has raised these concerns with me, too. I am in no rush for marriage, and you know as well as I do, as a young titled gentleman I have a lot of leeway. And as a widow, she at least has a bit. We are taking it step by step." His mother did not need to know he had a limited amount of time to convince Charlotte of his true intentions. He drew a breath for fortitude, knowing his mother would balk at his next statement. "I need to prepare you, Mama. I am in love with her, and I do hope to wed her if I can convince her to have me."

His mother looked stricken.

He patted her hand. "I believe you have much in common and would enjoy her company."

"I have become somewhat acquainted with

Charlotte. And yes, I do like her. As a friend and a contemporary—of *mine*. Not as a marriageable prospect for my *son*." Ruth frowned at him.

He shrugged again. "That is a beginning. Hopefully you shall come around to the rest."

He stood to leave.

Ruth stood and faced him, square shouldered. "William, I forbid you from seeing her. You must court marriageable ladies your own age."

"Really, Mama?" His laugh had a bitter, angry edge to it. Inside, he was outraged at her audacity, and insulted that she thought this was appropriate for a man of one-and-twenty. After his patient and courteous answers to her questions, he couldn't believe she was going to try to play parent.

"I am serious." She folded her arms.

"As am I. Hear this. I am a grown man." He stabbed the table with a finger. "You do not get to tell me what to do any longer. Nor can you forbid me from seeing who I want, when I want. I love you, and I will gladly help you and the rest of the family in maintaining our way of life. I am grateful for everything you have done for me. Please do not fight me on this. You will not win. Enjoy the scones. Good day, madame."

He bowed and strode out before he broke something.

Chapter Twenty-Three

Charlotte whipped her head around when he stomped through her library door. Although he'd been announced by Austin, his gait was surprising.

He came around to buss her head with a halfhearted kiss before stomping the length of the room and back.

She rose and came around to meet him. "What is wrong, William?"

"My family. They are all wrong. Wrong to me, wrong about me. Simply wrong."

Her mouth twisted in wry humor. Not a helpful answer. She tried again. "Right, then. Or, ah, wrong, as the case may be. Tell me how?"

"I know my mother has good reason for her sense of duty. I've done everything I can to relieve some of her burden and will continue to do so. But she does not have the right to tell me what I can do with my free time."

Oh no. This was about her. Charlotte felt sick again.

He halted and faced her, giving a bitter laugh. "You'll like this part. She wondered what you would see in me. The sophisticated widow with the callow youth. You always worry the other way around. She'd appreciate that you call me 'puppy.'" The pacing resumed.

"I presume some part of why she is upset is because

I am in all likelihood barren." She kept her tone matter-of-fact. This was why she should have never have allowed this thing between them to start. Then, restart. Now she would hurt both of them.

He rushed over to her, kneeling in front of where she sat, hands reaching for hers on her lap. "Mistress, you know I don't care about that. I simply want to be with you."

"But she is right, William. You are wasting time with me, when you should be looking for someone younger who can give you children. Heirs."

"No. I am a grown man, and I shall choose how and with whom I spend my time, dammit. I do not give a fig what society has to say on the matter. You claim not to, either. And my mother likes you."

"Your mother likes me as a friend of hers. Not as a potential daughter-in-law!"

He ignored her echo of his mother's words. "Mistress. I wish only to serve you and make you happy. Were you truly happy these past months? Did you find other men who suited you better than I do? Because I don't see them here. Instead, I am here, and I am begging, as I only do for you."

It was her turn to stand. "And then what? I will not marry you."

"You promised me until next Season. I am holding you to that promise. Children, even heirs, are an abstract thing to me. *You* are not. I am in love with you."

She gasped, tugging on her hands where he held them and frowning.

He held tight and continued, "I need you in my life. I do not feel as though I need children. In fact, now that I think of it, I'm not sure my bloodline is worth passing on anyway. But either way, please. I am not asking you to wed me this minute"—because he knew she'd refuse just yet, even before this quarrel, and especially as her eyes had gone wide at the word "wed." "Please just spend time with me. Think of it this way. As a young— what was your term?—rakelet, no one cares a whit what I do, you shan't harm my reputation. Indeed, someone as accomplished and beautiful as you, with a title higher than my own, would be considered a coup."

"Will—" She didn't even finish his name before he was on her, not asking permission or waiting for direction.

His mouth covered hers. He kept it soft, pleading in his own way. His lips moved against hers, requesting consent without words. Licking at her lips offered service. Sucking her lower lip gently between his teeth tugged on her heartstrings as well as her flesh.

She sank into him, her hands coming to his hair.

He thanked her by rubbing his tongue along hers, cupping her head as he tilted his for better access. Placing his other arm around her back, he drew her against him.

The dratted man. He knew that she could not resist when his youthful flesh pressed into her. His muscled arms and chest, his thighs, hard from riding, and that stiff poker between them pushing against her belly. All offered their service, hers to command.

She yanked his hair to tilt his head back.

"What have I told you about touching without permission? Now you have a punishment. Your cravat, please." She held a hand out between them.

His hands released her and leaped to the knotted tie, his grin stretching his face wide. "Yes, Mistress!"

* * * *

Two nights later, Charlotte surveyed the ballroom as she entered. She did not mind them as much now but was still grateful there were fewer during the little Season.

There was the usual wall of matrons and clusters of débutantes, a few matrons lurking near their daughters. Against a second wall, the orchestra was setting up. In another corner stood the usual litter of would-be rakes, tossing their hair and hands as they jostled for power.

Where was her rakelet?

She scanned again, not seeing Ruth among the women or William among the men. Given her nerves about seeing the one and her anticipation of seeing the other, she needed champagne and a minute to gather herself.

Finding only punch, she helped herself, then strolled, glass in hand, greeting a few acquaintances.

The aroma of spiced rum wafted to her. She turned, and her puppy stood there grinning at her. "William, are you stalking me?" Her brow arched with the whispered question.

"Mistress, never. I paused for a moment to admire the view before I intended to greet you." A dimple and the cheeky grin made its appearance.

Charlotte flushed.

He bowed. "Will do you give me the honor of a dance, Mistress?"

"I might. If you behave." She rapped his arm lightly with her fan then peered behind him. "Did your mother accompany you?"

"Yes, she's somewhere about. D'you want me to help you find her?"

"No, more like I prefer to be warned," she muttered.

He threw back his head and laughed.

"Go play with the other cubs." *Gah, I am mixing animal species.* "Find me for a dance."

She made another round of the ballroom, finding herself more relaxed than ever before. Her balls as a débutante had been nerve-wracking. Later, she had Charles, and they preferred salons, their few ball appearances spent ensuring they spoke to everyone they had not seen recently. Then came her first balls as a widow. She'd realized how few people she had kept in contact with as she mourned, but she'd also met William.

Now, two years later, she needn't feel anxious. She had rekindled friendships, and she knew who she was going home to that night. Whatever happened here did not matter as much.

The orchestra finished warming up, and the first dance was announced. His delicious aroma of spiced rum heralded William's return, and she smiled even before she turned.

He bowed and held out his hand for hers, then led her to line up for the dance.

Close, then back, then turn, then handed off to another partner, watching him across the square of four couples. *Gracious, he rounds out breeches beautifully. I may have to bite that bit later.* He caught her watching him and smiled, and she licked her lips when they came round to face each other again, causing his eyes to flare at her.

As the dance brought them to partner again, he whispered, "Mistress, I am behaving. Dare I say, *you* are not, however."

"And? What are the consequences?"

"Well, I only had to behave to earn a dance, which I

have done. Now, if you do not behave, then nor shall I, which means *this*." As the song ended with a flourish, he twirled her twice and they were on the edge of the dance floor near a hallway.

He grabbed her hand and stepped into the shadows before pulling her behind him to an open doorway. Peering inside to ensure the room was empty, he whisked her through the door, shut it, and pushed her up against it.

Her gown was midnight blue with a pattern of abstract flowers in silver. It had a deep square neckline, deep enough that she should have worn one of the newer style of corsets. As she did not own one, she had donned her lowest cut satin stays, and had skipped the chemise. The satin saved her skin from chafing without a chemise.

Licking his lips, William put them behind her ear, and trailed them down the side of her neck. With a shudder of pleasure, she remained still, her hands on his shoulders, allowing this touch without permission. His punishments were wickedly fun for both of them, and she swore half the time he deliberately misbehaved to earn them.

Tracing the wide edge of her gown, his lips paused a mere inch from her nipple to tug on the neckline. When her bare breast popped into view, his head reared back a little, and she could hear a guttural whisper of, "Oh, Mistress."

Then his lips were on her nipple and the warmth that had flared at the first touch of his lips exploded into a fireball, pulsing in her belly. She shivered again. Then realized her reaction was in part because he'd drawn her skirts up, catching them against his knee to pull them further with a second tow. His fingers skimmed the skin above her stocking.

She moaned. However, being seen in public together and being caught disheveled and rumpled coming from a room together would cause very different gossip. The first, she was willing to handle. The second she was not ready for. That thought doused her desire, and she put her hands on his chest, pressing into the door at her back. "William, no. Not here, please."

He whined a little in his throat, making her smile at the puppy-like sound. At last, he raised his head, letting her skirts drop. His gaze roamed over her before he tugged her gown back up, covering her wet, rosy, stiff nipple.

"Come, let us mingle for a bit, then I will have you at my mercy."

"Yes, Mistress." He sounded grumpy, but complied, stepping away and adjusting his trousers.

He held the door for her.

Charlotte had not thought to ask him to check that the hallway was clear.

It was not. Two young men from the pile of rakelet puppies in the ballroom lingered in the hallway at the edge of the ballroom.

One glanced at her then past her to nod. She realized the youths were about William's age and knew him. The man's gaze slid back to her, and his eyes widened. He dug his elbow into his companion's side without finesse.

Fighting panic, Charlotte stiffened her spine, raised her head, and marched past them as though she did not see them. Beyond them, she slowed her gait to hear their greeting to William.

"Stanton, well done. That dame looks good for her age."

Another voice added, "Come, gents. She's a tempting armful, but you can do better than an older widow, if you want to sneak off to the library for some action."

She fled, not waiting to hear William's response. Would anything he said make a difference?

No one wanted to be the target of gossip, but having already held a title, she understood the ramifications. Her fears were not only for her reputation, but William's. He needed to maintain relationships among his peers in order to stay abreast of Parliamentary activities that could help or hurt his financial holdings.

Separate from all of that was her hurt. Call it pride, call it vanity, but the young men's disparaging comments sent shafts of pain through her. His mother's presence meant that she would hear about this, thus William was likely to be caught between them again.

Why had she agreed to continue until next Season? All this pain and fear would only worsen each time this sort of thing happened, and for what? They still had an expiration date.

* * * *

Needing time to regain perspective, she told him she had a megrim and needed to go home and sleep it off—alone.

When the butler came in to announce a visitor the next morning, she assumed it would be William.

"My lady, the Countess of Harrington is here. Shall I show her in?"

"The—what?"

"The—"

She shook her head. "I heard you. I am just shocked."

Could she decline the countess? No, better to get this

over with.

"Show her in, please, and have the kitchen bring a tea tray."

Violet skirts rustled as Ruth stepped in behind Austin, coming forward to clasp hands with Charlotte and exchange cheek kisses. Charlotte was glad she'd chosen one of her nicer day dresses in a moss green.

"Ruth." She couldn't very well say it was an unexpected pleasure, so she settled on, "'Tis lovely to see you. How are you?"

"Charlotte, thank you for seeing me without notice. I've been well, dear. How have you been?"

"Fine, thank you. Please, have a seat. I've rung for tea."

"You did not stay for the presentation on rubber at the salon. I found it illuminating. William told me the next day that you weren't feeling quite the thing."

"I was sorry to miss it. Sometimes these things cannot be helped." Charlotte shrugged, a list of questions running through her head that she could not manage to frame in an acceptably polite way, starting with *Why are you here? Get to the point.*

"I understand. William tells me he is courting you."

Charlotte clenched her hands to stop herself from fidgeting under his mother's gaze. This was worse than being a débutante. It was being treated as a débutante when she was a decade older than one. "For lack of a better term, I suppose."

The countess's eyebrows drew together. "Might there be a better term? Come now Charlotte, we are both smart women. I am sure we can solve this dilemma together. You're likely closer to my age than William's. I know you loved your husband, which is lucky in many ways, but difficult when tragedy strikes. I thought this might be a step in your recovery—a dalliance with a much younger man? You are a businesswoman, as am I. Perhaps it would be best to negotiate terms, like length of contract." Ruth's expression was fierce now. A mama bear protecting her cub.

Charlotte was well past awkwardness to fury by the time Ruth finished. William wasn't her cub, and her overbearance was not welcome to a woman she'd just admitted she saw as a peer. No, William was not Ruth's cub. He was Charlotte's puppy. And while she knew she needed to let him off leash, no one else had a say in how, when, or why. She was indeed a businesswoman, and a master negotiator. She busied her hands pouring and doctoring tea for them both. Then she lounged back in her chair, crossing her legs and swinging her foot, the embodiment of casual ease.

"With all due respect, my lady, William is an adult. I am an adult. So—and again, I do not mean to be rude— I am not sure what business it is of yours…?" She gazed unblinking at the countess, not allowing herself to frown or clench her jaw as she wanted, trying to appear open to understanding but firm. It was a fight to keep her fingers gentle on the teacup and saucer, but she managed it.

"You are right of course, my dear. Generally, it is not. I simply want to ensure that you've thought of these questions, and your answers to them." Ruth paused to sip tea. "And I must speak plainly here. William will need heirs. Therefore, at some point, this will have to end. I like you. I don't want to see either of you hurt."

At the reminder of the heir issue, Charlotte's anger faded. There was no way around that hard truth, and she could understand Ruth's concerns after toiling behind the scenes for more than a decade to keep the earldom afloat and allow William time to finish university. She likely felt like he was throwing it all away.

Taking a deep breath, she ignored the slights from the mama bear. "I understand. He and I have discussed this—more than once. And I am certain we will again. Whilst I will not betray his confidence and share details of those conversations, I am sure you know better than I how persistent he can be when he wants something."

"Like a dog with a bone." Ruth said, unknowingly reinforcing Charlotte's vision of him.

A snort of laughter escaped Charlotte.

Lady Harrington gave a wan smile, her brow still furrowed.

Charlotte dropped both feet to the floor and sat forward. "I care a great deal for your son, Ruth. I have also come to like and admire you. I should like to maintain both of those friendships. Finding the right balance will be difficult, but I assure you, I will not stand in the way of William's path to the earldom or his need for heirs."

"Thank you, Charlotte. He has much to take on. I hope both of us can make shouldering those burdens a bit easier for him."

"I do have a request. As I said—and I feel certain he has as well—we are all adults here. Please leave the details to us to work out. I will come to you if I need help, just as William does." She raised her brows.

Ruth's lips tilted down as Charlotte spoke. After a moment, she blinked and nodded. "Yes. You have my apologies for the way I barged in this morning. I shall try to do better."

"Thank you."

Ruth hesitated rather than standing to leave.

"Did you want to discuss something else?" Charlotte asked.

"Ah, since I am here, do you have time to discuss these new developments in rubber manufacturing? Can I share my thoughts? Have you read anything on it?"

There was no time like the present to test their ability to balance this friendship. Charlotte smiled and settled in for a lively debate and education.

Chapter Twenty-Four

William was furious and distraught. More, he was overwhelmed and exhausted.

A letter from his solicitor had been waiting for him that morning. His father's investment from last summer was worthless. The shipment had not been stored correctly for the voyage. His father's friends liked to cut corners, which often resulted in total losses for investors.

The loss was sizeable enough to undo all the progress he had made and then some, bringing their estate finances to a dangerous low. He'd already cut their expenses to the bone to avoid having to send servants packing.

Now, he did not see a way around it. He was too angry to write a coherent letter, however. His father had made this mess, he should be the one cleaning it up. And where was his mother? She'd inexplicably gone out this morning, of all days.

William paced the library, tugging at his hair, vibrating with tension. Unable to get past his frustration, he whirled. Heading for the stairs, he called out one last directive to the footman hovering in the hall.

Upstairs, he pounded on his father's door.

When no one answered, he opened it, thoughts of South forcing him to wonder if the earl had even made it home the night before. Snores emanated from the bed. He guessed his father's valet did not bother to linger nearby this early. No matter.

He entered the room, tugging the bell pull for the valet before shaking his father roughly. "Wake up. I need your attention."

"Wha-? Oh, William." The earl moaned. "'Tis too early. Lemme sleep."

William had already moved to the heavy curtains and slung them open.

"Argh. What the hell?" The older man sat up. "What is the matter? Is Ruth all right? Emily?"

"Define all right, old man," William spoke through gritted teeth. "Get dressed and come to the library."

Ten minutes later, the earl had slung clothes on and slunk into the library. He aimed for the decanters on the sideboard as he asked, "Tell me, William, are the girls well?"

"Do you really care? And don't bother. The spirits have been removed for this conversation."

His father blinked at him, the anger in his words finally sinking in. His words came slower now, careful. "Of course, I care."

"You have an interesting way of showing it. You reached for a drink before you even finished your question."

"Now see here—"

"No," William cut him off. "*You* see here. You have ignored your responsibilities. Worse, you've squandered much of the funds needed to run the estates and put food on our tenants' tables. We never see you. In fact, the only time I see you is at your club, when you're drunk, so I could not even have this conversation with you."

"What has happened?" His father raised his voice, "Ruth?"

"She's out."

"What then?"

"The solicitor sent word about your investment with your drinking mate. The one I tried to pin down last summer? It was improperly stored and is worthless."

"Oh no." The earl dropped into an armchair and lowered his face to his hands.

"Yes. Now, would you like to choose who loses their job at the country house? And write those letters of referral?"

"Uh…"

"I thought not. Why would you start upholding your duties now?" William's tone was bitter. "What will it take for you to realize how much you are hurting the dozens of people who rely on you? To say nothing of Mama."

"Son, you don't understand…" the earl trailed off.

"I'm listening, but you do not appear able to explain yourself. I'll handle it, along with Mama, as we've handled everything else in your absence." His lip curled in disdain. "Can you at least manage to stop throwing good money after bad, to allow me to get us out of this hole?"

Not waiting for an answer, he strode from the room to pace the garden. He hoped it would cool his temper, as he still wanted to hit something—or someone.

* * * *

Dusk settled and supper time approached. Although it was not their normal visiting hours, William could not wait any longer to see if his Mistress's megrim was gone. Or, more likely, if she was still upset from those stupid gits' comments at the ball. Beyond that, he needed her more that day than any before.

His mother had returned from her outing and he'd summarized the situation and his conversation with his father.

Ruth had attempted to soothe him, but as his father had disappeared by the time William had returned to the house, and was undoubtedly drowning his sorrows at the club, William was beyond appeasement. They spent much of the day rehashing ways around releasing staff, but had not been able to find any. William's tension had worsened throughout the day enough that his stomach hurt from holding it in.

He ached for the soothing peace Charlotte wrought by lifting that mantle of control and placing it on her own shoulders. She quieted his thoughts and worries, and more importantly warmed his heart. Well, and other parts. His lips lifted in a half smile for the first time that day.

After being shown into the parlor, he stood, too tense to sit, too much in turmoil to even pace. His fists clenched and unclenched as he listened with his whole body for his Mistress, his salvation.

The swish of skirts in the hall had him turning. Taking a deep breath, he let a head-to-toe shiver run through him and dropped his shoulders. He already felt better.

Charlotte rounded the doorway, green skirts settling around her as she stopped just inside. Her hair was up—hmm, perhaps she'd let him brush it out and massage her scalp—and she was lovely from head to toe.

And unhappy, as her lips were pressed flat.

"Mistress, thank you for seeing me." He bowed over

her hand, bussing it with a light kiss, wondering if a touch without permission would spark her to the actions he needed.

"William. 'Tis a rather odd time to visit, is it not?"

He straightened. "I wanted to ascertain that you are feeling better. You appear well. No, you appear lovely, as always."

She nodded once, the skin around her eyes loosening a touch.

He led her over to her preferred blue armchair. Once she was seated, he declined the settee at a right angle to her, or the matching armchair across the rug and low table. Instead, he perched on the padded footstool directly in front of her chair, requiring him to look up at her.

"What excuse did you tell your friends about dallying with the spinster? Or was I more of a light-skirt in their minds?" Her tone was bitter.

Blazes. She was still upset. He wanted to beat both of the men, in addition to his father.

"I do not need an excuse. Nor will I tolerate you being spoken of like that, which is what I told them in no uncertain terms." He took her hand from her lap, kissing it. "Mistress, you cannot hold me responsible for others' words. Please."

"I do not. But you have heard it before, and we both know talk like that will continue as long as we are seen together. And they aren't wrong. You could do better." She combed her hand through his hair.

"Stop." He firmed his voice, straightening on his seat, as low as it may be. "I shan't hear that from anyone, including you. I disagree."

"Oh, William. How noble and caring you are. I worry

how much both of us will be hurt between now and next Season if we continue." She stopped caressing his hair, dropping her hand to her lap.

Alarmed, he swallowed hard, pained at her words. She remained focused on their end date, refusing to see that he wanted to be hers for the rest of his days. He needed her, for heaven's sake.

Tremors of anxiety ran through him. The urgency of his need for that evening, that hour, pressed against his skin as much as forever did. He could not bear it if she turned him away. He might explode, or go find South and let his friend lead him into all sorts of trouble, going the way of his father. It was all too much.

He ran his hands through his hair before flinging them wide. "I'm not leaving!"

"You must, eventually."

"No."

"Yes." Her voice firmed now, becoming more Mistress than Charlotte. "You must marry. You must have heirs. 'Tis your responsibility. You're the only son, there is no other option."

"I am tired of my responsibilities, especially today. I do not want to—I *cannot*—think about them. Please, Mistress, I love you. I need you." He stretched his hand toward hers again. It trembled.

"William? Are you quite all right? What happened today?" She was staring at his hand, reaching to meet it with both of hers.

"I don't want to talk about today. Suffice it to say it was terrible. To answer your other question, no, Mistress, I am not in a good frame of mind. You denied me the opportunity to comfort you last night, you continue to debate the wisdom of this. Yet all I can think of is you. I can't imagine courting someone else, much less marrying them. Please, I beg of you. I wish to be yours."

He slid to the floor and knelt, placing his head in her lap over their clasped hands. His shoulders shook with the vibrations of his fear, and he fought tears. He could not leave her.

She mustn't make him.

Chapter Twenty-Five

Strangely, his trembling calmed Charlotte. Seeing how the stress of managing his world was eating at him made her forget her arguments.

He bore so much responsibility at such a young age. Other young men his age were on their Grand Tours of Europe, enjoying all the freedoms of being newly independent adults. He was shadow-managing an earldom for a drunkard of a father, trying to manage his sister and a wayward friend, and learning it all along the way. No wonder he did not want to think of marriage or children. He perceived them as more responsibilities to drag at him.

Well, she refused to be another one. This, she could solve for him, and would continue to do so until the start of the next Season, no matter how much it hurt her. She'd survived losing one love, she'd find a way through the next loss. In the meantime, she could be his port in the storm.

She pulled one hand out from the tangled clasp beneath his head, and stroked his hair with it, raking her nails gently along his scalp.

He shuddered.

"Shh, William. No more talk now. Your Mistress is in charge. Let go of the rest of it."

She pushed at his shoulder, standing. "Stay right there." Going to the door, she opened it and stepped outside, asking Austin in a low voice that a note be sent to Ruth regarding William's absence for supper. Then she closed and locked the door before returning to her seat.

"Now…remove your coat, your waistcoat, and cravat."

"Mistress?" He glanced around.

His confusion was understandable. The first floor had always been their serious place, not their play space. She liked keeping him off-balance though, so that was about to change.

"Ah, I said no talking. Come now." She watched his reaction to her tone as it brought him into the mindset of their private relationship, pushing aside all the pent-up frustrations he had arrived with.

His pupils dilated, his shoulders relaxed a degree, and his mouth softened.

She sat back, shaking her head when he looked at her for permission to rise for ease of movement. She rather liked him at her feet.

He struggled out of his clothes, shifting back and forth on his knees. His delicious spiced rum scent floated to her. Dissatisfied at not being able to see his young supple skin, she added, "The shirt too, unless you are cold."

The shirt was whipped off over his head as he grinned at her.

Ah, there is my rakelet's smile. Glad her skills could unburden him and bring him joy, she returned the smile.

He gripped himself through his trousers, shifting to find some relief for his hard length.

"You may unbutton your trousers if you need a bit more room."

He rushed to comply, one quiet moan escaping as his swollen cock sprang free.

As always, she salivated at the sight. Her breasts pushed against her gown, anticipating his touch, and heat gathered between her legs. With a smile, she gave him more opportunity for creativity since his hands would be free.

"Right, then. You have one minute to get me in the position you want me, without getting off your knees. Then you must clasp your hands behind your back and focus entirely on me. You may speak from now on, and ask me to do things, but you'll have no guarantee that I'll do them. Your minute is ticking, puppy."

His eyes flared. He knelt up and twisted one hand in her fichu, ripping it out of its pins in her décolletage. Tossing it over his shoulder, he scooped both hands in and drew her breasts out over the neckline of her bodice.

Gracious. Shock at his aggressive actions was tempered with an added bolt of arousal singing through her veins.

Abandoning her upper half, he went to the bottom of her skirt, grasping a chunk of the hemline in each hand. His arm muscles bulged and his jaw locked.

Realizing what he was about to do, she opened her mouth, although she wasn't sure she would protest. Her dress was replaceable. His freedom to escape through this was not.

Regardless, she was out of time.

Rrrrriiiiippp.

His arms were spread wide, the hem of her skirt in each of them. He'd rent a split half way up the skirt.

Repositioning his hands closer to the top of the tear, he did it a second time, until the reinforced seam at the waistline of the bodice stopped it. Flipping the pieces to either side of her, he untied the tapes of her petticoat, and yanked it down and off her, not even needing her to raise her hips.

She gaped at him, blinking. He might have been harboring more frustration than she'd understood.

In an effort to save the rest of her clothing, she took back control. Always before deferring to her had helped him release tension, and she hoped it would this time. She was hot and bothered and ready for the next step. "Time is up. Hands behind your back."

He groaned, and put his hands behind his back, but did not sit back on his heels. Instead, he leaned in, braced a hip against her knee to avoid toppling, and claimed her lips with his.

"Mistress," he panted. "Touch me, please."

Ohh, she liked this. He could give her commands thinly veiled as requests, but she was still in charge. This was a new sort of play for her, and she found she was looking forward to where his brain would go now that she had refocused it.

She skimmed her hands over his shoulders, running them down his arms until she could not reach. Running her hands forward, she pinched the small flat discs on his chest, causing him to twist against her lips. He had reclaimed her lips, but at that touch, he pulled back, and still braced, bent further to lick and suck the hardened tip of her breast.

"Touch your other breast. Let me see you give yourself pleasure."

Happy to oblige him, she tweaked the nipple he

didn't have in his mouth, before cupping her breast as though to offer it to him.

He straightened. "Unh. Mistress, give me a minute." Panting, he squeezed his eyes shut, tilted his head and muttered.

Is he—is he conjugating a Latin verb again? It had been ages since he'd needed to do that during their play.

Then the verb registered.

Subsistere—to stop or withstand or resist.

She almost giggled, then upped the ante. Reaching out, she gripped his length in a firm hand.

His eyes flew open and he gasped. He twisted his hips, pulling away as though she was hurting him. His arms twitched, but he did not bring them forward.

She slid her hand slowly toward his tip.

"Mistress. Please. I cannot—you cannot—" He recognized the error of his phrasing. "Please let go of me, I want to ensure I please you. You come first."

At that, she did giggle.

He paused, and then after a minute, realized what he had said, and choked out a quick laugh.

She sat back, and he skipped all other preliminaries, sinking to sit on his heels and scoot closer, burying his head in her lap.

"Sit your hips forward in the chair and lean back, and hold yourself open for me, Mistress?" He half-commanded, half-asked. His puppy dog eyes peered up at her from between her thighs, his panting breaths gusting over her sensitive flesh.

That sounded like an excellent next step.

She scooted. She placed her fingers where he asked, his breath on her before she'd finished. Then his mouth was there, eating at her. His teeth grazed her as he nearly chewed in his eagerness before he remembered himself. Gentling, he nuzzled and tongued her through a smile.

"William…" His name came out on a breath, barely audible.

Bracing herself with her elbows against the chair arms, she shoved her flesh against him, moaning.

Lapping at her, he firmed his tongue and sped up.

She was lost. They could take their time later. She had a hazy thought of dining together but could not focus. She needed his cock in her as much as he needed to pound.

"I release you, William. Come to me."

He rose before she finished the sentence. Dragging her out of the chair, he pushed her in front of him onto the settee to kneel facing the back.

She grabbed the carved wood lip when he pushed her forward. Air wafted over the back of her legs as he tugged the remains of her skirt up to pile at the base of her spine.

He dragged her hips back a few inches to where he stood, shins pressed against the seat cushion.

Then he shoved into her, fast and hard, sliding the settee an inch and rattling a candlestick on the narrow table behind it. She gasped then groaned, shocked at how much she loved his forcefulness. She shuddered and wiggled her hips once as her body adjusted to the sudden penetration, her blood throbbing in her veins.

He needed no further direction. Having stepped forward to follow the settee, he tempered his force but increased the speed.

She set her teeth as his thrusts grazed her internal front wall, throwing logs on the already-leaping flames of her desire. She keened as the pleasure spiraled through her.

His sac slapped her most sensitive flesh and they both moaned in sync with each impact. She had no idea how he was refraining from exploding, but she could not worry about it. She was too busy chasing her own ecstasy, as every muscle tightened and stretched toward the sensations only he could wring from her.

He reached around to cup her breast, thumbing her nipple, and she jerked at the lightning bolt shooting from her tip to her core.

He leaned in to nibble on the side of her neck.

"Ah, ah, William!" The contrast of gentle and rough sent her into an unstoppable slide.

In another moment of role reversal, she heard, "Mistress, yes. Come with me."

She obeyed. Her muscles clamped down on him and she shook under him, surrounded by him. Her breasts grazed the brocade of the settee, and her hands dug into the wood. Each piston slapped her hardened nub and sent a fresh pulse of heat through her, as though his cock touched her fingers, toes, ears, and everything in between. Sagging in his arms, she rode the wave until it ebbed.

His hips jerked hard, and the pulsing of his cock inside her prolonged her ride.

Vaguely she felt him reposition them both. As they lay, her on him now, prone on the settee, it was clear that for the short term, William needed her.

She might be simply an outlet for the moment, but she was a much-needed—and much-satisfied—outlet. She grinned against his chest.

* * * *

It was a sign of her urgency that Belle had forgotten

a disguise. She burst through the back door in full courtesan regalia. A scarlet gown—*such a cliché*, Charlotte smirked—makeup, hair up in an elaborate coiffure, musky rose scent wafting.

"Good morning, Belle. This is an unexpected but lovely surprise. Tea?" Charlotte motioned for a servant to bring another place setting and teacup and saucer.

"I may need brandy. You should have brandy." She collapsed into William's—and her usual—chair.

Charlotte's brows rose. "Always so dramatic, Belle."

Gathering herself, her friend sat up straight and took two deep breaths. Leaning forward, she took Charlotte's hand and sighed again.

"Right. Now you are frightening me. Whatever is the matter?"

"You have not yet heard the news. Right, then." She eyed the newspaper across the room on the desk.

"You know I like to have my breakfast in peace before facing the newspaper, correspondence, and the like."

"When did you last see William?"

Charlotte tilted her head and looked at her. "Two days ago, why?"

"Have you heard from him since?"

"No. He had something urgent he needed to handle for the family that was complicated, and there was a late meeting of his acquaintances after Lords last night. He planned to come tonight. Why, Belle?"

"His father passed." Belle sat back, grim-faced.

"What? No. When? How? He is barely fifty! No." Charlotte was not quite sure what question to ask first.

Oh, William. She wanted to hold him and protect him from the mantle of responsibility that weighed so heavily on him. Just as she knew he wanted to do for his mother and sister.

"Explain, please." She needed to hear more.

Belle gestured toward the desk. "There is not much information in the newspaper. A formal note of his death, due to 'a heart condition,' which we all know was whisky-infused, and William's new title."

"Oh, puppy," Charlotte murmured, her heart hurting for her young lover's increased burdens. Then Isabella's last words registered, and her own heart shattered.

She could not help him any longer. He needed heirs sooner rather than later. They were out of time.

Chapter Twenty-Six

William stood in the front pew of the church. His mother stood beside him, his sister on her other side. Percy and his family were beyond Emily.

I am out of time.

There would be no more joint decisions, no more sharing the burden with Percy and his mother. Of course, he'd always be able to ask them for their advice, they'd always support him, and they'd prepared him well. And really, he'd been managing it all for months.

He could not even regret his last conversation with his father. His father was out of time to fix himself and his relationship with his family. He never hugged his wife or daughter or son one last time to tell them he loved them—and perhaps even that he was sorry. No, William was too angry still to mourn his father.

He mourned his freedom. And, he feared, his Mistress.

The decisions, the fate of his family and all the families who depended on the earldom for their living, indeed the weight of the earldom, sat on him like a heavy cloak. He bowed his head, only to have his mother poke him and whisper, "Head up, please, Lord Harrington."

He snapped straight.

Right, then. Full steam ahead and all that. No time

for grieving. He knew she mourned, though, and her sorrow caused him pain, even if he did not understand her grief.

Her reminder of his new title was unnecessary. He felt the magnitude of it as a millstone and dreaded the fight he knew he'd face with Charlotte. As he strained under the burdens his sudden ascendency, the one he worried about the least would be the one that remained uppermost in her thoughts: the requirement of heirs.

To him, children were an abstract part of his future. He had enough to juggle at the moment. The worry of it all made him itch, his shoulders tightening. His skin felt too tight, and he struggled to focus on the vicar's words. His thoughts spiraled, thinking of the cost of the funeral, the roofs that needed repair on his lands, the village children who could benefit from more books for their school. And above all, he worried that his Mistress would not allow him to turn himself over to her, to love her as he wished.

His mother appeared outwardly serene, her only tell the handkerchief she twisted between her hands. Was losing his father more or less painful to her than watching him throw their happiness away with each drink he tossed back? At least she no longer had to bear the responsibility of finding the funds for her family and beyond, or managing the estates with limited ability to influence change.

No, those are all mine to worry about now. Then he would cycle back through the chain of emotions.

It was not enough that he had found out three days ago about his father's unsalvageable loss. He'd been about to write his stewards and housekeepers at the family holdings to have them each release several servants when his mother had entered the library white-faced with the news of his father's collapse. Of course, it had happened at his father's club.

She had not yet raised the obvious solution to their problems. In the time-honored tradition of the aristocracy, the quickest way to steer them back to solvency was to marry for money. As long as that lady could also provide the necessary heirs. If he had not met Charlotte, he might have considered it. Now, however, his heart was fully engaged, and he would never settle for second best.

He sighed. He had wanted to tell Charlotte in person, but there had not been a moment he could call his own. Then he'd received a formal note from her addressed to the Earl of Harrington, which arrived with a separate note in the same handwriting addressed to his mother.

He needed to hold Charlotte, even if he could not play, could not serve his Mistress, could not read Latin with her or discuss a news article. He craved her in his arms, her honey curls against his neck and chin, her arms slipping under his coat to rest closer to the warmth of his skin. That little sniff she took, thinking he did not realize she was smelling him, and the resulting smile which bloomed each time, that he could feel against his chest. He needed Charlotte, the love of his life, more than his Mistress.

After the service, the family filed out of the pew first, following the coffin, as the rest of the mourners and supporters stood. He spied South and Folly at the far end of a pew, South appearing gray but sober, Folly in an ill-fitting jacket. They nodded to him as he passed. As he led his mother farther up the aisle, he caught honey curls and sable eyes. Charlotte!

She looked immeasurably sad, her mouth grim and her eyes big pools of cocoa in her pale face. He was sure he looked much the same, actually. As he approached, still holding her gaze, she tore her gaze away, plucking at her gown before turning her head completely.

No!

His hands fisted where they hung clasped in front of him. She was his last vestige of freedom—and if he could convince her, his wife. His shoulders hunched another inch, and his head bowed, weighed down by the chains of his life.

Tears pricked at his eyes. Tightening his hand on his mother's where it lay on his arm, he bit the inside of his cheek to avoid embarrassing himself.

He straightened, a new determination rising in him. He had dragged the family out of debt once, he would do it again. He had won other arguments with Charlotte, and he'd find a way to win this as well. He just had to strategize. If he could handle the title of earl, he could handle this.

* * * *

William pored over the accounts. The loss of that shipment was a setback, but nowhere what it would have been had he not been investing. And that investing had happened with the help of his Mistress. To say she had a knack for it would be putting it mildly.

He hated having to let staff go, but he had forced himself to finish the letters to his stewards, offering good letters of character and severance pay, despite the family's circumstances. It did not seem fair to punish other people for his father's bad judgment. Although they might have been selling off jewelry and other family heirlooms if not for Charlotte. She had introduced him to her man of business, but more, she had talked through her strategy of mixing industries and her thorough research into anything before investing in it. She was more comfortable with simple business ventures: a hair product shop, a few imported goods, shipping. For the last, she had joined a group of investors who funded a shipping company with several ships and had spread their outlay across those ships. The company had to find other sponsors to share in each ship, but everyone had less risk, albeit possibly less reward. He wished he could hand over that side of managing their finances to her, even without marriage. He could picture her at the other desk in the room, where his mother worked now, as they acted together to share the duties and have more time for themselves.

Now, he frowned over the ledgers, trying to find ways to recoup their losses, as well as estimate how long it would be before he could bring the country estate back to full staff. He knew his mother would like to go there when it got warm, although the longer he delayed selecting a wife, the longer his mother would stay in London to prod him.

He loved her dearly, but there were occasions when he wished for a more traditional mother, one who would have already retired to the dower house in the country and let him catch his breath before badgering him about marriage and heirs.

Sitting back, he envisioned working, the patter of young feet in the hall, a boy with honey curls bursting in to hide between his feet under the desk, before his fairer-haired sister chased inside looking for him, followed by—*Mistress*.

Propping his elbows on the wood, he buried his head

in his hands. Sadly, children with their coloring were improbable if not impossible. He wanted to weep for the loss. She would excel at motherhood, just as she had at everything else.

Without lifting his head, he stared at the paperwork scattered across the desk, his skin itching again. Being an earl felt like a life sentence in prison. Hellfire, it *was* a life sentence, but it should not feel like this. Every document he read seemed to require an opinion, every letter a decision, every tenant guidance. It was exhausting. Finding a wife or fending off his mother's prodding was another burden.

These past months as he had unofficially performed much of this role, his outlet had been Charlotte. With her, he could relax. No decisions were needed after the first one, to bow his head and submit to her will. His brain was quiet, his soul was at peace. More, his heart was happy. He trusted her and adored her.

How could he convince her of that? He needed to find a way to be with her, despite the issue of heirs. However, she would not let him in. He'd tried for the past two nights, and he could not find time to formulate different ways to woo her when dozens of mouths depended on his ability to provide their food and livelihood.

Scribbling off a note to Charlotte's—and now his—business manager, he set it aside to be delivered, and refocused.

* * * *

William slumped on the pub bench, South and Folly watching him across the table. They hadn't spent time together in weeks. Both men looked rather grim, almost as grim as he did, as he shared the news about the ruined ship's cargo.

Folly shook his head. "'Tis horrid, like one last slap from the grave, if I may say so." His friends both knew William had lost respect for his father once he saw the state of the family's estate and how hard his mother had to work to get him through Oxford. Only memories of his very early childhood saved him from hating the man. His sister did not have those but neither had she been forced to deal with the repercussions of his abandonment of his responsibilities.

South swung a hand with a glass and a cheroot in it. "Well at least 'tis the last. Hear, hear." He raised the glass and they all toasted.

William was sure that anyone listening would have thought them—him, especially—the coldest of men, but he could not give a fig. They did not know what he had had to deal with, nor did they understand what he faced going forward.

He sighed. "He's undone over a year of work. I am just thankful I had gained enough ground that we aren't begging on the street."

"Yes, well done, chap. I confess I must have missed that class at university, I've had nowhere near the returns on my investments that you have." South made a quick air toast before sipping his ale again.

"Perhaps you drank more of them away?" Folly murmured, and got an elbow in his ribs.

William smiled, although the curve of his lips was tinged with sadness. "'Twasn't Oxford, South. 'Twas Charlotte, Lady Peterborough to you. The lady you doltishly addressed as a wench in her own home."

South rolled his eyes. "I apologized for that, old chap. Are you ever going to let me forget it?"

Folly jumped in, getting back to the import of William's statement. "You are saying that Lady Peterborough helped you invest?" His voice was incredulous.

"Yes, actually. Why is that so hard to believe?"

"Are you sure they weren't her husband's investments?"

William frowned at his friend. "Her husband died three years ago, Folly. The steam locomotive had not been invented then, as one example. Yes, I am quite sure."

"Right, sorry, Will. Hmm…"

South tossed his arm around William again.

William watched his friend's beer. The height of sloshing liquid told him it was still only his second or third, a remarkable feat for this time of evening. The funeral must have sparked sobriety.

"You know, we haven't seen you here much these past months. You've been at the ever-so-lovely Lady Peterborough's." South and Folly toasted his overly careful reference and snickered. "Why are you not there now?"

William shook his head, lips turning down. "She won't see me. As far as I can tell she is not even home."

"Wait, do you mean that she found you inheriting an earldom awful enough that she hied herself off somewhere?" South snickered, while Folly raised his brows.

"What, was her first marriage to an earl so horrible it put her off for life? Or is she wealthy enough to want to keep a string of young men to play with, but never wed?" Folly added.

"Watch it!" William sat up. "I'll not have you speak

of her like that. Do you really think I'd be someone's plaything?"

Folly shrugged, muttering almost to himself, "If the sex was good…"

South roared with laughter, swinging his drink dangerously again.

William shook his head at them. And his Mistress called *him* a puppy? She would have their attitudes straightened out in no time, not that he wanted them anywhere near her. "Ugh. You two. Seriously, I should like nothing better than to continue to court her, even to wed her. But she'll have none of it. I'm open to ideas to get her back."

"Why did she turn you away?"

"Heirs."

"Riiiggghhht. She was with Peterborough for almost a decade." South prided himself on knowing details of Ton gossip. "And whilst heirs are a vague, future concern when you have all the time in the world, they become much more real when you gain the title. Credit goes to the lady for being honorable. Not all ladies—or gents for that matter—would willingly step back from someone they liked."

"No one could ever doubt her character." William's lips twisted.

Folly shrugged. "Tree climbing was the extent of my knowledge for how to win a lady."

South's glass swung again, albeit a little less wildly. "There are plenty of fish in the sea, Will. The lovely countess aside, marriage does seem like the expedient solution. Heirs and blunt, what?"

William glowered. They were supposed to help him win Charlotte back, not agree with his mother. He'd have to find his own way.

Chapter Twenty-Seven

Despite their romance being at an end, Charlotte considered both William and Ruth friends. She attended the previous earl's funeral service to support both of them. Avoiding William as best she could so as not to encourage him, she skirted the procession offering condolences outside the chapel. She would offer her sympathies to Ruth later, one widow to another, in both written form and even later in person.

Ruth caught her gaze, though. Charlotte nodded solemnly to the countess.

I am sorry for your loss. I am here for you. I know what needs to happen now.

Ruth nodded back, then glanced at William. Charlotte wagged her head once in the negative, gave a shallow curtsy and made her way down the side of the steps and home.

Once home, she attempted to draft two more notes, one to Ruth and one to William. In Ruth's, she offered her ear to commiserate whenever Ruth might desire, and said that she would see if she was open to a quiet social call in a fortnight. William's was more difficult. Her own devastation interfered with finding empathy for his. He was also likely more miserable over her distance than the loss of his father, which was not ego but based on her knowledge of his frustrations at his parent. After several heart-rending tries, she gave up, unable to find words beyond the stilted condolences and best wishes for his new role she'd parsed together in her first missive.

There was nothing more to say, although that thought filled her again with despair. Whilst her grief might be different than his, it was nonetheless as deep. This felt worse than the loss of her husband. Her bereavement now had the added fillip of watching the person she had lost move around London, even as her heart felt as though he was gone as thoroughly as Charles was. The fact that she had gone into this willingly, knowing the outcome, made it worse. She'd brought it on herself.

How could she stand it?

Unable to focus through the pain and seeing the ghost of William everywhere she looked in her home, she scribbled a third note and asked the servant to wait for a response. While she waited to see if Belle was available for a call, she paced, holding her hand to her mouth as though it would force back the tears.

After what felt like hours, the servant returned, and she called for the carriage. Speeding over to Belle's, she found her friend waiting with open arms and several bottles of sherry sitting on the sideboard for their evening.

"Belle." She collapsed into those arms, and let it all go. Sobbing, sniveling, dripping from eyes and nose on her friend's dress, she could not seem to stop. Taking heaving breaths in between, she tried to speak. "I…he…Belle…" She wailed again.

Belle held her and rubbed her back. After an hour or a week, she let go with one arm and led them to the sofa. "Shh, dear. I know. I am sorry."

"Oh, lud. Why?" Charlotte frowned through her tears. "Why did you encourage me in this?"

"Because you deserve him."

"I did not deserve this heartache, which we always knew it would come to."

"No, you do not. But I used present tense. You still deserve him. We just need to convince you of that."

"Ack, I cannot argue with you right now, Belle. Please? You know my reasons, and they are the right ones. Please, let us not discuss this. I can't bear it." Leaning her head wearily against the back of the sofa she sat sideways on, facing her friend, Charlotte closed her eyes for a second, exhausted.

"Right, then. Sherry? That was the plan, I believe." Belle rose to pour them each a rather large glass, and they proceeded to work their way through the bottle as they talked about anything other than William. Much later that night, Belle poured Charlotte into a guest bed at her house to sleep it off.

Unbeknownst to her, Charlotte had hoped to sleep there to avoid William.

As Belle was between paramours, Charlotte wallowed, sending for a few items from her home, and spending the days playing cards, discussing investments, and drinking vast amounts of sherry with her friend.

On the third morning, morose but resigned, Charlotte picked at her apple cake as her tea grew cold. The end of her courtship with William had been a foregone conclusion. She had regularly reminded her rakelet of that fact. She'd expected to have time to plan, to see the end coming, but she'd adjust.

Belle sat across from her, watching her move crumbs around. "You know you're welcome to stay with me forever. You might be invited to participate in a threesome now and then, but I've no doubt you can handle that. I think you will be more comfortable in your own space, though, to move on with your life."

"I know," she answered with a wan smile. "Thank you for having me these past days. I appreciate you letting me hide. And yes, I admit I've been hiding. It so happens I packed this morning."

"I still think you should—"

"Please. Not again." Charlotte waved a hand. Belle had been harping on the possibility of marriage to William sporadically, despite Charlotte's protests. She was too tired and too sad to have the argument again. There was no getting around the risk she could not bear children. "I am grateful for your support and encouragement. But having dealt with the aristocracy at one level or another for more than a decade, I know 'tis not the right thing. The correct thing is to ensure the continuity of the title to his children."

"What about his estate?"

"Of course. The estate and the title go together."

"Not necessarily. Not if he cannot afford to maintain the estate—or estates, as I believe there are a few properties that are sellable, beyond the entailed assets."

Charlotte frowned. "I knew funds were scarce, but I thought William had started to turn the corner."

"My source—"

Charlotte snorted. "Your source? Do I even want to know? Is the source connected to the footsteps I heard in the hall last night?"

"Pish, a girl has to earn a living." Belle snickered, before resuming her intelligence sharing. "My source tells me that his father's most recent investment failure has made their circumstances rather more dire."

Oh, puppy. Another burden for you to bear.

Belle watched her closely. "If only he had someone he was interested in marrying who could solve the financial issue, to help him keep the estate whole."

Her lips flattened. "Belle. Do not start again, I beg you."

"Hmph. What have I told you about that word? Do not use it around me unless you mean it."

They both laughed at her favorite joke.

When Charlotte returned home, she started a note to Ruth to follow up on her note after the funeral, paused, and put down the fountain pen to pace. Thinking hard, she returned to the note with fresh words of invitation in mind.

* * * *

Charlotte slid a nervous glance to the hall mirror to check her hair. She had dithered over her appearance all morning after receiving Ruth's acceptance of her invitation yesterday.

Not wanting to appear ostentatious, she had chosen a simple gown. Her earrings had only small gems in them. She had contemplated removing some of the more valuable art from the parlor, but realized Ruth had already seen it. Besides, she was proud of what she had achieved—with Charles's help, of course. Ruth had not had that, at least in recent years, but this was her house and her life, and she was not going to hide it. Indeed, it put her in a place of being able to offer a new friend help.

She swung into the kitchen to ask them to prepare a tea tray with pastries, and then to the parlor, where she fidgeted with the two versions of Homer. She had been unable to focus on reading this past week, but promised herself she would not stop learning just because she did not have her favorite tutor any longer.

Voices murmured in the hall, and the butler announced the Countess of Harrington before standing aside for her to enter. Charlotte stepped forward to greet her, grasping her hands and leaning in to buss her cheek.

As they sat, Charlotte said, "Thank you for coming, Ruth. I am sure this is a difficult time for you."

"It is, although in some ways, I had lost my husband years ago, I'm afraid. As 'tis common knowledge, I may as well discuss it freely, at least away from the gossips." She shrugged.

"I never thought of it like that. I suppose your grieving has been spread out over these past years then."

"Yes. But I do appreciate your offer of support. Shared perspectives, and all that."

"Ruth, I may have a way to offer you support in…a more tangible way." Charlotte was not sure how to frame her idea. Fidgeting for a moment, she finally looked up. "I am sure you are aware of the speed with which rumor flies about the Ton?"

Ruth nodded, cocking her head, no doubt wondering what tale Charlotte was referring to.

"I have heard that your family may have been hurt by the latest damaged shipment the papers mentioned last week?"

Ruth straightened. "Why do you ask?"

Charlotte leaned forward. It was now or never. She hoped her good intentions would get her through, even if Ruth was offended. "Ruth, first let me clarify. I have not seen William since the funeral, nor do I intend to. I do understand the…unsuitable nature…of our relationship given William's change in station. However, I care about him and about you, as my friend. And I am in something of a unique position. My jointure from Charles was generous, and above and beyond that, Charles's brother gifted me this London townhouse, as it was my favorite place."

Ruth tilted her head, her brows furrowed.

Charlotte sighed and spoke plainly. "Even before then, I—we—invested. Since then, I have added to my portfolio using that jointure and have…been very successful. Frankly, given my lack of children, I have more than I could ever need." Her words came faster as she battled nerves at being so forthright. "I should very much like to loan your family any funds you may need to get back on your feet. I know that William is a very astute investor, and I have no doubt you will recover sooner rather than later. But I also know that he worries a great deal about his tenants and servants. I should hate for him to lose sleep over someone dependent on him being affected by this loss."

Ruth opened her mouth, but seemed unsure of what to say, and Charlotte held up a hand. "One last thing. My only stipulation is that William not know where the funds come from."

The older woman closed her mouth, nonplussed. She narrowed her eyes at Charlotte.

Charlotte gulped a breath, unable to discern if Ruth was angry or offended.

"Why?"

"Because he will try to take advantage, using it as a reason to continue our relationship. He might even see it as an overture on my part." Or worse, he could take it as Belle had, and think she was buying his services. But she was not going to share that with his mother.

After a long moment, William's mother said something Charlotte had not expected. "You appear to understand my son quite well."

"Perhaps. Likely not as well as you." Charlotte did not want to talk about her and William. "This will depend on you being able to mask the source of the funds successfully. Can you do that?"

Ruth snorted. "He still does not know why I put up with his father's drinking all these years. I am confident I could manage that aspect, if I accepted."

Charlotte's curiosity was peaked. "Since you raised the subject, may I ask why you did?"

The new widow sighed, her back bowing as her head lowered to look at her lap. "That is a long story, and not well done of me. But given your generosity and care with my family, I shall share the short version. William's sister is more than three years younger than him. It took us that long to have a second child, although we both would have liked her sooner. Then, three years after her, I became pregnant again. It only lasted three months, and I nearly died when I lost the baby. The physician said any more pregnancies were dangerous. Fred had always wanted as many children as possible. He was devastated. That and almost losing me put him over the edge. He was always more sensitive than me…For the first few years, I thought he would get over it. He'd drink until he didn't need to any longer. But he never reached that point. By then, William was older, and it just did not seem right to make William grieve our loss as well."

"Do you believe that now?"

"No, not at all. William is like me. Strong enough to do what he must. To shoulder the needs of the family and ensure they are met. Too, I saw their previous father-son relationship fall apart. And more recently, I've come to realize that without understanding the reason behind it, Fred choosing drink over him hurt him terribly. I regret not telling him."

"'Tis never too late, Ruth." Charlotte leaned over and held her friend's hand.

"I know. I will, soon, now. Better late than never, I suppose. But I digress." Ruth pulled herself up and looked straight at Charlotte. "You made me a very generous offer, one I never could have imagined, and I have not even addressed it to offer my gratitude. I cannot thank you enough...I am not even sure I have words."

She sounded choked up, and Charlotte rushed to spare her further discomfort. "Please consider it. I really do mean it, and I really do have enough to do it comfortably."

"Very well, I shall consider it. May I call on you in a few days then?"

"'Twould be my pleasure, Ruth."

Chapter Twenty-Eight

William flung the book of Catullus's naughty poems across the room. He could not even concentrate enough to find something fitting. Poetry was fine as a method of wooing when he was miles away at university. Now he could not stand being close yet unable to see his Mistress in person, even if it was to debate the merits of their relationship.

He needed her. Not the stress relief that she brought. He was learning to handle that. The essence of her—her smell, her fingers in his hair, her wit and raised brows and teasing. The little frown when she was beleaguered by a Latin verb. The smile of satisfaction when she'd helped more women start businesses. All of her felt as essential to him as air, and he was gasping for lack of her.

He glared at the book lying spread-eagled on the floor. Even Catullus did not have the words, so what would William manage to say if she did permit him entrance? More to the point, how would he even get an audience? Her doors and windows were locked to him.

And what response would he get from a poem? He was Penelope in Ovid's *Heroides*: "This your Penelope sends to you, too-slow Ulysses; A letter in return does me no good; come yourself!"

No. Whatever else I am, I am a man, and I must fight for her like a man. How do I balance fighting and giving her control, as I have in the past?

He stared blindly at the wall, the idea of marriage circling. A servant's knock interrupted his musings. At his question, the butler called out, "Your mother requests you in the library, sir."

"Right. I shall be down momentarily."

He found his mother in the seating area by the fireplace, and settled across from her as she poured him tea. "William, I need to tell you something that is long overdue. I've been remiss in sharing information with you that was pertinent to your relationship with your father."

"I don't understand, Mama. And why now?"

"Because you deserve to know, and it may help you understand my actions as well as his."

Ruth shared with him the loss of her third child, his father's reaction, and her attempts to wait it out, manage it, and finally accept that she'd lost her husband in addition to her baby.

He sat back, tears in his eyes, as his mother held both his hands in hers. "I beg your pardon, William. There was just never a good time, but that is not an excuse. I was a coward."

Leaning in, he hugged her. "Mama. Never a coward. You simply had too much to deal with and had to prioritize. I am sorry for the loss of the babe." He shuddered at the thought. "To be devastated and not have a partner to turn to, the person you thought would be your mainstay through thick and thin."

His mother nodded and clutched his hands. "Thank you for understanding, William."

He straightened, the connection made. His parents' bond is what he wanted—nay, *had*, with Charlotte. They were partners, in every sense of the word. He could not care less if they never had children, although he realized that his mother would. It did not matter. He needed his Mistress. He would not have children without her, because he would never wed someone else. No one else would be his safe harbor in times of trouble as well as the first person he turned to when he had something to celebrate. Without her, *he* would be a ship lost at sea, never mind the finances.

There was no time like the present to start his battle for his Mistress. "I never understood how you could still love him. I mean, I assumed you stayed with him because there are not many choices for women, but I saw your patience with him, and struggled."

Ruth snorted. "You know me better than that. I could have made my own arrangements if I wanted to live separately from your father. 'Twas not lack of choices, or even responsibility to those depending on us. 'Twas an actual choice. I was lucky enough to wed someone I loved, and whilst not everyone can be as strong as you and I are, I understood why he did what he did. He felt too much sometimes."

Stifling his snort of impatience at his father, he took advantage of the opening. "I may have a touch of my father in me, then. I also feel too much sometimes. I have never allowed you to witness the tremor in my hand when I signed a document with significant impact on our family or the estate. But Charlotte saw. More, she helped me recenter myself, and regain my strength whenever I wavered. She is as much or more of a partner to me as Father was to you, and I cannot do this without her,

Mama."

"William, no. It cannot be, my dear." Ruth's mouth pursed, although he could not tell if it was sorrow or anger. "You need heirs."

"Without Charlotte, there will be no heirs anyway. I will not shackle myself to some chit merely for children—or money. Do you recall the conversation when I gave you that brooch?" He gestured to the starling she wore every day.

She nodded.

"Who do you think helped guide me to those investments? Charlotte is smarter than me, perhaps even smarter than you, Mama, without so much as a day at Oxford. She researches and evaluates opportunities and then directs her man of business to invest where she wants. All I did was follow her suggestions, right down to using the same investment manager. Without her help, we would have been far worse off when father's latest investment failed. We would have been selling properties, as you know from reading the ledgers."

"But—"

"No buts. I thank you for sharing your story with me. I know it must have been difficult to tell, but it clarified my priorities. I will wed her, or not at all. And that is final, as earl." He swept out, intent on getting to Charlotte to have the same conversation with her as quickly as possible.

* * * *

William continued to knock on Charlotte's front door. After the first five minutes, the butler had opened the door a crack and asked him to remove himself from the premises, that the lady of the house was not at home, nor would she be for the foreseeable future.

Quite sure that was a bluff—Charlotte always preferred London after all, no matter what the season—he shrugged and said he'd keep knocking until she changed her mind.

He caught curtains twitching at two of the neighbors' homes and smiled over at them as he persisted, switching hands to alleviate the soreness.

In the brief pause, voices exchanged muffled words just inside.

The door opened all the way, the butler stepping back just in time to avoid William barreling into him.

Following his Mistress's skirts as they turned into the parlor, he declined to wait to be announced, following her with rapid strides.

She turned to glare at him.

"Mistress, thank you for seeing me."

"You are ever so welcome, William. How polite you are." Her lips twisted sardonically.

Ignoring her sarcasm, he grabbed her hand and pulled her in for a cheek kiss. He released her easily when she tugged her hand back.

"Mistress—"

"William—"

"Ladies, first." He sketched a shallow bow.

"I am very sorry for your loss."

His lips twisted in a half smile. "So you said in your letter. Anyway, as you know, my father was lost to me a long time ago."

"Yes, but he was still your father. I also meant the loss of your freedom. I realize you had expected to have that for quite a few more years."

His face softened at her understanding. "Interestingly, I have come to a realization. That is why

I am here." He followed her over to their customary seats. Glancing at the footstool for her chair, he rejected it for the settee. Today was not the day for blind subservience.

When he did not continue, Charlotte prodded, "I assume you came to actually *share* that idea with me…?"

"I have concluded that being an earl gives one rather more privileges than being the son of a misbehaving earl." His smile was grim. "I have come to see that I had all of the responsibility but none of the benefits before. Now I have both."

"I suppose. I still do not understand."

"Y'know, my title requires me to do all sorts of things. I must wed, I must fix the family's financial predicament, I am required to produce heirs. But," he took a cleansing breath. He needed her to see how serious he was. "Not every earl does those things. Not every earl has the ability to invest wisely, or the friends to help him do so…" He nodded at her. "Not all marry or have children, or some end up with only girls. There are more ways than one to dig for money. And to keep an earldom in the family."

"William, have you spoken with your mother about this?" Charlotte asked, a note of concern in her voice.

They both knew his mother's grip on family affairs would not be relinquished easily.

"Let us be clear about something, Mistress. 'Tis not up to my mother whom I choose to wed." His voice was sterner than he'd ever used to address her.

Her mere presence, even when they were arguing, calmed him. His shoulders loosened, dropping away from his ears. He breathed easier, and sat forward rather than slumping away from the piles of responsibility. His heart beat fast, but that was for his Mistress, and with the need to convince her of his sincerity. He would never admit it in words or expression, but he'd fully expected to be refused on this first visit. Thankfully, he was stubborn (his mother's word)—or rather, persistent (his word).

His gaze narrowed. "Do you understand what I'm saying?"

Her head rose at his firm tone, meeting his stare, a brow arched. "Enlighten me."

His mouth went dry at her command, said in her Mistress voice. His heart thumped harder and his cock twitched. Knowing that part of him was not likely to be satisfied that day, he took a slow breath for patience.

"I have options, choices. And as I said, they are my decisions to make, no one else's. Marriage will of course require two people to decide on each other. I came to state my intention." Without breaking eye contact, he reached for her hand and squeezed it before continuing. "I choose you."

She opened her mouth to respond and he raised his free hand to stop her.

"I shall continue to choose you. You may decide not to choose me, which is your prerogative. But I choose you. Forever."

She shot to her feet, yanking her hand away to twist her fingers together at her waist. "William, no. You do need heirs. We've been over this. Not only for your family, but for your own sake. Besides, society will make your life miserable."

Prepared for this, he came to his feet to face her. "Mistress, with a father who was in his cups more often than he was sober these past years, do you think that society doesn't already whisper? I could care less. What is important to me is having the right partner for the rest of my life. Someone who will support my decisions, who will even help me make them. Who will manage some aspects of the earldom as I manage others, to give us more free time for each other. A person I can learn with and from. And who can help me forget my worries at night and soothe me through her love. You."

She blinked back tears, still silent.

He sent his first shot over the bow. "So, Mistress. I have had my say. The choice is now to you. What say you?"

"I cannot." Charlotte was wringing her hands again.

Ouch. He'd expected her answer, but it still hurt. He rubbed his fingers over his chest, then dropped his hand to his side.

Bowing, he smiled and gave her fair warning. "I accept your answer. For today. Tonight, and every night thereafter, I shall return to ask, again and again, how may I serve you? I am certain you remember how tenacious I can be."

As he straightened, he threw his shoulders back. This would be fun. He'd always enjoyed a challenge, and he'd won the first battle, gaining entrance this day. His last question was hopefully his path to her brain, as he suspected her heart was already on his side. He was almost positive he could win this one.

Chapter Twenty-Nine

Charlotte stood where he'd left her, watching him go.

He spoke and moved with a new confidence. As he'd declared himself, she had thought for a moment that her puppy no longer needed his Mistress. But even his assertion that it was his choice to make showed her how much he valued their dynamic.

Then he'd left, and she'd wondered if he'd wanted the challenge, given his newfound self-assurance. She worried about the loan she'd offered Ruth and her stipulation. That had been done with the assumption she would not see William again, but of course his tenaciousness knew no bounds.

Now, she lay in bed, unable to sleep, book thrown aside after having read the same paragraph four times. Gracious, he was more delicious than ever. His new strength held a unique appeal. The young university student at her command had been fun. But to have an earl, among the most powerful men in the country, at her behest was another level of reign. It might be irresistible.

No. He was what was irresistible. Their conversations, their fit. She'd promised Ruth she'd do the right thing and step back, however.

Unable to reconcile her desires with her conscience, she put her thoughts aside and waited for him, basking in memories and planning what she wanted to do when he arrived.

Given his forcefulness, she thought he might break a door or window if she tried to keep him out tonight. However, there was no reason to make it easy for him. The doors were locked, as were the ground floor windows.

She smiled to herself.

If he still wanted to climb the tree or whatever he had used the prior year to get to her room, then so be it. One could say that an earl's behavior should be more circumspect, but he had made his disdain for the rules clear.

She was itching to touch herself, her blood racing since his brief visit that afternoon. Her body had hummed with arousal all evening, her nipples chafing her chemise, her hips twitching with electric pulses sparking between them.

But after another hour passed with no sign of him, she sighed and rolled over, away from the window. Blowing the candle out, she counted backward from 100.

Some time later, the smell of spiced rum wrapped around her, tugging at her consciousness. No, those were arms. Her heart would have recognized them as William's, even without the delicious scent.

"Did you think I bluffed, Mistress?"

The rumble of his quiet growl at her ear sent a shiver through her.

Still fuzzy from sleep, she shook her head, aborting even that small act as William's head pinned her hair to the pillow. She tried to stretch, finding that the movement arched her body against him, her thinly-clad bottom pushing back into a stiff club that poked at her.

Placing her hand on the arm around her middle, she discovered linen. She frowned, confused. He was still at least partially clothed. Then his breath sighed over her ear, pointing her nipples and quickening her blood.

But it was his whispered words that undid her. "I choose you. How may I serve you Mistress?"

All her muscles went limp, and she slumped against him.

His hand swept the bed covers down and skimmed up her leg, bringing her nightshift with it. He traced fingers over the dip at her waist before gripping her to thrust his hips against her once.

Her breath caught, sparks racing along her nerves. This was a different William, no longer her puppy waiting patiently for instruction. His knowledge of her pleasure points enabled him to press his suit without guidance.

Feeling unsettled, she attempted to regain control, by tugging her head forward, signaling for him to lift off her hair.

"Nay, I think it is my turn to have you pinned in place. Tell me how I may serve you, or I shall have to guess." He did not lift his head to make his demand-request. Instead, he trailed his hand upward under her nightrail to cup a breast, a finger back and forth over the tip, not enough firmness to give the pleasure she sought, just enough to tease.

Arching forward, she tried to increase the pressure. She did not trust herself to speak, her thoughts ricocheting between knowing she should make him leave and wanting to see what he'd do with whatever control she gave him. Her body pulsed, her core heating and clenching, wanting his shaft where it could do more good.

Beyond the physical, her heart panged, remembering how right this felt, wishing she could have him wrapped around her every night. He'd caught her at a weak moment, half asleep.

His finger remained steady, a too-gentle metronome against the tight, sensitive furl of her nipple. Defeated without a spoken word, she sighed and gave in, bending her top leg and sliding it forward.

He squeezed the point between thumb and forefinger, teeth sinking gently into the top of her shoulder.

As though to further pin me.

Wet warmth gushed between her legs, surprising her. She wanted to squirm or reach for him, but could not. On the other hand, his question had given her the option of assuming control. She could take over at any time, or her silence would act as permission for him to move at his own pace. She lay quiet and waited.

He ran his hand down her side, around her hip, and down her bottom to probe careful fingers between her nether lips, opened by her canted position.

Her slippery swollen folds revealed her acquiescence, but wanting to be clear, she lifted her bent leg an inch higher on the bed.

Again, he proved he was her perfect match, checking in with her at each step. "Nothing to say, Mistress? I shall assume I am serving you in an acceptable manner then."

She gasped at his words as much as his fingers, heat stealing through her, centering in her chest. Around her heart.

Stroking through her wetness, he found the tight bundle of nerves and strummed it as she'd taught him.

Her hips twitched, then thrust toward him. She

moaned.

He gathered her closer, pressing his whole body against her. His cock poked her bottom, nestling into the cleft.

The sparks flickering through her flared into flames, his cock and fingers and flutters of breath over her hair all fanning them. But now a layer was added. His clothed body wrapped her in a warmth more emotional than temperature driven, cocooning her in a world of love that excluded all their worries.

Then his hips mimicked hers and the flames took over, burning away existential thoughts. He made tiny circles around her nub with his finger.

All her muscles tightened at once. "William, William," she breathed, unable or unwilling to verbalize the command she wanted to give.

He understood her wishes anyway. "Mistress? You need more? I am happy to serve."

Her body was taut from head to toe, hands clutching the bed linens, spine arched to hold her bottom still to ensure he would stay just there, there. She panted.

Just as the ecstasy grew and gathered into a ball of need, his hand left her.

A puppy whined, needing attention. Gracious, that was her. Appalled, she cut it off.

"Shh, I know. I shall provide relief in a second."

His hands fumbled between their bodies at his waist, then he was up against her again, his shirt pulled up and trousers down. Now he was naked where she was, her nightrail still scrunched up around her ribcage.

He reached between them to line himself up then tugged her hip backward as he thrust forward. His cock speared into her, impaling her all the way to the root in one smooth motion. The crisp hairs at his groin rubbed the crease of her legs.

She wriggled, seating him a fraction deeper. She wanted more friction, his bollocks against her sensitive flesh. But no, the angle was wrong. She writhed again, still not ready to vocalize commands, enjoying this rare shift in their dynamic.

He groaned and squeezed her hip then grabbed her bent leg. Guiding it up to rest on his thigh, he let her foot fall behind his bent knees. With her thus spread for him, he snaked a hand forward over her hip to circle her nub.

Her hips snapped, her hand reaching blindly for his hip to help him piston in counterpoint. She bit her lip, humming a moan in her throat. This was the friction she'd wanted. They'd never done this before, but her puppy knew her well. Her stomach muscles clenched, her thighs working to brace against his more forceful thrusts now. Lud, she was so close, so close.

He shifted to change the angle, and she was gone. Her head and shoulders rolled forward as she tried to curl around the orgasm, everything in her tightening and reverberating. Her nub, hard as a pebble under his finger, shuddered against him and she milked him with her internal muscles, every plunge and withdrawal extending her pleasure. Ecstasy threaded through her limbs.

Before her climax had fully abated, he barked a short, muffled yell behind her and thrust hard twice.

The pulses of his orgasm extended her own pleasure, and a rush of heat bathed her inner walls.

Limp, she lay in a twisted heap as he rose. She stifled a giggle.

He had not removed any of their clothes, just shoved them out of the way. Her puppy had been more eager than his control had implied. Happy to see what he did next with his freedom to lead the way, she watched him.

He wet a cloth and cleaned her, as was their custom. Then he cleaned himself with it, and righted his crumpled clothes.

"Mistress." He bowed. "Sadly, my duties as earl demand an early day tomorrow, so I shall see myself out the way I came. I will choose you again tomorrow."

It took Charlotte a long time to go back to sleep after he climbed through the window. His visit had undone any healing she'd been attempting these past weeks. She wallowed, bereft without him to snuggle with, a circumstance she was certain he'd intended, to show her what she was resisting.

* * * *

The next night, Charlotte sat in a chair by the window, reading. Well, attempting to read. She remained in her day dress, determined to uphold her promise to Ruth and do the right thing, allowing William to find a mate who was more likely to bear him children. She had reinforced her resolve by once again limiting his point of entry.

Nonetheless, he arrived earlier than the night before, undaunted by her challenge of locked doors and windows below.

A soft knock on the window preceded his entry, accompanied by a smirk. "Good evening, Mistress. Lovely to see you. I thought I might find you at home."

She shook her head at him. He was incorrigible. But she could not resist smiling despite her sarcastic retort. "Hello, William. Thank you for calling."

He chuckled, stepping in to lean over and buss her cheek. Then he dropped to his knees before her, repeating his new mantra. "I choose you. How may I serve you tonight, Mistress?"

Her fingers itched to comb through his hair as she loved to do. Clenching her fist, she asked, "William, this cannot continue. Do you not have an earldom to manage?"

"By day, I play the earl. By night, I am your servant." The puppy grin was out in full force, more confident than ever.

"Please, William, you know this is not tenable." His verb choice was not lost on her, but whether or not he viewed it as playing, he *was* the earl.

"We've found a way to bridge the gap of funding, thankfully. I am ready to celebrate, especially as it means shorter workdays and more time with you."

"A wife would solve that."

"Agreed. Are you ready to choose me, then?" His reply was quick and eager.

She'd walked right into that. Sighing, she pressed her lips together and sent him a stern look to quell his puppy tendencies. Changing tack, she reminded him, "I am very happy for you and Ruth. I know that takes a weight off your shoulders, especially as you struggle with people's livelihoods depending on you. But that does not eliminate the need for marriage and heirs, William."

"I know your concerns, trust me. Please, I beg of you, may we take tonight to enjoy this boon without going over these arguments again? I promise tomorrow I will debate with you to your heart's content." Puppy eyes begged her better than words ever could.

Why am I so susceptible to this man? There are many other handsome intelligent gentlemen. Why must I be addicted to this one?

Mute, she stared at him, unwilling to voice her capitulation.

"Right, then. You know the rules from last night, Mistress. If you do not speak, I will serve you as I please." William stood, and shucked his coat, shoes, waistcoat, and cravat.

At his words, she realized she had remained silent due to an unconscious desire to see if he'd toe the line between submission and control as well as he had the prior night. Distracted, she gasped when he hauled her out of the chair, spinning her around. His hands were halfway down the fastenings of her gown before she realized his intent.

Her dress fell. Her corset. The pins in her hair pinged on the floor, then his fingers combed through her hair.

She dropped her head back to give him better access. *Unfair, puppy.* He knew having her hair brushed by any means was a weakness of hers.

He lifted her arms and whipped her chemise over her head, rubbing the creases in her skin where the corset had pressed the chemise into her.

She smiled, memories of Charles and more recently William always taking care with her skin in such a way filling her with tenderness. She had not thought of her husband in days, her mind and heart consumed with William. Stroking the pendant laying warm on her breastbone, she knew that if circumstances were different, she'd be more than ready to forge ahead with a new partnership.

Her petticoats dropped, then each stocking, and she stood nude, her back to her puppy, waiting for his next move.

His warmth dissipated as he stepped away and she

turned to see him drawing back the counterpane. Returning, he led her to the bed. As she lay back, he tugged his remaining clothes off, then sat on her thighs. Supporting himself on one hand, he leaned in to brush a kiss over her lips, his free hand skimming down her arm then up.

"Mistress, I am going to kiss every inch of you. Then I shall start all over again."

And so he did, bringing her to the cliff of pleasure three times, only to back off and begin slowly again, building her sensitivity and arousal to new heights. Finally, she could not bear it.

"William. Please…" she lost her train of thought.

"Ah Mistress, I am yours to command. Always."

"I need you in me. Now." She managed to refrain from begging, firming her voice at the last minute to make as close to a demand as her thoughts could form.

"Yes, Mistress." He knelt between her thighs, and leaned forward again to kiss her, just as he had started. This time, though, the tip of his cock teased her opening.

"William—more. Faster." She dug her heels into his hips. Her voice was stronger now, her need greater. He hadn't filled her, instead lingering near her entrance. While he'd technically obeyed her command to be in her, he was going to earn a punishment if she could find the strength.

"Yes, Mistress." He sped up, but kept his thrusts shallow.

Narrowing her eyes, she started to formulate various forms of retribution.

He flipped her over and tugged her hips up. When she was on her hands and knees, he nudged her around to kneel sideways on the bed.

"Perhaps this angle will help." He sank into her and stayed still. "Deep enough, Mistress?"

Her breath left her in a whoosh. A spike of pleasure shot through her as he grazed all her nerve endings inside. His bollocks tickled the sensitive nub in front of where they were joined. She wanted to collapse her arms and rub her breasts against the bed, to reach back and fondle his testicles or bounce them against her pleasure center. She wanted him to somehow kiss her and pinch her nipples and stroke her nub and thrust into her all at once. Needing to start somewhere, she gritted out, "Yes. Now move. Please."

"I shall in a moment, Mistress. First, look up."

Lifting her head, she froze at their reflection in the cheval mirror in the room's corner. Ohh. Gracious, he was beautiful. All floppy hair, youthful toned muscles, and big hands holding her hips as he took her in. His gaze was strong but respectful, raking over her as though she was the most exquisite thing he'd ever seen, but from above, enjoying his power over her pleasure.

"I want to see your beautiful face, even as I touch you as deep inside as I can. I want all of you, Mistress."

It mirrored her thought of a moment ago. She wanted all of him at once. Her lips twisted. From his words and actions every night, she *had* all of him. However, she'd left him uncertain.

He slid out then surged forward, robbing her of all thought. The angle rubbed the ridge below the head of his cock along an extra sensitive spot on her front wall, and she moaned at each thrust, pushing back against him.

He sped up, one degree at a time. Watching in the mirror to gauge her pleasure, he tried tilting his hips and hers.

Pressure built in her, edging toward an explosion. Her arms shook, her mouth went dry as she watched them. Her breasts swayed in the reflection and she felt an answering impact of him against her most sensitive flesh. His nipples hardened, and hers buzzed with sensitivity. His face flushed, and heat wafted over her.

Watching their bodies intertwined added another layer of intimacy, as though adding another sense to the act opened a pathway to her head and her heart. The eruption of pleasure building within her felt bigger, wider than ever before.

He leaned forward to press his chest to her back and threaded his arm around to slide his fingers through her folds. Gathering wetness that dripped from her, he rubbed it around before sliding a finger on each side of her raised flesh and squeezing in time with his thrusts.

His eyes on hers, he vowed, "I love you."

That was the last layer of kindling on the fire. The blast flared outward from his fingers and his cock, arrowing straight into her heart, and she convulsed.

I love you I love you I love you.

She bit her tongue, still not quite ready to take the leap of faith to verbalize her feelings, as her hips bucked wildly and her internal muscles spasmed around him. She dropped to her elbows, unable to hold herself. The bed linens chafing against the pointed tips of her breasts extended the pulsing explosion. She keened through her teeth, and tears came to her eyes.

He thrust once more and then grunted, throbbing within her. His eyelids dropped to half mast, but he held her gaze throughout.

It was the most intense, intimate interaction she had had in her life. As they panted in the aftermath, she wallowed in ecstasy. She'd not only been intimate with two men, she had loved two men, each of them teaching her and loving her in return. The strength of her connection to William superseded even years of marriage, but her husband would want her to be happy. And she was beginning to wonder if everything in her life had led her to this generous, smart, tenacious young man.

Chapter Thirty

A fortnight later, William had chosen his Mistress every night, but had yet to convince her to reciprocate. However, he considered it progress that she did not turn him away each night. They were at an impasse, back to the secret relationship they'd maintained between his years at Oxford.

He would accept this for now, seeing her every night. But he missed spending the night in her arms, and he might need one night to catch up on sleep. He yawned a third time.

"Late night, William? Were you at the club again?" Ruth asked from her spot across the breakfast table. Newspapers were strewn between them, traded to scan the news and gird themselves for the coming day.

"Sorry, Mama. Briefly. Mostly, I was at Charlotte's." She frowned.

"'Tis not for you to worry about, Mama." He raised his teacup to finish the last of his tea.

Ruth sat back, contemplating him, her own teacup and saucer in hand. "I wasn't worrying, William. I was debating with myself."

"Oh? Who won?" He asked with a grin.

"Har har. I did, of course." She smiled. "Never mind, let me think on it some more. Now, what is first for our day?"

An hour later, William looked up from his desk. He'd taken over his father's workspace, dominating one end of the room. His mother's desk was halfway along it, perpendicular to his. She'd chosen to face the room, rather than pushing the desk against the wall. This room was all about business these days, although they often ate and worked at the table and chairs in the other corner.

His mother was still toying with the same letter she'd started with, the end of her pen in her mouth.

"Mama."

She looked up, her gaze distracted.

"'Tis clear you have something on your mind. You'd feel better if you simply came out with it."

Ruth's movements were stiff. "I do not like to betray a confidence. In fact, I do not believe I ever have before."

"That seems like a good rule to live by." William slid his chair back and crossed one ankle over the other knee, patient. He refused to coerce his mother into sharing secrets.

She appeared to weigh her words carefully when she spoke. "In this case, I think the greater good will be served by me sharing information with you, however."

"Oh? If 'tis information that will help me, then I can be persuaded to waver on the good rule theory."

"That loan from a friend…"

When she did not continue, he considered the circumstances of the loan more. He'd been busy still learning, and so focused on whatever time he could find to be with Charlotte, he had not given it much thought.

Despite her role of managing their family situation for years, Ruth's friends were mostly women. Women, especially wives, generally did not have enough funds for the loan they'd received. He contemplated titled gentlemen with enough of a generous spirit to do that. But they would have come to him, man to man, decision maker to decision maker, would they not? Perhaps his mother had an admirer already.

Ruth was still speaking, albeit picking her words. "As you know, the one request by this person was that I do not disclose the source of the funds."

William frowned. A lover of hers was sounding more likely. He'd be happy for her if it was, but when could she have found the time, and why the secrecy about the loan?

His mother had more to say. "However, I think it is vital that you know the source, given the situation, William."

Vital? What situation? He was lost. "Thank you, Mama. I can see 'tis hard for you to break your word, but I trust your judgment. If you think I should know, I am certain I can maintain the confidentiality of the arrangement."

She took a big breath in. "'Tis the Dowager Countess of Peterborough."

"The Dowager…do you mean Charlotte?!" His voice rose on every word until his Mistress's name came out in a yell. The two women he trusted most in the world had conspired behind his back like he was a child? Worse, Charlotte had felt he'd needed rescuing, rather than treating him like an equal. Shoving back his chair, he punched his fists onto the table and leaned over. "Why would she do that? And why with you? And neither of you told me."

"William, I—"

"I thought we were partners in this, Mama."

Ruth frowned at that. Flapping her hand at him, she commanded, "Sit down, William, you know I do not like when you loom over me."

He growled and came over to her desk.

She raised her brows at him, waiting.

He sullenly subsided into a chair.

"I am telling you now. I needed time to think about it, especially given her request for secrecy, but also because 'twas embarrassing to accept help from a peer. If it were not for otherwise releasing staff, I might have declined, knowing you would turn things around in the long term. But I knew that weighed on you as much as it did me. As for Charlotte, you'll have to ask her."

Why would his Mistress go to his mother but not to him? Blazes, she was determined to keep her distance, to maintain that they were unsuitable, but this was untenable. If she wished to help any other earl, she'd talk to him, not his damned mother. A muscle ticked in his jaw as he clenched his teeth. His anger at her evasiveness warred with hurt at her actions. Above all, he missed her, no matter how wrong he felt her approach to helping was.

His mother watched him, giving him time to consider all aspects of this information.

He straightened in his seat as a question occurred to him. Also, slouching was not going to promote confidence in his maturity. "Why tell me now and breach her confidence?"

"I believe your words were 'I shall wed her or not at all.'" She tapped the wood between them.

He stared at her. She'd accepted that? Relief bloomed in him, and his shoulder muscles eased. They'd always been a team, and he hadn't realized how much this disagreement had worn on him. Needing confirmation, he asked, "You've accepted that?"

"You made your point, *Lord Harrington*. You are, indeed, earl. And yes, your father's and my age gap was similar, albeit reversed. More to the point, I know you. In addition to being a grown man who can make his own decisions, you've always been mature for your age. Once you settle on a path for yourself, 'tis nigh impossible to sway you. A fact that I hope she's recognized." She grinned. "Getting to know her as a friend of my own helped me see how well you two fit, as well."

"I must say, it is no surprise to me that you two became friends. You have much in common. It is out of my love and respect for you that I was drawn to her to begin with."

"We need to address the issue of heirs, though."

He nodded. "I understand. I've given that a lot of thought. Percy is a good man, as a start. I'll outline my ideas for you over tea, shall I? But oh, Mama, thank you for understanding and supporting me in this." He came around the desk to hug her.

His mother smiled against his chest as she returned his hug.

After his discussion with his mother, he'd address the loan with Charlotte. He needed to calm down first, though. If they could get past this difference, he'd still need to convince her to marry him.

Chapter Thirty-One

Charlotte held out for a week, then two. Each night, she was torn by her desire for him and her desire to do the right thing. But he and Belle had addled her mind enough that she was no longer sure what the right thing was. And not responding when he declared his love hurt her almost as much as it hurt him.

She needed to speak with Ruth.

Worried about William's presence, she sent a note to Ruth asking for a private conversation and welcoming her to call on Charlotte if that was acceptable.

Ruth agreed and arrived the following afternoon.

Calling for tea, Charlotte poured and passed.

Before she could begin, Ruth said, "I told William about the loan yesterday. I'd say I'm sorry, but I suspect 'tis why you requested this visit."

"You are correct, I was rethinking keeping it from him. How did he take it?"

"He is angry with me for making decisions without him now he's come into his majority."

"And me, I suppose."

Ruth nodded. "William told me he's been spending much of his free time with you. And has made it clear that he will not marry anyone except you."

Charlotte sucked in an apprehensive breath. Where

was Ruth leading with this?

Oblivious, Ruth continued, "You know I was opposed to it, and why. But Charlotte, I see he is serious about this. And he's right, I have no say in who he marries. What I do have a say in is how I handle it, and how I welcome the next countess into the family."

Charlotte exhaled in a gust to ask, "And how do you feel about a countess who may not be able to provide the next earl?"

Ruth rose, and Charlotte hastened to do the same. "Your willingness to step back from him, followed by your kind offer to support him in a way you hoped I'd find acceptable showed how much you care for him. To a mother, that is the most important thing. The rest of this conversation belongs between you and my son. You know my circumstances, Charlotte. They are why I firmly believe love should come first; there are enough hurdles in this world. You have my blessing"—she grinned—"despite my son insisting you don't need it."

Swallowing back tears, Charlotte hugged her before seeing her out.

She only hoped William would visit later that night despite his anger.

* * * *

She chose to remain in the library, fondling rather than reading the book of Catullus's poems, trying to find words to explain her reasoning to William.

He stalked in behind Austin, his mouth pressed into a flat line. Bowing, he muttered, "Mistress," and waited for the butler to leave.

Charlotte stood.

"Why?" His one-word question forestalled any explanation she could begin.

"Your father had just died, and I was trying to free you to find someone more suitable to marry. You cannot tell me you would not have jumped at my offer of a loan as a sign I wanted to stay connected. You've taken advantage of every opportunity to press your suit and even created some. I stepped back to try and do the right thing."

His gaze narrowed on her. "You treated me like a responsibility, made decisions for me."

"No. We were not together—"

"Only by your choice!" His words came through gritted teeth as though he was holding back a roar of anger. He clenched his fists by his sides.

"Please, William. I only wanted to help. Your father was the one making decisions for you that had long lasting repercussions. I saw what your concern for your employees did to you. I thought to bridge the gap until you could manage it without the cloud of his bad choices hanging over you," Charlotte cried, wringing her hands. Gracious, she'd never seen him truly angry. Would he ever forgive her for this? She'd never expected to be trying to win him back even if he'd found out about it. Now, she wanted more than forgiveness, she wanted her lover, her future.

"Madame, I am an earl and a man. I have always been ready to assume responsibility for my family and staff. I came to you—have continued to come to you—as a man, wanting a partnership. But this is not that." He sliced a hand through the air.

"William, please, I was attempting to balance the scales, not treat you as anything less than you are. You are indeed a man. You take care of your family, your friends, me." She was begging, a ball of fear in her throat.

He had to forgive her. He loved her still, didn't he?

"Then why?"

She gulped. Her conversation with Ruth had cleared the way for this, but it was still hard to say after losing her first love. However, the words were long overdue, the reason she'd felt guilty and torn these past weeks. "It was a gesture of love. I am in love with you."

He unclenched his hands, staring at her with wide eyes. "Charlotte?"

Oh no. He was using her name, not her honorary title he always used. "Please, William, you must know I would never have gone to Ruth rather than you if we had been together. Please, I see you. You are strong enough to take care of all of that and still allow me to command you. You are my puppy, my rakelet, yes. But most of all, you are the *man* I love."

He strode to her and scooped her into his arms to hold her tight against him.

She released a breath and sank against him, clutching his jacket in relief and adoration.

His body shuddered against hers.

"William, I truly am sorry. And I love you more than I thought I could love someone. You are the best parts of me. Please forgive me." She'd continue to beg until she was sure she was absolved of her gross misstep.

He didn't answer, but his throat moved against her hair.

He needed soothing. How could she have forgotten how tense he could get? She smoothed her hand up and down his back, content to hold him. Forever. She knew she wanted that, but they still needed to talk about children, Ruth, and everything else.

Chapter Thirty-Two

She loved him.

Thank heavens. All the rest they could work out together. His emotions finally under control, William lifted his head. Knowing his eyes were wet, he checked her hair and smoothed it, commenting, "No snot, just tears, I promise, Mistress."

A small giggle escaped her, as he'd intended. While his joke signaled that he'd forgiven her, he needed to clarify with words.

Charlotte led him over to the seating area and took her favorite chair. He poured them each a much-needed sherry and plopped onto the footstool in front of her. His intent was to show her he did not need their entire dynamic to shift.

"Mistress, there can be no more secrets between us."

"Agreed." Her eyes were uncharacteristically lowered to her lap.

"Look at me, please."

She shot her focus to his face.

"We are equals, partners, yes?" He raised his brows and waved a hand between them. "All this is mutually agreed upon. Always, we've exchanged and shared ideas."

"Yes, William." Her hand rose and hovered.

He took it and placed it in his hair, where they both wanted it.

"Whilst we will both make mistakes, forgiveness is part of a relationship. Thank you for explaining. I understand the circumstances were unique. *And shall not recur*." He narrowed his eyes and firmed his tone.

"Yes, William." Her fingernails scratched with just the right amount of bite.

He nearly hummed in pleasure but forced himself to remain on the subject at hand. "I forgive you."

She dropped her hand to his shoulder and leaned forward to kiss him. "Thank you, William."

Knowing she was not quite ready for a betrothal, he tempered his next statement. "And I can court you. Publicly."

"Yes, William."

Damnation, she was compliant. What else should he ask for? No, this was all he needed to win this battle. The war would be his in no time.

"Then we can talk about heirs tomorrow. For tonight, how may I serve you, Mistress?"

Chapter Thirty-Three

Charlotte and William fell back into their routine of attending salons together, then discussing their learnings in the garden in good weather, or the seating area in her bedroom on more inclement nights.

As she'd met South, albeit briefly, he wanted her to meet Folly.

"Would you like to have them both to supper here?"

"Thank you. I would like that but not for your first meeting. Folly is unused to the Ton's conventions and whilst I know you are very accommodating, I think he might be nervous in such a formal setting. Would you be willing to come to a pub in Soho with me?"

They sat in the men's usual corner She was quite entertained by the prospect of a new experience, as well as meeting William's closest friends. She was also curious about the man who crafted the metal parts of the leather cuffs and other items she bought from the Orfords.

Folly slid onto the bench across from them, and William performed the introductions.

"Please call me Charlotte." She gave his friend a warm smile.

"And I am Nate. Or Folly, I suppose."

"Beth Orford has told me about you." She winked as

William whipped around to stare at her. "But I shall call you Nate."

"How do you know the Orfords?" Nate asked.

William's eyebrows were near his hairline as he jumped in with his own question. "Charlotte, do you mean you know Beth and Robert Orford?"

"Yes." She patted his leg under the table.

"Oh, so those…" His face went red as he trailed off, shooting an embarrassed glance at his friend.

Folly guffawed, holding the table to avoid falling off his seat. "Well, Charlotte, you certainly know how to break the ice."

Charlotte grinned at him, ignoring William's pinch to her leg. "To answer your question, I know Beth through mutual friends. Sophia, the current Countess of Peterborough, is close to her."

Still red-faced, William asked Folly, "Where is South?"

"I haven't seen him since the last time the three of us were here after the funeral. Have you?" Folly asked.

"No. Blazes. I'm worried. I shall try to catch him at home tomorrow morning."

"Let me know if I can do anything," Folly offered before turning to Charlotte. "Now, milady, tell me about how you two met. William has been stingy with the details."

William stared at his tankard, spinning it by the handle.

Charlotte withheld a snicker. Of all William's friends, Nate would appreciate the cravat in the garden meeting. But all she said aloud was, "We met at a few balls, after which young William was bold enough to call on me."

"Was it perchance via trellis or tree?" Folly asked with a grin.

"Why, yes, it was. Do I have you to thank for that?" Charlotte was snickering.

William groaned into his drink as Folly nodded.

They lingered over drinks, the men shooting frequent glances toward the door, but South did not appear.

William appeared distracted as they navigated the stairs at her house.

"I am sorry you are still worried about your friend."

"Thank you. 'Tis yet another weight on my shoulders. There do not seem to be enough hours in the day. As it is, I see less of you than I'd like."

"I thought you were adjusting to the rest, despite your father's last poor investment."

"I am. You saw my mother, though. Some days it is easier than others to move forward without feeling like I must report back to her. Some days I need to check in because I'm still learning. And Emily is getting wilder by the day, disappearing from the house who knows how many times. Twice I've caught her sneaking back in as I've come from here. She's not quite as wild as South…yet."

They gained her bedroom, and Charlotte turned to him. She could not help him by day, but she could assist in quieting his worries at least for a time. "Strip, Puppy. You are going to get a massage. Perhaps it will relax you. I shall also be naked, though, so perhaps not."

His smile blinded her and warmed her heart.

* * * *

Charlotte strolled into the tea shop through the door William held for her. Someone on the street called his name as she swept inside. Glancing back, she nodded to him, granting him leave to return the greeting and linger outside.

Perusing the treats, she reflected on the past two months. They had attended salons, lectures, and even the theatre together. They had browsed bookstores and even visited with her brother-in-law and Sophia when the couple was in Town from Peterborough. She had not been sure she was ready to interact with people outside her intellectual salon circle as a couple, but the dinner had been enjoyable and, once she relaxed, even fun. Edward and William discussed all things Parliament and horses. Sophia, always warm and welcoming, disarmed her and quizzed her on William's courtship.

Nights were largely spent at her house, despite his daytime commitments as earl. But their lessons had lagged due to his new responsibilities.

Sophia had mentioned the possibility of finding a lady—who could have imagined?—who knew Latin and even Greek to help Charlotte pursue her studies. Apparently, there was more to Roslynn's salon group, including Sophia and Ruth, than Charlotte had realized from her first few meetings with them.

During that period, William had grown from a puppy to…well, a more demanding, assertive puppy. He remained eager to serve at her slightest command, however. She could not imagine life without him. Somewhere in those two months, with him coaxing her out to one event at a time, simultaneously protecting her and proudly parading her at each, she had fallen even deeper in love. She had been swept off her feet by Charles at nineteen. This love, due to its complexity, her life experience, and their roles, was far more complex and layered, although nothing would negate her feelings for her first husband.

William had explained that his mother was comfortable with Percy inheriting the earldom, if need be, but that no one had given up hope that Charlotte might still become pregnant. After all, he'd preened, he was young and potent. She'd punished him for that, making him waste his seed on the sheets that night.

He'd been taking things slowly so as not to frighten her, but she also suspected he did not like money between them. Then a few days ago, he had entered with a triumphant whoop and announced, without even a hello, that he had the payment for her loan.

They had formatted the agreement with no payments due until a few of his other investments matured—or, in the case of the shipping group investment Charlotte had encouraged him to join, provided a return. She had not yet received word from their man of business of the next quarterly payout, but William had. And the successful arrival of more than enough ships to meet the investment pool's requirement was what he had needed.

He dragged her out of her chair, bouncing on his toes while she donned a pelisse, and marched her down to the financial manager's office. There, they both signed the loan document as paid in full, to be held and filed by the manager.

William had sped them back to her house where they retired upstairs for a celebration, complete with champagne he'd brought. He deemed it a no-clothes-allowed party and it became quite rowdy. They'd needed a servant to change the sheets before they could sleep that night. The bed linens had been soaked in spilled champagne from them sipping it off their favorite spots on each other.

Now as she stood in the tea shop reviewing everything, Charlotte nodded. She was ready to choose him. To spend her life with her puppy. There was no doubt he loved her and was impatient to start that life together. They had his family's support. But given the dynamics of their relationship and recent events, she suspected he was loath to push her too hard.

It was time for the Mistress to make her feelings known and direct him as she loved to do. Her relationship with Charles had begun quite differently. But who she was now, so dissimilar to her nine-and-ten-year-old self, was in large part due to Charles's love. The whole situation was unique, and she rather thought Charles would find this approach amusing.

She tucked her pendant inside her dress, pressed her lips together, and crinkled her brows to make lines form on her forehead and around her mouth. Her clothing choices had been deliberate—a more conservative dress with an older style coat and hat—to appear more matronly. If this scheme did not work, she'd think of another.

"Madame, what can I get you and your son?" the shop assistant fell right into her hands.

William stiffened, having turned to shut the door after entering. He whirled and took a breath to correct the girl.

The young woman looked surprised at his countenance. Regardless, it was the opening Charlotte needed. Snaking her elbow back, she gave him a gentle jab and took a half-step forward.

"Thank you. I shall have one of those miniature cakes please. And this"—she gestured to William—"is not my son. He is the Earl of Harrington, and I am the future

Countess of Harrington." She lowered her chin, raised her brows, and stared at the girl, afraid to look around at William. This might be the boldest act of her life, even more than tying a strange puppy's wrists in the garden of a ball. Nerves raced along her skin, raising gooseflesh on her arms, as she waited for both of their reactions.

"I beg your pardon," the girl said, wide eyes ricocheting between her two patrons.

"Mistress—" William's gasped whisper underlaid the girl's apology. But he stopped on that word.

She turned to see him sway and grabbed his arm, alarmed.

He shook his head once to clear it, then swung his hand around, reversing their grip to hold her arm. Turning her to face him, he whisper-yelled, "Truly, Mistress?!"

"Quiet, please." She kept her voice low but gave him a wide grin. "Yes, William. I've chosen my cake, and I've chosen you. Now, I'd like my cake, and then you may take me home and shout at me all you'd like."

"Shout? I shall dance, I shall cry." He turned to the worker, grabbed the cake, and thrust several coins at her, never letting go of Charlotte's arm with the other hand. He dragged her out to the street, hustling them along at a near-run.

"Puppy, really now. You know the rules about touching without permission. Dragging me about the street warrants a further punishment." She was reveling now. She'd done it. *They'd* done it. He was hers to keep, they just had to work out the logistics. "Walk with dignity, for heaven's sake. You're an earl."

He laughed at her, nearly skipping, and she could not help her own ecstatic giggles.

Chapter Thirty-Four

Ignoring his Mistress, William continued to drag her home as fast as her steps allowed.

She can punish me all she wants; she is lucky I don't pick her up and run with her.

Realizing he'd crushed the bag with the cake, he sighed and softened his grip a fraction.

His Mistress was his for the taking! She had chosen him. He'd grown more and more impatient these past weeks, envisioning all sorts of scenarios in which he proposed. But none felt right. She'd said she loved him and ventured out with him and introduced him to friends and family. However, he'd been waiting for her clear signal that she'd chosen him.

He was relieved and grateful that he'd put his eagerness to good use and prepared for this. After their last visit with the Earl and Countess of Peterborough, he'd managed to corner Edward in White's.

"Lord Peter—"

"Ah." Edward tsked. "Remember? 'Tis Edward to family and friends."

William nodded once, feeling tongue-tied. He'd been so eager to have this conversation he'd neglected to consider how to phrase his questions. His Mistress would shake her head at the puppy-like behavior. "My apologies, Edward. Er, speaking of family and friends…"

Edward arched a brow at him, letting him stew.

He fidgeted.

"William, if you cannot say it, you are not ready for it," Edward admonished, grinning as he crossed one leg over the other.

That phrase broke William's apprehension. He laughed loud, heaving guffaws of merriment.

Edward stared at him with a puzzled look.

"Is—is that a family phrase, my lord?" he gasped out.

"Not that I am aware of." Edward was shaking his head, but then understanding dawned. "I take it Charlotte said it to you?"

He nodded, clearing his throat and sobering.

Under his breath, Edward murmured, "Why am I not surprised…"

Mind focused, William found his words. "Fine. I shall say it. If one was—if *I* was to ask Charlotte for her hand, who would sign the marriage contract?"

Edward's grin stretched across his face. "I thought that might be it. Congratulations. Or, I suppose, for now good luck. However, I do not think you shall need it."

"Well, she's given tacit permission."

Edward rolled his eyes. "Of course, she has. Hellfire, I think you might need wishes of luck for the marriage, never mind the proposal."

William smiled. "I would not have it any other way."

"Good, good. You are well-matched, and all teasing aside, I am sincerely happy for both of you. To your question, the signature on the marriage contract will be mine as head of the family, but that is a mere formality. As you can well imagine, she is the only person whose opinion matters, and is well able to negotiate on her own behalf. I daresay she knows what she wants and what she doesn't in a marriage."

"I would not have it any other way." William repeated.

Now, as William slowed in front of Charlotte's house, he patted his pocket. He was ready, he'd just been waiting for her signal. They turned into the parlor, Charlotte calling for tea. He hoped she was not anticipating the cake too much, as he suspected it was ruined.

Impatient, he paced until the tea arrived, then held the door for the servant before shutting it firmly and twisting the simple lock.

Charlotte did not notice as she was sitting to pour tea.

Advancing on her, he chose the settee.

She offered tea and he waved it to the table.

He produced the small velvet bag he'd been carrying for days and dug in it for the first thing he wanted to offer. This one was the gift he was least sure about, but he felt it was important to lead with it.

"Mistress, I love you with my whole heart, and I know you love me." He took her hand in one of his, still holding his gift tight in the other closed fist. "I do not ever desire to replace your first husband in your affections, nor do I think I could. Indeed, I am grateful to him for molding you into the perfect fit for me."

Her hand trembled in his.

He squeezed it once before opening his hand to show a filigree setting for around the heart pendant she wore, the fine gold design dotted with a few tiny diamonds. "I offer you this to enhance your pendant. In some ways, Charles is at the core of what we now have. We've built on it and expanded it to make us what we are. And the diamonds are for the stars in the sky that first night I met you, the same ones which will light our nights as long as we live."

Charlotte was crying silent tears, her lower lip quivering with each breath sucked in as her gaze flicked between his face and the setting and back.

"Oh, Mistress, no. Please do not cry. I should have said this sooner. If you are not comfortable changing your necklace, I will return this to the jeweler, and you can pick what you want. I simply wanted to show you my respec—"

Her finger on his lips stopped his words.

"William. It is lovely. Both the sentiment behind it and the piece itself are absolutely beautiful, like your soul. I could never have imagined such a thing, but 'tis perfect." She was sobbing between words and he slid to the edge of his seat, alarmed. "Thank you for this. I know you don't mind references to my prior life, but hearing those words lightened something in me."

He leaned in to kiss her, wiping her tears with his thumbs.

Why had he thought that was the hard part? Asking someone to wed them, even when she'd as much as said she would, was intimidating at best, and terrifyingly vulnerable at worst. He gulped a breath and slid to the floor, forgoing the footstool to kneel at his Mistress's feet.

Chapter Thirty-Five

Charlotte gaped at him. Now what was her puppy doing? She needed him to hug her before they began their games. Reaching out to run her fingers through his hair, she yanked her arm back when he twisted back toward the settee.

He'd left the velvet pouch there. Now, he grabbed it and produced a folded piece of paper, handing it to her.

If to delight man's wish, joy e'er unlooked for, unhoped for,
Falleth, a joy were such proper, a bliss to the soul.
Then 'tis a joy to the soul, like gold of Lydia precious,
Charlotte mine, that you come to delight me again.
Come yet again long-hoped, long-looked for vainly, returnest
Freely to me. O day white with a luckier hue!
Lives there happier any than I, I only? a fairer
Destiny? Life so sweet know ye, or aught parallel?

She read through it again, noting his substitution of her name in the poem. Just as the diamonds on the filigreed pendant symbolized the night they met, this Greek poetry was the epitome of their path to love. Their discovery of shared interests and intellectual pursuits.

More, it was the method he'd used to entice her into what had felt like a completely unsuitable relationship, more alluring than any restraints she'd used to seduce him.

He was shaking the velvet pouch into his other hand. "Mistress, if I may give you this small token…"

She gasped.

A gold sparrow brooch, encrusted in garnets, lay in his hand. Again, her puppy had chosen the perfect gift for its beauty and symbolism. They had long discussed Catullus's use of the sparrow in his poems to his lover, and the significance of it. In the end, both of them had believed it represented the lovers' feelings for each other that they considered precious and fragile, with which they wanted their lover to take special care.

Still kneeling, William reached for her hand. "Please, Mistress. Will you do me the utmost honor and allow me to serve you for the rest of our lives together? To give you happiness, engage your brain, and support your independence in every way I can think of—and more, every way you direct? Will you be my Countess as well as my Mistress?"

Charlotte was weeping again before he finished his first question. She clutched his hand, unable to find embarrassment at her uncharacteristic mawkishness, but also unable to answer him through the emotions clogging her throat.

He sat motionless, unblinking, awaiting her response.

She wasn't sure he was breathing. She'd best answer him.

She began, "William, I went to that ball to start to find something that would at least substitute for what I had in my marriage. Instead, I found a young puppy, brash but eager to please, smart but willing to follow, helpful but supportive of my independence."

He blinked. He breathed.

She continued, "You are more than I could have ever hoped for, more than I likely deserve, and I am in love with you in more ways than I knew even existed. I will give you all of those things, along with punishments, encouragement, and the odd financial advice"—she winked—"for the rest of my life."

He chuckled but grew serious again in a moment, standing to tug her upright. Wrapping his arms around her, he clutched her tight, his body trembling against hers.

Charlotte clung to him, one hand still holding the paper and brooch.

"Thank you," he whispered in her hair. He sniffed and wiped his hand over his face before releasing her.

"You did well, puppy." She smoothed his hair with her empty hand. "I did not expect you to have things arranged in readiness, although I suppose I should have."

"I assume—as Edward does—that you will negotiate the marriage contract." His smile was smug.

"Gracious. You really were prepared."

His smirk lingered.

"However, none of this negates the fact that you dragged me several blocks without permission." She attempted to look stern.

He bounced on his toes, eager as ever for whatever she had in store for him. She bit back a smile.

"I locked the door, Mistress. And as you referenced punishments as part of our vows a moment ago..." He dropped back to his knees. "How may I serve you?"

Her smile blossomed. This second chance at a

lifetime of love was going to be fun.

* * * *

After a week of William cutting his work days short to dine with her morning and night, Charlotte shooed him home to refocus on managing his family's affairs. She hated them living separately, but that would change soon, also. The first two banns had already been posted, and they would review wedding plans and living arrangements that evening over dinner at his family's home.

Ruth had issued the invitation days ago, but Charlotte had not been feeling well. She still wasn't, but she was determined not to cause any further delays for the Stantons in settling their future.

She lingered over her morning toilette before going down to nibble on toast and sip tea. When this stomach upset came on, she'd suddenly craved ginger marmalade on her toast, which she had always taken with butter alone or a dash of strawberry preserves. The ginger helped settle her nausea, which she assumed was the reason.

Unable to face the newspapers that day, she wandered listlessly into the library and to the settee in the small seating area there, carrying her tea and toast with her. She stared at the unlit fireplace, contemplating what she needed to get done that day if she could find the energy. Correspondence, following up on one investment, perhaps scheduling a visit with Belle. Still considering where to start, she leaned back.

Jerking awake at a knock on the library door, she checked that she wasn't still holding her teacup. Thankfully it was in its saucer on the low table in front of her.

Her butler stood by the door. "Apologies for disturbing you, madame. Miss Rossi is here. May I show her in?"

As he finished the question, Belle pushed past him. "Thank you, you needn't bother. I know the way." She winked and nudged him on the way by, outrageous as ever.

Her gaze found Charlotte on the settee, still loose-limbed against the back cushion, and her jaw dropped. She hurried over. "Are you all right, Char?"

"I am fine." Charlotte struggled upright from her half-prone position.

Belle leaned over to feel her forehead. "Hmm…no fever. Do you want to have a lie-in?"

"'Twouldn't be much of a lie-in as I've already been up." Charlotte muttered bad-temperedly. She hated people fussing over her, although if she had to choose, her puppy's fussing was the least invasive. *And most cuddly.*

"Well, then." Belle wandered over to the table, made herself a cup of tea, and returned. "What is the matter? And is that ginger marmalade?"

"My stomach has been upset for days, and I haven't been sleeping well. It seems to like the ginger sometimes." Charlotte shrugged.

Her friend's expression went from curiosity at her sudden change in breakfast preferences to contemplative. "Anything else? Fever? Chills? Headaches?"

"No. Just the queasy tummy. And the sudden ability to sleep in place whenever I sit still for more than a few minutes, except when I am in bed, where I toss and turn for hours."

"Even with puppy there?"

Charlotte smiled. "Less so, but yes, even then."

Belle had a strange smile on her face. She tilted her head at Charlotte, as though searching for something in her expression or answers. "Could it be your womanly time?"

Charlotte squinted and cast her mind back. "Perhaps. I last remember that…huh. Just after the funeral, but then I must have had it since. That was nigh on three months ago, was it not?"

"Yup." Belle's lips smacked, making the word pop. Her grin threatened to split her lip.

Charlotte frowned at her in question, still running through the weeks in her head, trying to remember her last menses.

"So. Three months ago." Belle's tone was provoking, like Charlotte was supposed to understand something.

Not in the mood for games, she pushed back at her friend. "Belle, could you just spit out whatever is going on in that head of yours, please? I don't know what you're getting at."

"You haven't had your flux in three months. You've been having untold amounts of sex with a virile, and may I say divine, young man. Now your stomach is queasy, particularly in the morning." Her eyebrows raised. "When you catch up, you may state clearly and often that I. Was. Right."

Charlotte frowned, thinking. Then with every word of Belle's last sentence, her eyes widened and her brows rose. She fluttered her hands, something she'd never done in her life. "Belle! It cannot be. No! Belle? Fancy that!"

Belle smirked.

Charlotte wanted to jump for joy, but then worried if that was permissible. Her hand crept to her belly, and she imagined William's reaction. A smaller puppy to love. Or oh gracious, he'd be putty in a daughter's hands. She laughed even as she began to cry.

Belle waved her hands, her palms facing Charlotte, rolling her eyes. "No, no, no. None of that. Gah, I forget how emotional women in your condition can be."

But these were happy tears. And scared tears. And tears of wonder. She could not believe it. Should she call a physician to verify? Belle would know. "Please. Don't tease me. What other symptoms would there be?"

"Are your breasts more sensitive or swollen? Any change in appetite or food preferences, like, oh, say, marmalade? I don't know much more than that, honestly, but I can get my physician here within the hour I suspect."

Charlotte grinned and nodded through her tears at each question then reached out to clasp her friend's hand. "Yes, please. Let us do that. I want to be sure—well, as sure as we can be. And to know what to do to ensure I stay healthy." Her hand remained cupping her stomach, still flat, to protect the life that might just be growing in there.

"Gracious. Could it really be?" Her tears intensified as hope burst within her. She thought she'd had everything she wanted. But she'd felt guilty for robbing the Stantons of their legacy.

"Oh, no. What if it's a girl?" She'd giggled at the idea of a daughter, but William needed a son.

Belle tsked and Charlotte realized she'd asked that out loud.

"Then nothing will have changed. You will wed the

second love of your life just as you'd planned. And maybe in another year, you are blessed with a son. William has made it clear he does not care either way." Belle reached for her hand and dabbed at Charlotte's tears with her rose-scented handkerchief. "I am so happy for you, Char. You deserve William. You deserve this. And Charles would have been beyond ecstatic for you."

"Yes, I believe you are right. I have thought about that a lot these past months and I know he would have wanted all this for me, just as I would have for him." She took the handkerchief from Belle to wipe her face, then reached for her hand with a solemn look. "I know this goes without saying, but please do not tell anyone until the physician confirms it, I tell William, and we are sure it 'tis going well."

"Of course. If you do one thing for me."

Charlotte nodded and, bracing herself, took a deep breath in. "You. Were. Right."

The women laughed uproariously until they lost their breath, still holding each other's hand.

Chapter Thirty-Six

William stared at the tree. Charlotte had been acting strange the past week, and then had given him some story about creating anticipation for their wedding night by denying him entrance these past two days.

However, his shoulders had begun to creep up around his ears with concern over what was bothering her. His fears had escalated to worrying that she would leave him standing at the altar. The result was that he needed to see his Mistress tonight.

She knew locked doors had never stopped him, but he admitted that he was glad tonight would be his last night of tree climbing. 'Twas unbecoming for an earl. He snorted a dismissal and began his ascent.

At her window, he found her pacing the length of the room. Concerned at that behavior from his usually serene Mistress, he hastened over the sill.

She turned and he gave her his best innocent puppy grin.

Sighing, she set down the teacup she held.

The cup was also unusual. He'd only ever seen her drink wine or sherry at night. He sniffed, smelling ginger.

"Mistress? Are you quite all right?"

"Puppy. I suppose it was too much to ask for two and

a half days? I suppose I should feel flattered." She was shaking her head.

He could not detect whether she was truly upset at him or simply distracted. Going to her, he tugged her over to the chairs. As she sat, he grabbed a decorative pillow off the bed and knelt on it at her feet.

"Please answer me. Is anything amiss? Are you having doubts about tomorrow?" His throat closed over the last question and his voice was muffled.

Her hand went to his hair, soothing them both with the familiar action. "Oh, no. I am sorry to worry you. No, I have no doubts whatsoever."

He gusted out a breath.

She smiled at him.

"I am certain you have had something on your mind this past week, though. If we are to be partners, I hope we will share everything—hopes and dreams, yes, but also concerns and worries. I can serve you best when I am informed."

"You are right." It was her turn to sigh. "I apologize. I needed time to absorb it myself and then I did not want to…worry you."

"Well, like it or not, I *am* concerned. I shall fret less if I know what to worry about. Is it bigger than a bread basket?" He asked with a smile.

She giggled.

Ah, that sound made him happy. He placed a hand on her knee to encourage her.

"Not yet, but it will be." Her hand twitched under his.

Huh. "'Tis something that grows that has you dithering."

She had not stopped grinning since his question. Now, she cocked her head and clarified, "I suppose I stated it poorly. I did not want to…get your hopes up."

He squeezed her hand once. "An investment perhaps?"

"Hmm. I suppose you could call it that. 'Tis certainly the result of a deposit." And she was off into peals of laughter.

He frowned in concentration. "So 'tis financial."

"No, the heart of it is not, although there are financial repercussions."

"Mistress! Please, stop teasing me." He threw his hands up. "I've been plagued by anxiety these past days. And I'm guessing you've had this…information for that long."

"Right, then." She took a breath. "You should sit up here for this."

His eyes widened as she patted the chair next to her. He obeyed, but asked, "Why?"

"Because 'tis something that we are both equally responsible for and shall be for a very long time." Now that her hand was free, she slid it over her lower belly.

He watched her, waiting for her to reveal this mystery that had her pacing the floor for a sennight.

"William, we are expecting a baby." It was her turn to watch him.

"A what?" His thoughts stuttered, struggling to absorb this. After all their planning, her assumed barrenness…a baby. Unable to stay still, unsure what to do, he stood, then sat, stared at her for a second, then stood again. "Mistress, are you sure? A baby? Really?"

She was nodding, her eyes sheened with tears.

He threw himself to the ground before her, resting his head on her lap, his arms going around her hips. His Mistress had part of him in her, that would grow into a life they'd made. He was not sure he was ready to be a father, but blast, he hadn't been ready to be an earl and he was doing fine for the most part. They'd learn it together. And his mother would be over the moon.

She combed her fingers through his hair again.

"This is the second happiest day of my life. Thank you." He turned his head and kissed her belly.

Her hand in his hair stopped moving. "The *second* happiest?"

"Tomorrow will be the happiest. I have told you I need you more than heirs, more than air."

She began crying then.

"No tears, please, Mistress? Even if, as I hope, they are happy ones?"

"Belle says 'tis the pregnancy that makes me more emotional. And before you ask, she is the one who discerned the condition. I thought I had a simple stomach ailment."

He laughed as he tugged her down onto his lap on the floor, surrounding her as though protecting her. When she'd calmed a little, he used one finger to tilt her chin up. "How do you feel about it?"

"Oh, William, I am beyond excited. Like you, 'twas not something I expected or needed, but as soon as the physician confirmed it, I realized it was something I wanted with every fiber of my being. I cannot decide if a miniature puppy or a daughter to help me keep you in line would be best to start."

He gulped. He hadn't thought of that. "Oh, no. A son, please, a son. I am not sure I could serve two Mistresses at once. That sounds terrifying."

She giggled more. "For my part, 'tis vastly entertaining to picture."

Smiling despite his trepidation, he pinched her gently then stood with her still in his arms. Laying her on her bed as though she was the most fragile china, he knelt and asked, "Mistress, how may I serve you and our baby-to-be?"

Epilogue

They'd decided to wait to tell his mother and sister about Charlotte's condition. William desired a few more weeks of freedom from another layer of his family's emotions centered on him and Charlotte could understand that.

A week later, she was very glad they'd remained at her London townhome in lieu of a wedding trip, as she did not want witnesses to the dispute that was brewing between the newlyweds.

William had been treating her like the most fragile of flowers. She could not stand up without him leaping toward her to ask what she needed then fetching it for her. She had to sneak downstairs for fear he'd offer to carry her. In bed, he'd insisted on her lying back and accepting pleasure without effort on her part, so as not to disturb the baby. They were still enjoying all the intimacies of marriage, but he held himself back during the act of sex. Up on his hands, he'd enter her slowly and then make shallow thrusts, often kneeling up to take her over with his finger on her pleasure button as he moved, then fisting his cock to empty it on her belly.

At first, she'd enjoyed the royal treatment. Then she tried to be patient with him. Now, she was done. She would strangle him with his cravat before the baby arrived if he tried to tether her movements for another five or six months.

In addition, she craved reclaiming control. She'd been surprised and aroused by his occasional dominant behavior in the past, particularly when she had not felt well. It was another layer of service but with an added core of strength, and it was not something she'd had in her first marriage.

However, she was an independent woman who had led her whole world, in and out of the bedroom, before she'd met him. His control over her movements, her body, was at an end, as was his authority in the bedroom, at least for the foreseeable future. Her world was out of balance, and her puppy was out of order.

Before she knew she was pregnant, she'd bought a leather flogger from Beth and Robert Orford as a wedding gift for William. She was eager to see if he'd enjoy it, as they had not played with the edge of pleasure and pain much. Apparently, she would need to cuff him for that, though, or he might try to object to her wielding the flagellator. She needed to set the tone for the remainder of her pregnancy, and hopefully for future ones as well.

After supper, she poured herself a sherry and him a whiskey and took them upstairs. Puppy behavior in full force, he followed at her heels.

Placing the drinks on her dressing table, she glanced over her shoulder. "Unlace me, puppy."

"Mistress, would you like to sit down?"

"Not tonight."

"But—"

"I think tonight there will be no talking—"

"But—"

"—on threat of punishment."

"Yes, Mistress." He bowed his head and made fast work of her dress and stays.

Her core heated, trailing through her to bead her nipples and plump her nether lips. This, this was how they'd fallen in love and what she needed now.

She turned toward him, brushing her hip against him. Excellent, his trousers were already tightening over a growing bulge. Whether he was willing to admit it or not, he'd missed this too. Now she needed to ensure he understood where concern ended and irrational behavior began, and that she would not tolerate the latter.

"Puppy, sit on the edge of the bed, please."

He opened his mouth, probably to invite her to sit with him.

She arched a brow.

He subsided, perching on the bed.

Handing him his drink, she sipped hers. "You always ask me to tell you what I need."

He nodded, his whisky forgotten, clasped in his hands between his spread knees, his full attention on her.

"I need more freedom than I've had this past sennight. Not from the marriage"—she added when he looked alarmed—"but from you shadowing me. I appreciate your willingness to wait on me hand and foot, but you must realize that when we return to our daily lives, you will not have time."

He was frowning.

She continued, "We have servants if I am too tired to fetch something, but I am perfectly healthy and for now at least, can go about my life. The physician even approved me riding for the near future if I choose, as long as I am not racing or hunting. I understand you are concerned, but women have babies all the time and I will be careful. I want this child as much or more than you do, William. I promise I will take care of myself and the child. I need you to trust me to do that, to give me back control."

William slid to his knees. "Mistress?"

"Yes, William? I am sorry, I should not have decreed silence, this should be a discussion." Her fingers started their habitual combing through his hair.

"Please, Mistress. I worry about everything. Your health, the baby, being a father, everything I'll need to teach him or protect her from."

Her brows raised and she tightened her fingers' grip to tug his hair. "I dislike that you think of teaching a son and protecting a daughter, but we can address that another time—"

"No, Mistress. I mean, yes, I understand. And truly, I have visions of teaching her Latin or whatever else she wants. But that doesn't worry me. Besides"—one side of his mouth tipped up—"my visions included you teaching our son or daughter, too. I promise they were not as antiquated as they sounded. I am excited for our future together. 'Tis just that some aspects worry me more than others. For the time being, the only thing I can manage is your health. Please, don't take that away from me." His voice was strangled on his last words.

"Well, now I am sorry I waited so long to have this discussion. And you will be sorry you waited as well. You know this is punishable behavior." Her fingers resumed combing. She should have realized he would have begun to list the duties as earl that would come with fatherhood, on top of the normal nerves about impending parenthood.

"Yes, Mistress. But please, first, I need your reassurance."

She tilted her head. "William, think about what you have told me about the dynamic of our relationship."

He tilted his head.

"One of the aspects you enjoy most is letting go of your decisions and responsibilities by deferring to me. You can do the same with your worries. Not because I am older or wiser. Because this is how we are most comfortable. Trust me to give you some release from your concerns and to take good care of myself and our child. Please?"

He considered her statement. "I shall try. I ask for your patience, and I cannot promise not to fetch things for you or the like."

"Fair enough. I think if we regain balance in the bedroom, some of our anxiety outside it may be reduced."

He nodded. "Mistress, I beg your forgiveness. How may I serve you?"

With that signal that he had acquiesced and was ready to play, Charlotte nodded, pulling her hand from his hair. "You are forgiven, but I think tomorrow you shall wear the ribbon."

He moaned. Tying his cock with a ribbon had become a favorite torture of hers, to keep him thinking of her all day. He did anyway, of course, but that tether kept him on edge contemplating what she'd do with him that night. His persistent cockstand distracted him from work, but he wouldn't have it any other way.

She added, "Now, I have something I bought for us that I'd like to try. Please keep an open mind."

He looked up.

"First, remove your clothes, puppy. I want to see this body that is mine forever." As he flung clothes aside, she added, "I shall never tire of this view."

She shrugged her loosened dress off, then stepped out of her stays, leaving her in a chemise and petticoats. Untying the petticoat tapes, she withdrew cuffs and the flogger from a drawer.

"Have you seen one of these?"

He stared at it, then nodded.

"Really? Where?"

"Folly had a copy of the catalogue from the Orfords, as he supplies the fasteners and such."

"Ah," she murmured. "We should view it together one of these days."

"I was interested in a few things in the catalogue but did not dare buy them for you." He wagged his eyebrows up and down and teased, "Now that I have you at my mercy for the rest of our lives, I shall have to reconsider."

"Hmm. That sounds promising. Other than the fact that *I* have *you* at my mercy. Now, watch," she said. She wielded the flogger against the mattress in a figure eight pattern, the smacks getting faster and firmer after every few rounds.

"Does it hurt?" William's voice was hoarse. His cock bobbed and he grabbed it, squeezing.

That was a hopeful sign. Not everyone would be willing to even explore impact play. She'd had to practice when she first bought it as she had never used one. This would be new for both of them, a concept that added to her excitement.

"It does not. However, if I slapped it harder and faster, it might. This one has strands wide enough and short enough that it should not cause real pain or even leave lasting marks. Others are cut differently. 'Tis also important to aim for well-padded areas, either with muscle or otherwise." She twisted a hip to portray her bottom as an example.

He chuckled.

"Here. You try it on your leg. Move your wrist with it and work up."

He took it, testing the motion in the air first, and then against his other hand. When he caught his wrist, he winced.

"Be careful of your wrist and start with a slower motion, less of a snap."

His glance at her was questioning.

"I spent a lot of time practicing once I bought this, as I've not tried it before either."

His expression echoed her twinge of excitement at exploring a new intimacy together, as he looked between the instrument and her with a broader smile.

"We will need to talk through it all, especially this first time, as I dislike the idea of either receiving or giving pain. For me, the hope is that we find that edge and ride it together."

He moaned and grabbed his cock again as it nodded in agreement. "I admit I am unsure whether I'd prefer actual pain to your punishments of prolonging pleasure, Mistress."

"Hmm. Your cock says otherwise, my puppy. Now let me see how hard you like it." She gestured to the flogger, liquid pooling between her legs as his muscles rippled, anticipation of perusing the catalogue together sending a shiver of excitement through her.

They had so many intimacies to explore, topics to discuss, and books to read. And hopefully this time around, a lifetime to enjoy them together.

* * *

335

Want to read about Belle & South's shared carriage ride, which introduces their book Lyon's Lover, out December 2024?
Get this hilarious bonus scene at the link below (includes newsletter signup):
https://BookHip.com/PVHFFBA

Other Books by Maggie Sims

<u>The School of Enlightenment Series</u>
Roslynn's Rebellion (prequel novella)
Sophia's Schooling (Book 1)
Penelope's Passion (Book 2)
Althea's Awakening (Book 3)
Beth's Behavior (Book 4)

<u>Spin-offs</u>
Helen's House
Ann's Angel (a Christmas short story)

<u>The Control Series</u>
Lyon's Lover
Folly's Folly

<u>Spin-offs</u>
Duke's Diversion

Books written as Debbie Charles

<u>The Texas Tornadoes Series</u>
Second Chance Puck (exclusive newsletter novella)
Dances with Pucks
Net Pucks and Chill
Spicy as Puck
Intentional Offside

For Love or Money (a spin-off novella)

Acknowledgments & References

This book was an education. Even if I had taken courses in the Classics, it would have been a few decades ago. For this, I relied on fellow authors and friends Jenna Bigelow and Emily Anderson, who directed me to all sorts of gems to incorporate here.

Critique partners Jena Doyle, Jennifer Britt, Helen J. Conway, and Sonia Bellhouse helped a ton in streamlining this story's timeline, as did my editor, Misha Robinson of Verity Ink Editorial.

Always, my real-life romance hero, my husband, gets the biggest thanks of all.

Translations of Catullus's poems and related vocabulary interpretations are taken from:

SPQR Study Guides: <u>Gaius Valerius Catullus Carmina, Latin & English & Vocabulary</u> developed by Paul Hudson, which in turn had its own bibliography.

This was removed from Amazon before I could purchase it and has no copyright, so has a semi-permanent spot in my Kindle Unlimited library.

About the Author

Maggie Sims began her love affair with romance before her teen years, drawn to the Regency by her mum's British influence. In her twenties, she did her best to live the Carrie Bradshaw life in New York City, albeit with less expensive shoes and more books.

Despite reading hundreds of romance novels in her life, she was still blown away when she met the love of her life, an ex-Marine cinnamon roll with creative woodworking and culinary skills.

Having retired from corporate life, they live in Central Texas and are parents to a varying number of dogs and cats. When not writing, Maggie is a wine enthusiast, a travel junkie, and a romance reading fiend. She also sporadically crochets for KnotsofLove.org and does just enough exercise for that second glass of wine at night.

To find out more about Maggie's latest reads, favorite wines, and travel destinations, sign up for her newsletter.

~*~

Contact Maggie at
www.MaggieSims.com

www.ingramcontent.com/pod-product-compliance
Lightning Source LLC
Chambersburg PA
CBHW071230300726
48975CB00002B/358